Two
for the
Seesaw

Haunting Memories and Aching Souls Collide,
and a Family Evolves

BILL HEITLAND

PAGE PUBLISHING, INC.
New York, NY

First originally published by Page Publishing, Inc. 2018

ISBN 978-1-64214-916-6 (Paperback)
ISBN 978-1-64214-917-3 (Digital)

Printed in the United States of America

1

A Rocky Mountain Confessional

C onsidering what I was about to do, I couldn't help thinking about the moment I knew I had something in common with Tim Brown. Our fathers had a strong influence on the way we saw ourselves and those around us, bestowing nuggets of wisdom at critical junctures. There was something that set us apart, however. It became clear when Tim related a story that had a profound impact on his life.

"Dad hired this guy who seemed down and out," said Tim shortly after we met as reporters at *The Southeast Missouri Bulletin Journal* newspaper.

"When he told me the guy openly admitted to spending time in jail, I couldn't believe it," he continued. "I asked Dad why he picked him when there were plenty of men who looked cleaner and had more impressive references from previous employers."

"Okay, so what did your dad say?"

"He said he had a hunch honesty was probably the only thing the guy had left, the one thing that couldn't be taken from him."

I knew there was more to the story.

"But what was it that gave him this hunch?" I said, sensing he was making me fish.

"Well, I'm thinking he passed the handshake-eyeball test," he replied.

"Oh okay, you mean he was looking for a firm grip and eyes that weren't bloodshot," I said, disappointed that the explanation was so easy.

"No, he looked for calluses in the hands and an unwavering eye toward intense physical labor. Dad called those two factors his real references."

"Okay, so that's what did it," I said, just to make sure the expedition was over.

"It should have, but another candidate was equally impressive in the way he passed the test," he said. Before I could complain, he held a hand up and said, "I know, you think I'm jerking you around. I'm not. What finally separated the two candidates was the eye contact and a gesture from the guy who spent time in jail," said Tim.

"Dad said there was nothing desperate or intimidating in the look or gesture. I think he said they strengthened the man's chances of being hired because they appeared genuine."

"What exactly were the look and gesture?" I said, wondering if there was an end to this story.

"He said there was a kind of fierce hunger, a determination that became clear when the man tapped lightly on the left side of his chest. He told dad, 'If you want to know what's in here, give me a chance out there. You won't be sorry.' Dad figured if a man paid for his crime with time, money, and a soul-searching determination to do better, he's earned a second chance. The next day, Dad hired him with the understanding that there would be a thirty-day trial period."

There was no smug demeanor as Tim said this. Rather, I detected a look of quiet fascination and admiration for a man he was beginning to know as a friend who happened to be his father.

I was happy to be the hooked fish.

"After that I started to pay attention to some of the guys he hired," noted Tim. "Dad's gift, if you could call it that, was in reading people by their body language, especially the message coming out of the eyes."

I realized at that moment that Tim pondered life's complexities from a more sophisticated vantage point. He had already come to an understanding about issues I was still questioning.

Yet another discovery was that I was the only one who could answer my own questions. And there were many.

What stirs a man to make such a gamble with much to lose? Were these nuggets our true inheritance, to be passed on to the next generation? Or was it incumbent on us to turn own experiences into anecdotal advice that would enrich the lives of our sons and daughters? How long would I wonder and wander before I came to the decisive confidence of such seasoned men as these? It would take a considerable amount of time to answer them.

For the present, I sensed Tim was someone who could help me become a better reporter and perhaps a more skilled writer.

"Did the guy let him down?" I wondered aloud, anxious to know the outcome of such a fascinating story.

Tim shook his head, saying, "He ended up being one of his best workers. And laying down carpet is grueling work, installing tile an even tougher test of a man's fortitude, especially during the dog days of August, when the heat invades every room in the house and makes staying hydrated difficult. Dad called it the back breaker, the mental and physical test few could pass."

I had to know more.

"Okay, so how long did the guy last?"

"He was there for a few years. He was promoted twice, leading crews on his own."

"Your dad's hunch paid off," I mused.

"Yeah," said Tim. "Deep down we want to back an underdog, but few come through as well as that guy did. Makes you wonder how many are out there but never get the chance to prove what they're made of."

Honesty and facing up to harsh truths were traits I sorely lacked when Tim put his reputation on the line for me.

The letter of an apology and follow-up phone call should have settled things between Tim and me. He said as much when I called.

But I suspected something was not quite right. It was in the tone of his voice—polite yet distant—that left my need for atonement feeling unresolved.

Although he did have a forgiving nature, I would have felt better if there was an argument. That would have brought whatever was festering to the surface.

Was he reluctant to discuss the mess I made because, as far as he was concerned, our friendship was not what he once thought it was?

Perhaps a face-to-face meeting would provide the closure I desperately needed.

He did want to know how Anna was doing. In fact, the only thing I *was* sure about is that we had an open invitation to visit Tim and Patti when we got the urge to travel from St. Louis to Colorado Springs, Colorado. I wondered if they were more interested in seeing Anna than me.

When I voiced my concerns with Anna, she leaned back, rolled those pale-green eyes, and with a look of exasperation, said, "If he said things were okay, then they're okay." When I explained why that probably wasn't so, she protested for several minutes before giving in, saying, "Looks like we're about to take the ultimate guilt trip."

"We're doing this to make things right," I reminded her. "I'm going along, and it will be good to see Patti again, but *you're* the one who needs to make amends," she corrected with a challenging gaze.

Then, with a hint of sarcasm, she added, "Don't Catholics just opt for the nearest confessional? It's way cheaper than traveling 830 miles."

"Usually they do, but this is a special deal," I said, mindful Anna was raised Presbyterian.

"Saying a few Hail Mary's and Our Father's won't mend what I broke," I admitted.

"You think there's no telling the extent of the damage until you check it out," she surmised. "Something like that?"

"Yes, exactly," I said, taking comfort in her willingness to understand the importance of this trip. God, how many ways could I tell her how much I loved her for understanding all of what I told her—not just about the damage to my friendship with Tim Brown, but the real reason I lost my job at the university. And in the end, she was willing to talk it all out. It was rough, even painful at times, but we endured and are better for it today. I was relieved there was no more fear of the truth because that is what brought us closer. I wanted to say the same about my relationship with a former colleague. Tim told me more than once that my plea for forgiveness was enough and he was willing to move on. Would he be as kind face-to-face? Probably not.

What could I say to make it right? Was this beyond fixing?

If I could adequately measure Tim's mood, I might know how to begin. Was he waiting for the right moment to bring up the incident that threatened our friendship? When we arrived at their new home in Colorado Springs, he seemed calm, even happy to see us.

"Can I offer you two something to drink after such a long drive?" he said with a smile that appeared warm, relaxed.

Too easy, I feared. He wants us to drop our guard, then move in for a stinging jab or an uppercut we wouldn't forget. He knew something about the sweet science. The feature he wrote on amateur boxing was one of his best, the column that followed even better. He felt there was more to be learned from the struggle than the outcome. He said in defeat the soul is undressed then fitted in threads of truth; in victory it wears the raiment spun from fairy tales.

This felt like a torturous struggle. And yet there was no turning back.

Had to take a chance. Just had to. But when? I waited until the wives paired off and it was just the two of us.

Once sports, politics, and rehashing old war stories from the newsroom were exhausted, it was time to get at why Anna and I traveled from St. Louis to Colorado Springs.

Since this didn't involve Anna or Tim's wife, Patti, I saw no reason to interrupt their conversation. The energy they spent on reminiscing and filling in the gaps created by a ten-year separation was positive proof their friendship was on solid ground. I hoped that Tim and I could be there as well.

I was determined to bring up the press box fiasco but didn't know how or where to begin.

"You know, one of the things I miss most about Cape Girardeau is the Playdium," said Tim, showing no sign of ill will.

"Oh, that was my favorite hangout," I agreed, gently rubbing my chin with thumb and forefinger, a sign we often used during our journalism days to signal a private meeting was in order. "With Beav behind the bar and the locals coming and going, it was *the* place to go to relax," I agreed, surprised that Tim wasn't picking up on the sign.

"We practically wore the cover off the pool table," Tim recalled fondly, showing no sign of catching my signal.

"Yeah, I haven't played in years," I said, feeling like a third base coach being ignored by the batter.

"Oh, I meant to tell you during the phone conversation," he said with a wistful look, "I was watching the Division II national basketball championship game and remembered that great quote from the coach you covered during the Elite Eight. Where was that at? Springfield, Mass?"

I nodded.

"Yeah, Springfield."

"If memory serves me right, the coach was asked by another reporter if, in his wildest dreams, he ever thought he would end up playing for a chance to win the Division II title, and he said, 'Whoa, hold on there. My wildest dreams have nothing to do with basketball.'"

We erupted into the kind of laughter we must have shared countless times when we were journalists.

But when that subsided, we were left with the stark realization that this couldn't be brought up numerous times in the future. Better to be stored in the attic of our minds. It was something we could reflect on quietly but not rely on to fill the gaps of boredom and loneliness that comes with old age. It was good to share that wonderful memory of the past, but now it was time to press on.

Much to my chagrin, I realized that the time spent apart and the betrayal eroded a deep friendship I probably took for granted.

We were essentially starting over. What an empty feeling. Someone needed to break the heavy silence. Tim was always one you could count on to do that. Thankfully, he still had that touch.

"Well, it just so happens I have a new table downstairs," said Tim, leading the way to the basement. "Care to play a game?"

"Sure," I said to the friend I once thought of as my mentor.

When we reached the basement, I could tell they were still sorting through the clutter that comes with moving. Seemed odd since that happened six months ago. Chairs and tables were covered in see-through plastic, and boxes were still unopened. The smell of fresh paint told me they weren't completely settled in.

There was some travel literature, several issues of *National Geographic*, and untidy stacks of books in small clusters along the side wall. One box was marked "miscellaneous junk." I wondered where he kept his awards. None were on display.

Did he still care about that?

"Tim, before we get into a game of pool, I want to tell you to your face how sorry I am about what happened in the press box," I ventured, knowing I was opening a wound that had not healed. "I betrayed your trust, and there's no excuse for that," I admitted. "If you want to pop me in the mouth right here and now, I would gladly take the hit because I deserve it."

Finally, the stoic posture peeled off. Tim's jaw clenched, his brows pinched, and the eyes that were shut tightly popped open as if giving way to a gust of anger he could no longer hold back.

"When I understood what happened, words couldn't describe how damn furious I was," he roared. "I would have slugged you, and yes, you did deserve it. But now that I've had time to think about it, I figure there had to be an explanation for such a stupid thing like that to happen. At this point, I don't really care."

I should have been relieved he was giving me an easy out, but this didn't seem right.

"I *want* to explain," I stressed. "You see—"

Tim held up his hand and continued calmly, "I'm not sure I need to hear it now. It doesn't matter because the new publisher was intent on getting rid of old farts like me. So the disciplinary action didn't have anything to do with the early retirement, if that's what's making you feel so guilty. Maybe it would be better to just let it go."

Perhaps it was the hurt look I saw or didn't see or the gnawing sense of a deteriorating self-image that led me to want to fight for something that once was.

"The truth is I used your position to gain a favor," I admitted. "The sole motivation for getting the press passes to the Cards-Cubs game was getting out of having to pay someone the full amount owed," I explained. "I violated a sacred trust and you paid the price."

Tim reacted the way I hoped he would, dropping the stoic posture and meeting me halfway.

"But why? It just doesn't make sense," he cried, running fingers through a shock of thick black hair. "This isn't the guy I knew in Cape. He never would have done that. What the hell happened to you?"

He still cared enough to question. That was encouraging.

"You're right. The guy you knew in Cape wouldn't have thought of doing such a thing," I admitted. "What I did was as careless and reprehensible as a firefighter dropping a lit match on dry timber."

Tim seemed open to hear me out. This was what I wanted. So why was it so hard? I had to carry it through.

"A lot happened during the downward spiral: bad decisions followed by panic, then a realization that there was no going back to what once was," I said, mindful that I was setting myself up for another fall.

"Tim, the full explanation is complicated," I added, desperately searching for the right words. "I need time to tell the whole story."

He closed his eyes and held both hands up.

"Stop it," he shouted with a look of exasperation. "I didn't invite you into my house to hear you grovel like some shallow, pathetic con artist."

I lowered my head.

"I deserved that," I said. "I deserve that and more. Keep it coming," I urged.

"Oh no, you don't," he declared vehemently. "We're not going there. As shameful as all this is, I'm not giving you the satisfaction of punishment," he continued. "I decided there's no point in holding a grudge. The lengthy letter of apology and phone call were enough. Let's just forget it and move on. I mean, didn't Cookie once say if you spend too much time looking in the rearview mirror, you'll miss what's right in front of you?"

"Yeah, what a wise woman. I ran into her at Broussard's when I went back to Cape Girardeau to talk to you," I said.

With a pensive look, Tim said, "I always thought Cookie would have made an excellent feature story, but when I asked her if she was interested, she said there was too much dark stuff. I never knew if she was kidding about that." What followed was an awkward moment of silence. Tim moved toward the cue rack and reached for a cube of chalk.

"The reason I suggested we play pool is I wanted to tell you away from Anna that she looks great," he said with the same warmth that met me at the door. "Not that she looked terrible the last time I saw her. She sometimes reminded me of a long-distance runner: intensely focused, locked into a conversation with herself, and prepared to endure a long uphill climb. She rarely allowed herself time to kick back and forget the troubles of the world."

"I know," I said with a twinge of regret. "The reason for that is she was trying to keep everything from falling apart while I chased fame and fortune. While I was doing my best to become then next Bob Woodward, she was doing her best to perform as a grade school teacher and overburdened parent."

Tim moved closer and placed a hand on my shoulder.

"Man, it's okay. You don't have to beat yourself up over it," he said with a look of empathy. Then, with a glint of mischief, he added, "I know how you can make amends, though."

"Yeah, how?"

"We're going out to dinner tomorrow night," he said. "When the check arrives, I will be stricken with alligator arms so only one of us can reach far enough to pick it up and insist it's his treat."

"You've got it," I said, feeling relieved. What a brilliant way to resolve this.

"But I *will* take issue over thinking you were going to be the next Bob Woodward," joked Tim. "Would it be so bad having to settle for Bernstein?"

We had a good laugh over that one.

"Seriously, we did some decent work with that series on gangs," I noted.

"Yes, we did," he said solemnly.

"I guess what I'm trying to say is Anna never got to do what she wanted until now."

"Oh, you mean writing grant proposals," said Tim, recalling what Anna told him shortly after we arrived at their home.

"Of course," I said. "Teaching gave her some satisfaction, but she wasn't using everything she had to do the greatest good. That's what makes her feel whole."

"Okay, I get that, but you two seem closer," he said with a searching gaze.

"You're right," I agreed. "After Danny's essay, we became closer as a family, and Anna suggested we start communicating the way we did early on." I noticed a look of doubt.

"You're telling me that an essay by a high school student had that kind of power," challenged Tim.

"It was insightful," I assured him. "He took us back to an understanding of the essence of family by recalling a poignant moment at Circus Flora." I could see he was intrigued.

"Hmm, interesting. Okay, give me more," said Tim earnestly. "Oh, and you can hold the ketchup, mustard, and relish."

He was referring to my tendency toward embellishment on feature stories. He would tell new reporters I had a habit of turning chicken shit into chicken salad.

"You sure you want to hear about it?" I asked. Tim nodded. "This will be an honest account from beginning to end. But it will take a while," I warned. "If you want to know why a powerful wind storm felled one tree yet left another standing, you should go all the way to the roots.

"It's not just a story about Danny's essay. There's Annette's contribution too. She did more for my ability to see than the gifted surgeon who fixed my right eye. And when Anna revealed a secret she held inside for many years, an enormous weight was lifted."

"Wow, you've got my full attention," he declared with enthusiasm. "I really want to hear this. You're here for the weekend. We've got the time. So lay it on me." That was a phrase he often used when I told him about a tip for an investigative story. We were on solid footing once again.

"Okay, well, to tell the story properly, I'd have to go way back, all the way to grade school," I explained. "To know how Danny's essay came about, you'd need to know something about my grade school essay and about two classmates whose ordeals shaped my outlook on class and ultimately race. Then there's this thing my high school football coach called the test. Not the classroom test given after you've had plenty of time to prepare. This would be unannounced and could occur when least expected. He said that in the game of football, like life, there will be a critical moment in which character and mental strength will be measured. The amount of time and effort put into practice will become a factor, but at the end of the day, it's who you are and what you're made of that will determine how well you meet the challenge."

Tim flashed a knowing grin.

"Well, you passed plenty of tests as a journalist. I can tell you that much."

"As it turns out, that wasn't my greatest test," I assured him. "I'll tell the story, and you decide when that was. You *sure* you want to hear all of this?" Tim settled into an easy chair and nodded.

"Okay, I'm going all the way back to the '60s. The country was still reeling from the assassination of JFK, and racial strife was rampant throughout the country. I was still struggling to find a sense of self. I hated the darkness that comes from not knowing."

Tim quickly stood and said, "I could use a beer right about now. Hold that thought."

2

A Grade School Crucible

When I was doing time at Presentation Grade School, Sister Gordiana called my name at the end of class and handed me a sealed note addressed to my parents.

"Don't forget to give it to them," she warned sternly, wagging a bony index finger as crooked as her smile. I recognized the school logo in the top left corner of the envelope: the fleur-de-lis. That meant this was official business.

I remembered hearing that *fleur* meant flower in French and *lis* stood for lily, a symbol of purity.

The contents likely had nothing to do with flowery innocence, however.

I feared the worst yet hoped for the best. After all, didn't I reach the semifinal round in a recent spelling bee? Then again, Sister Gordiana knew what I knew: that I could have won the thing had I not missed on purpose.

I stared at the white envelope with a sense of dread. What if this was another reminder that the signs of loneliness were showing up more frequently and in darker shades of gray?

A similar message came from teachers at Mount Providence, the first school I attended before transferring to Presentation at the tail end of sixth grade. The idea was to give me a chance to meet new kids so I could look forward to seeing them at the start of a new school year. I lacked the guts to inform everyone it didn't matter when I was enrolled in a new school. I had a better chance of playing major league baseball than being lucky enough to fit into a new setting.

Didn't they know the introverted behavior couldn't be helped, no more than you could make Donna Stearns grow or transform Jimmy Davidson into a rich kid?

When my sister Claire saw the note, she broke into laughter.

"What a dope," shrieked Claire, only a year older yet light-years ahead when it came to street smarts. "Are you telling me you didn't even open the thing before you got home?"

After a slight pause, she added, "And what in the world made you feel like you *had* to give it to them?"

When I didn't answer, she shook her blond braids and said, "Shoulda brought this to me. I could have saved you a lot of grief."

I don't know if she learned this from courtroom dramas on television, but Claire knew at an early age that you only admit guilt when you have no other choice. I envied her sense of independence and fearlessness when confronted by authoritative figures.

Cynthia, two years older than me, was more understanding. She was the family referee, doing her best to restore civility before things went too far.

"He didn't know," she said judiciously. "Give him a break."

Cynthia understood that the quarantine I was subjected to via a fenced-in yard put me at a disadvantage, like a runner starting a race long after the gun sounded. She also understood that the death of Ellen, the sister we would never know, was the reason Mom thought sequestering me would prevent pneumonia or any other disease from taking another of her youngest.

What she failed to consider, however, was what that might do to my mental health. The note warned that I was too much of a "happy-go-lucky kid" with no indication of ambition.

Sister Gordiana took me aside one day and said If I didn't shape up, I was headed for years of mind-numbing labor instead of a more challenging career in an office. Sister Gordiana did her best to steer boys away from wanting to drive a truck or dig a ditch, pointing out that these were lesser jobs for folks who failed to further their education beyond parochial high school.

If I was thinking of attending the public school just a few blocks from my house, I was destined to drive a truck, dig a ditch, or both.

"Strive to use your brains, not brawn," she preached, baring coffee-stained teeth that reminded me of a rickety wooden fence that depreciated our modest but well-kept neighborhood.

I was now sure about the direct motivation behind the note. It wasn't that I didn't want to win the spelling bee. I enjoyed working with words and testing my ability, but not in front of an audience. Each stare felt like a burning candle held so close to the face that dripping wax would eventually scald me. The only solution was to take a seat before I made it to the final round. When one of the girls saw how easily I blushed, she nicknamed me Pinky. That made me more self-conscious and sent me deeper into an abyss of introversion.

Pink was also the color of calamine lotion, considered at the time a trusted cure for poison ivy. I only had to look at the dreaded leaf, and it was more layers of calamine.

One summer my neck, arms, and legs were caked in so much calamine lotion, I looked too hideous to be seen in public. It was frustrating. If I wasn't blushing my way into self-imposed seclusion, I was itching my way there.

If I had the nerve to set the record straight in school, I would have admitted my lack of classroom participation and the decision to disqualify myself had more to do with inhibition than Sister Gordiana's assessment that it was due to apathy or lack of ambition.

Sister Gordiana put Jimmy Davidson in a more humiliating position, calling him out in front of the entire class for failing to comply in earnest with the new policy of wearing a crisp white handkerchief in his right front pocket.

This was to be the first of many gentlemanly lessons, and Jimmy was easily made into a poignant example of what could go wrong if anyone gave in to what was deemed mischievous urges.

What Sister Gordiana failed to recognize was that Jimmy was not looking to turn this into a prank.

It was widely known among students in our class that Jimmy's family was poor and could only afford to give him a Kleenex. But Sister Gordiana had a way of casting a cynical eye on events that other teachers would have deemed honest mistakes or moments of innocence. Once she believed a student was up to "no good," a grudge was established, and practically nothing could change her mind.

Thus, to her, Jimmy was trying to parody yet another class exercise, his first Catholic felony perpetrated during the Stations of the Cross.

The traditional Stations of the Cross lesson occurred in the church adjoining the school. It was within the hallowed walls of the Presentation Church that we would learn about the series of fourteen carvings that represented incidents during Jesus's ordeal from being condemned by Pontius Pilate to his crucifixion and burial.

Jimmy rarely participated in class discussions, but there was something about this exercise that piqued his curiosity. When she finished the lesson, Sister Gordiana asked if there were any questions.

In addition to having poor hearing, Sister Gordiana's eyesight was also fading. She slowly gathered her things and was about to lead the class out of the church when Michelle Olson said, with false sincerity, "Sister, Jimmy has a question."

"Oh yes, what is it?" said Sister Gordiana, squinting to find the pale raised arm.

"Um, if Jesus is all knowing and all that, wouldn't he know of a better way to get his message across?" said Jimmy meekly.

Sister Gordiana appeared stunned.

"Exactly what are you trying to say, young man?" she demanded, her hands and head shaking with such force, she appeared on the verge of an apoplectic fit.

"I mean a way that wouldn't hurt so much," he said softly, his determination to complete the student-teacher exchange losing steam. "All that pain over and over, I don't know . . . I just . . ."

Sister Gordiana's withered face puckered further into intense scorn.

"Your parents will hear about this, young man," she declared with quivering lips, fixing her pale-blue eyes on a boy who appeared more confused than ever.

"This is a *Catholic* grade school. We're not here to *trash* religion," she shouted, staring him down as if he were a disciple of Satan.

The decrepit nun went through a similar tirade upon witnessing the Kleenex in Jimmy's pocket.

"I'm sending a note home to your parents *again*," she barked with the glowering finality of a judge sentencing an unrepentant career criminal.

Michelle, who knew how to flaunt silky brown hair, striking facial features, burgeoning breasts, and legs that looked like they could dance all night, found Jimmy's new predicament with the Kleenex amusing, holding her hand against her mouth to keep from laughing out loud.

Paul Biggerstaff's reaction to most anything that didn't feature him was to display a look of pronounced boredom that reeked of arrogance. It started with eyes rolled back, an exaggerated show of annoyance via fingers drumming the desk, then the heavy sigh. The finishing touch would be repeated glances at a glistening gold Bulova watch that looked more expensive than the one my Dad wore to work.

Here was this sharp mind continually dulled by the slow-witted pace of those who inhabited his surroundings.

It didn't take much imagination to see how Michelle and Paul were deemed the school's Barbie and Ken, on display as the ideal couple at every school dance or Elvis movie at the Gem Theater.

In fact, they masqueraded as Elvis and Ann Margret during a Halloween dance that took place in the church basement.

Their costumes looked so authentic, I believed them when they announced they were ordered from a Hollywood movie catalogue.

If any boy other than Paul had the audacity to think he had a chance with Michelle, she would quickly quash that notion, pretending to be distracted by something just beyond his shoulder as he moved into her field of vision.

Paul was so intent on keeping his thick, flaxen hair perfectly coifed, he reached for his comb twenty times a day. When he wasn't preening for his trophy girlfriend, Paul was showing off magic tricks he learned from a professional magician. If there was a chance that a Biggerstaff might be mistaken for a member of the mundane, tricks and strategies had to be formulated to make sure that didn't happen.

The class king and queen set the tone for most events by an expression of approval or disgust.

I found these chastisements by Sister Gordiana confusing. I was taught that the teacher was the wisest person in the room. As much as I was tempted to pretend I was also amused, deep down I could see how my deficiencies as a stranger in a strange land made me as vulnerable as Jimmy.

Students like me, Jimmy, and Donna Stearns were essentially invisible to Michelle and Paul. The only time they did pay notice was when our frailties became material for their amusement.

I was the painfully shy one, Jimmy was hardscrabble poor, and Donna suffered from a physical deficiency that kept her body from maturing. I learned from students who enjoyed feeling superior to Donna that she was as elfin a figure in fifth grade as she was in first.

Her arms jutted out of her body as if she had inherited stunted appendages that forgot to grow.

Although we were linked together by our shortcomings, I considered my condition temporary because my problem stemmed from a lack of emotional growth that could be conquered with experience.

When Jimmy fought back tears upon hearing Sister Gordiana's latest threat, Donna fidgeted with the blue ribbon in her hair and said, "Isn't anybody going to . . . ? Oh gosh, darn."

She began tugging at her blond curls as frustration spread across her pudgy, strained face.

The only other time I had seen a kid look so distressed was when Jimmy was chastised for his curiosity during the Stations of the Cross exercise.

I asked Dad if it was a sin to be poor. He leaned forward with a look of astonishment.

"Who told you that?" he queried with an annoyed expression.

"Nobody, I just sort of guessed it." I finally told him about the ordeal Sister Gordiana forced on Jimmy.

"Maybe you misunderstood," he cautioned. "She's the older nun, isn't she?"

"Yes."

"Sometimes older people get things mixed up, and it comes out wrong," he said with a look of deep concern.

"I happen to know Jimmy's father from church and he works hard," stressed Dad. "He wants Jimmy to get a good education so he can do better. You should know that some people have it harder than others, and if we are better off, we should help those less fortunate when we can. It gives a kind of balance to things."

Much later I decided that given her religious background, Sister Gordiana should have taken Dad's attitude toward the poor. Wasn't this one of their vows? And wasn't Jimmy's question during the Stations of the Cross a teaching opportunity rather than cause for a severe rebuke?

I had to spend some time processing all of this. Eventually I understood that Sister Gordiana was too old to be working with young minds. As one kid put it, "She flat out lost her marbles."

Stories quickly circulated among families and administrators about her emerging senility. With just three weeks left in the spring term, she was replaced by Sister Rose Joseph, who, by consensus, "had all her marbles and then some."

Sister Rose was the antithesis of Sister Gordiana. Her almond eyes were vibrant and alert, holding the attention of the class by rendering it hushed and hungry for the next development of a story she routinely read at the end of class.

Initially I saw her as a welcome relief, a sharp contrast from the nun who instilled fear and loathing with ominous signs of ill will. The corners of Sister Rose's mouth would not twist and writhe and constrict into bitter forms of hatred and discontent.

Gone were the penetrating stares designed to police our thoughts and imaginations. I would no longer have to look at the loose skin hanging from jowls and throat, reminding me of the Thanksgiving turkey. The liver-spotted fingers that pointed accusingly at one student to the next were being replaced by slender digits that would point to information written on the blackboard or encourage student participation.

In addition to a vacation from the harsh reality of Sister Gordiana, however, I wondered if this was an opportunity.

Wasn't I good enough to establish myself as relevant instead of invisible? Not just for the teacher's acknowledgment that I occupied a seat, but to admit to some worth, some promise measured in what I said or did.

Just one look at her searching eyes was enough to embolden my desire to do more than wish.

Her Latin-shaped nose centered exquisite high cheekbones, the nostrils flaring out slightly during a lively class discussion. I imagined her unadorned yet delicately shaped lips as portals to a nurturing soul. When she smiled, her teeth reminded me of the sparkling white keys of the organ in Our Lady of the Presentation Church. Those keys had the power to fill the air with bold strokes of melodic certainty, stemming the tide of despair and loneliness.

The shiny silver cross that hung from her neck sometimes reflected tiny glints of light, lending to her form a quiet mystery that fed my imagination. The black rosary beads seemed stirred into an enlivened energy, click-clacking in a lilting cadence as she darted about the classroom.

There was something compelling about the way she took long strides to the blackboard or moved with urgency toward a student struggling with an assignment. It had this compelling effect of drawing you in and inspiring participation.

How could someone be all of this? I was willing to risk ridicule from my peers to set a plan in motion.

For the first time, I felt like I could relax and focus freely on the lesson at hand. I had a strong will to learn the gospel according to Sister Rose.

I was so spellbound by her wondrous pageantry, I spent hours going over every detail.

Her caramel skin was so pleasant to the eye, so compelling, it knocked Michelle down to number 2.

If Michelle was an early bud just beginning to show signs of blossoming, Sister Rose was in full bloom. I knew I was having what Father Sullivan called impure thoughts, but there was a hormonal army on the march, and I didn't have the strength or will to stop its forward push.

I wondered about the areas covered by robe, tunic, scapular, and cowl. What did her hair look like? Was it long and silky like Michele's? Were her legs as curvaceous as those of the girl who could dance all night? Were her breasts as full and hypnotic as the ones I saw in Johnny Miller's basement? I'll get to that later.

At that point, I knew I would have to settle for her ability to quench my thirst for knowledge.

Her teaching method was perfect for young, inquisitive minds. On her first day, Sister Rose took a deep breath, cast a glance at the shuttered windows gathering dust, and frowned.

"It's stuffy in this room, don't you think?" Some students nodded; others held back, peering intently at Sister Rose's face. Was she setting a trap? I wanted to believe not but still wondered.

"Well, it seems a shame not to let a wonderful spring day come in this classroom," she said with enthusiasm. "Let's open the windows and breathe in some fresh air," she suggested, pointing to students closest to the windows.

Shortly after the windows were opened, a cardinal swept down from a tree, flitted about, then hovered before landing on the ledge. The bird tilted its head from side to side, surveying the contents of the classroom.

"Well, I'd say the cardinal is as curious about us as we are about him," surmised Sister Rose as a warm smile spread evenly across her animated face. "Does anyone know something about the baseball team that goes by the same name? I mean something we might not already know?"

My hand shot up so quickly, I didn't have time to think over what I might say.

"Yes," said Sister Rose. "What is your name?"

"Doug," I said nervously. My heart was thumping so quickly, I thought I might lose my ability to speak. I finally thought of something Dad pointed out one Sunday. "Johnny Keane, the Cardinals manager, is a member of Our Lady of the Presentation Church," I said with halting breath, feeling as though an angel arrived in time to remind me of that fact.

"That's very interesting. I didn't know that," said Sister Rose, nodding appreciatively. "From the look of things, there are others who didn't know that as well," she added, looking at Michelle, who poked Paul accusingly. I thought I heard Michelle demand, "Why didn't you know that?" Paul reacted with a dismissive shrug then whispered something to his sidekick Mike McCluskey.

"Well, Doug, you came up with a very interesting fact," said Sister Rose with a look of approval. "Very well done. We can learn from each other if we're willing to share."

I never heard a teacher say that. I wasn't sure if I should admit that Dad was the one who fed me with that fact or the angel who reminded me. I wanted so much to savor the look on Sister Rose's face and the attention I was getting from the class; however, I decided to keep that to myself. Students sitting at the front of the class were straining to see who had just uttered a fact that impressed the teacher. It was as if everyone wanted to get to know a new kid being introduced for the first time.

If this was an indication of what could happen in the future, I should raise my hand more often.

Unlike Sister Gordiana's austere style of rote learning, Sister Rose employed a method that made participation and learning seem as fun as a trip to the Holiday Hill amusement park.

She handled a student's question as carefully as a jeweler examining a diamond. When she considered the question particularly interesting, Sister Rose would sometimes lean her head back slightly, tuck her delicate hands beneath her white habit, and gaze thoughtfully before speaking.

"Don't be afraid to ask about something, even if it may sound silly," she uttered with conviction. "There are no dumb questions in my classroom. The curious mind needs encouragement and challenge. I want everyone here to know that if they raise their hand, I will get to as many questions and answers as possible. Together we will learn about ourselves and the world around us. Our minds will grow from the challenging work, and I think there should be some fun thrown in there too. Don't you?"

I thrilled at hearing such a passage. She was putting us all on the same level.

Despite being draped in a stiff white habit and black robe, Sister Rose Joseph would be the focus of my imagination the following school year.

"I look forward to seeing all of you in the fall," she said with a soft smile. "Have a wonderful summer, and read as much as you can."

I sensed a transformation. I no longer had to dread how Sister Gordiana's dark, ominous thoughts might continue to stunt any chance at growth.

I was also able to break free from the cocoon of loneliness. Just three weeks before the school year ended, I was befriended by Matt Moreland, who introduced me to games like kickball, dodgeball, and dungeon tag, all played during recess.

"I haven't seen you in the cafeteria," he noted one day as I was headed toward home. I wasn't sure he was talking to me until I noticed there was no one else around us.

"Yeah, I only live a few blocks away," I said, uncertain what he wanted.

"Well, if you get back early enough, you might want to join us. We usually have an odd number of players, so one team has to play shorthanded," he added. "We could use another player. You're Doug, right?"

"Yeah, how did you know?" I said, surprised anyone would know my name.

"You knew about Johnny Keane," he beamed. "I'm a huge Cardinals fan. My whole family is. I told them what you said, and they seemed thrilled to know that."

"Anyway, I'm Matt. Hope to see you at recess. If you get there early enough, I'll make sure you're on our team."

Holy sweet Christmas, finally someone stood before me real as a holiday gift, holding the lost key to the backyard gate.

Just like that, I went from being invisible to having an invitation to be a part of something that looked fun. No one told him to be kind to me. His offer seemed as natural and simple as a pitcher throwing a ball to a catcher to start a game of baseball.

Then again, maybe Matt extended his friendship out of pity. At this point, it didn't matter. My desperation for friendship of any kind with a nonrelative forced a word of assent to the tip of my tongue as fast as a bullet blasting through the chamber of a gun.

"Sure," I said, trying not to sound overeager. Once I began the game, I tried to observe how others were behaving to get some idea what I should do. I didn't want to admit I didn't have a clue how I was expected to contribute.

Matt used his tall, lanky frame for both speed and power. He was no stranger to the art of deception, feinting and changing direction with the ease and confidence of a sleek animal who held himself to a level of excellence that elicited respect from both his peers and adversaries. There also seemed to be a code of conduct that would take some time to understand.

The school yard, which doubled as the church parking lot, was to Matt what a canvas is to an artist: an outlet for creative expression and release. His athletic instincts and understanding of how to play were so sophisticated, he knew when to lead and when to move to the periphery to complement someone who was having a better day. It was all about the team and what could happen if a collection of diverse personalities and multitiered levels of skill blended into unrelenting purpose and precision. This group was committed to squeezing success from whatever strategy or selfless effort was necessary. Slowly but surely, we secretly came to know there were subtle nuances that led to the climactic moment that made the difference in the score.

Over time I would understand two kinds of friendship: ledger and open. The ledger friend provides favors and compliments as if they were bank notes to be paid in kind. A loan from a ledger friend might come with more strings than a marionette.

An open friend offers comfort and companionship because it's what's needed, not because it translates into another IOU. An open friend considers trust and loyalty necessary elements of the bond. A ledger friend figures he has already paid for trust and loyalty. It's right there in column three, line eight.

In all my hours spent in the classroom, nothing came close to teaching me all of that.

When we played dungeon tag, it was important not to lean too far from side to side or duck too low to elude the gauntlet of outstretched fingers and hands attempting to score a tag because loss of balance meant a trip or slide onto the asphalt. This would result in scraped knees and dreaded holes in our navy blue pants. My parents were only able to afford two pairs of the uniformed pants and shirts, which were sold at just one store in the neighborhood: the Chix Shop.

Matt was among the few who didn't fear playing all out because he was skilled enough to avoid sudden slides or falls. Like Matt, Jimmy had amazing body control and was so small and light, it was difficult to catch up to him or get close enough to plant a tag. But just two consecutive trips home with holes in his knees was enough to force Jimmy to declare himself ineligible from future playground games.

"Mom ran out of patches," he lamented.

I could see I was not nearly as good an athlete as Matt, Jimmy, Paul, or Mike. In fact, most of the boys in our class were much more fluid and adept at scoring points or playing defense, but I was determined to improve, studying their moves and paying strict attention to detail. If I couldn't help the team, I didn't want to hurt its chances of winning.

Through Matt, I met Bobby Doyle and Scott Sanders. To them, I was a new player with Matt's stamp of approval. Nothing else needed to be said. I liked the simplicity of their unwritten code of conduct. Advancing the friendship beyond the athletic arena was up to me.

I envied their ability to cavort about without worrying what others thought of their behavior. I admired the unconditional camaraderie they shared and wanted to be considered a full-time member of their inner circle.

My days at school were usually tempered by caution and fear of ridicule after making a misstep or uttering something inappropriate—hardly the stuff of happy-go-lucky.

When I was in a game with my new friends, however, I began to feel less constrained. My hope for a positive change was gaining momentum. I dreamed of the day I would shed the constraints of self-conscious thought and begin to enjoy carefree days at school.

I bolted down my lunch as quickly as possible to allow more time to join Matt, Bobby, and Scott during recess.

When I arrived at the play area, the teams were already being picked. I could tell from Matt's troubled demeanor that something was holding up the selection process.

"Shoot, we're gonna be a player short today," he complained, counting the number of players again to make sure he was one short. Jimmy's parents told him he was no longer allowed to play, but he always lingered by the fence to watch the game.

When he was sure we would be short, Matt looked toward Jimmy and said, "You sure you don't want in?"

Jimmy shook his head reluctantly and replied, "I can't. My mom would kill me if I came home with another hole in my pants."

Paul tried to get the game started before Jimmy could be persuaded to betray the promise he made to his mother.

"Let's go," shouted Paul indignantly. "We'd kick your ass with or without that little turd."

Jimmy reacted quickly to the insult, pulling up from his passive stance and leaning on the balls of his feet. He was not going to let this demeaning remark go unanswered. The pallor that made him appear sickly at times was now replaced by a sudden infusion of bloodred anger. The reflexive ire hardened into a scowl. His green eyes intensified into hot emerald beacons, pregnant with purpose and cunning as they slowly surveyed the terrain and those who occupied it. It was like watching dying embers hungry for life catch a spark and grow quickly into a roaring, unrelenting fire. The transformation may have been triggered by insult, but it was growing stronger by something else. Was it a battered pride that needed to set things straight? A desperate need to climb out of Sister Gordiana's caste system?

For all the punishment he had to endure in the classroom, there must have been a longing to reverse the order of the day and turn abuse and scorn against his detractors, to feel the balm of catharsis administered by his own hand.

"I'm in," he declared, quickly joining our team. Before we could begin, however, Jimmy had a suggestion. "Instead of the normal game of dungeon tag, let's play kill the man with the ball," he challenged, directing a hard gaze at Paul.

"Oh, come on, that game has been outlawed by the principal," protested Paul.

"So you're saying you're afraid of getting caught?" replied Jimmy with a taunting stare. "Okay, let's play tag the man with the ball. How's that?" Jimmy said sarcastically, as if pacifying a spoiled child.

Everyone agreed to the amended form. The game would be played much like rugby. A player could pass the ball laterally, but we also allowed forward passes. The team with the ball would attempt to advance it from one end of the yard to the other without any player being tagged or having it pulled or punched from his grasp.

Jimmy seemed determined to make a statement. His spindly legs had a noticeable spring to them. From the outset, Jimmy looked like a seasoned athlete stretching and doing short hops to test his vertical leap.

When Jimmy was of an even temper, he was among the better players on either team. When he was upset over a misdeed or slanderous remark, however, he had the ability to take over a game. He found holes where none appeared to exist, causing both Paul and Mike to miss by a considerable margin. Jimmy would get close enough to make them look at his toothy grin, then flit away in an effortless motion, daring them to come up with a plan to tag him out.

"Catch me if you can," he taunted, holding the ball away from his body then quickly pulling it back before anyone could wrest it away from him or tag any portion of his diminutive frame. When he made Paul or Mike miss, Jimmy brandished a maniacal grin. I had never seen him this euphoric.

It was as if he were blessed with wings and the grace of a gazelle, threading his way in and out of danger at will.

Although it looked like Jimmy could win the game single-handedly, he was intent on making this a team victory. He would signal with his free hand whether he wanted Matt, Bobby, or Scott to look for a long pass, a short pitch, or a lob over the hands of a defender. Their ability to run just far enough or at the proper angle to give Jimmy room to thread a pass without interference was uncanny. When Mike and Paul found ways to cut down the angle, Scott and Bobby set screens to allow the runner with the ball to pick left or right for his escape route.

The marked contrast of fluid figures passing, leaping, and snaring the plastic ball in a precise yet unpredictable pattern against flailing arms and legs that looked like they were made of rubber made for comical theater.

When we took a short break, Mike and Paul huddled for what looked like a plan to exact revenge.

The lopsided display of talent against a group that appeared clueless caught the attention of several students, who stopped what they were doing to form an attentive audience. Donna was among the students urging Jimmy on, pulling the ribbon from her hair and waving it above her head, finding immense pleasure in his ability to frustrate Paul and Mike. Did Jimmy have what it takes to dethrone a king, to emasculate Ken in front of Barbie?

After a brief period of rest, the game resumed with Jimmy looking like he could dominate all day. Then something strange happened. Mike and Paul allowed Jimmy to dance past them without any attempt to tag or impede his progress. They wore impish grins as they continued to let him score points without the least resistance.

Then suddenly they came after him from both sides and had him trapped against the chain-link fence. When Jimmy attempted to run past them or find a teammate to pass to, they clasped hands to form a human hurdle. He leaped into the air and appeared about to clear their arms when they raised the hurdle slightly, tangling Jimmy's feet enough to send him tumbling backwards against the fence.

There was a moment of inchoate recognition in the arms outstretched and legs splayed, the tortured face, visceral images of something more real than anything I'd found in a book or movie. My eyes were riveted on the pain that seemed everywhere, beyond skin and bone to something I didn't even know, yet sensed I would know if I met someone who could interpret or explain it all. Maybe it was Matt. Or Dad.

I heard a loud voice—something about giving help. I felt as if I left then came back to another scene despite being there all along. Was I alone with these thoughts? Did anyone else sense this meant something other than what it looked like? Scanning the faces and trying to make sense of it all made my throat constrict and my mouth feel dry. I wanted to say something but felt powerless to do so. My legs felt rubbery, about to give way if I moved too quickly. I felt dizzy and scared. This was swallowing me up the same way the fenced-in yard had a hold on me.

Perhaps the others were more focused on the moment.

I closed my eyes then opened them quickly to refocus to find something positive from Jimmy's fight. I did see that Jimmy managed to keep from ripping any portion of his pants or sustaining an injury.

Mike walked up to Jimmy and extended his hand. Jimmy appeared wary of Mike's intent but offered his hand to be lifted. Mike pretended to miss the hand and ripped the left pocket off Jimmy's shirt, thereby sending Jimmy back to the ground.

The audience issued a collective groan as they watched in disbelief at what was an obvious act of malice.

"Oh my god, my mom's gonna kill me," cried Jimmy.

"Hey, my hand slipped," said Mike to the group of students voicing their disapproval. Paul pushed Mike aside and addressed the students who were decidedly behind Jimmy.

"Mike, what are you doing?" said Paul, shaking his head and bunching his lips. "This is a worthy opponent. We don't treat strong players like this. Here, let me help you up," said Paul, leaning down to grab Jimmy's hand.

Jimmy recoiled, appearing confused.

"Hey, wait a minute, where's my watch?" shouted Paul. When he moved toward Jimmy a second time, he pulled the disoriented figure close to his body and brushed his hand against the right shirt pocket that was still intact. "Why, this creep stole my watch," accused Paul, fishing his Bulova watch out of Jimmy's pocket. Jimmy couldn't believe what he had just witnessed.

"I swear I didn't take that," screamed Jimmy.

"Let's pants this creep," shouted Mike. Mike, Paul, and a few others overpowered Jimmy and pulled his pants down. His bone-white buttocks were bared to the entre school. The look of anguish on Jimmy's face was so intense, I suddenly got why he posed the question that infuriated Sister Gordiana during the Stations of the Cross.

"Whoa, he doesn't even wear underwear," shouted Paul.

"Well, what do you know about that." Tears welled up in Jimmy's eyes as he pulled his pants back up and ran until he reached home. Matt told Sister Rose that Jimmy was ill and had to go home. The excuse was allowed and that was the end of it, but there was no end to the look of defeat on Jimmy's face. Watching Jimmy ascend to such magnificent heights only to plummet once again caused a leaden sadness to descend on the core of my being, forcing some difficult realizations. Courage and talent don't always get their just reward. As much as I wanted to come to Jimmy's aid as Dad suggested, I didn't have the goods to enter that arena.

Matt waited until school was out and moved to within an inch of Mike's face.

"You ripped that shirt on purpose, and Paul planted that watch on Jimmy," screamed Matt as a vein in his neck appeared on the verge of bursting. "You know Jimmy can't afford to get another shirt. You've got enough shirts to last two weeks. You owe Jimmy a new shirt."

Mike didn't back away from Matt, matching the intense stare with steely dark eyes and fists clenched so tightly, they were turning white. The intensity of Matt's anger was evident in the swollen neck vein that looked like it might pop.

The scene came back to me when I saw two boxers on television glaring at one another during a weigh-in, each determined not to blink first.

I feared a fight would erupt at any second. Someone must have urged Father Sullivan to come to the school yard because he reached the two and broke them apart before a fight could erupt. They muttered something to each other and slowly walked away.

Nothing more came of the incident. At least that's what I thought until I noticed that Mike McCluskey was absent the next two days.

We were told he was sick, but I suspected he didn't want to face Matt. I asked Matt if he challenged Mike to a fight after school.

"He was supposed to meet me at Home Heights Field, but he chickened out," said Matt with an even tone. Nothing more was said about the incident. And Jimmy never played in another game from that day forward.

But everyone except Jimmy knew who stood up to Mike McCluskey, who quietly placed an envelope on Jimmy's desk, presumably payment for a new shirt at the Chix Shop.

The first thing Jimmy noticed was the names inscribed in the upper left corner of the envelope: Biggerstaff, Sanger, and White, attorneys at law.

He stared at the envelope grimly as if it contained the power to do him more harm. He pushed the envelope across his desk and let it fall to the ground then stuffed it inside his desk. Jimmy's family moved away from our parish in the summer. He would never benefit from the lessons of Sister Rose.

I knew I didn't have the courage or conviction that Matt displayed that day, but I could learn plenty from this group via osmosis.

I vowed to work hard to elicit sunny predictions from Sister Rose and find ways to score points for my team at recess. I spent the summer searching the library for books that would make me look smart in front of my sixth-grade teacher. I read Harper Lee's novel *To Kill a Mockingbird* cover to cover. I also read short stories by John Steinbeck and Eudora Welty. Mindful that they were celebrated authors, I knew they were offering stories that could teach me about life. Unfortunately, my lack of personal experience kept me from fully appreciating much of what was being presented.

The final days of August couldn't come soon enough for me. I was so enamored with Sister Rose when the fall term finally arrived, I raised my hand as many times as she posed a question, sometimes not even sure what the answer was.

A phrase she used more than once piqued my curiosity. It came up when a student asked Sister Rose how she knew she wanted to be a nun.

"It's been my calling since I was a young girl," she replied with a thoughtful gaze. "I knew I wanted to serve God with the talents he gave me. Teaching is my way of achieving that." After a slight pause, she added, "You will discover your own calling. It's just a matter of time before you know what that is." I wondered deep into the night what my calling would be. Could I be as sure as Sister Rose that it would allow me to do some good?

My grades improved dramatically, and so did my self-esteem. I now knew I was not as stupid as Sister Gordiana made me feel.

Dad rewarded my scholastic improvement with a new pumpkin-colored baseball glove and black bat. When I asked about an inscription inside the glove, Dad thought I was being funny.

"It says it's made of horsehide," I noted. "How much hide did they take from the horse to make the glove?"

"You come up with some good ones," he said, poking his head out of the sports page with a wide grin.

The bat and glove were timely gifts, coinciding with a dramatic achievement by the St. Louis Cardinals, who clinched the pennant on the last day of the regular season. Sister Rose announced to the delight of everyone we would be allowed to watch the 1964 World Series between the Cardinals and New York Yankees on a black-and-white television.

If a test existed on Cardinal baseball, I felt confident I could ace it. I recited the lineup as if the players were part of my family: Tim McCarver behind the plate, Bob Gibson on the mound, Bill White at first, Julian Javier at second, Dick Groat at shortstop, Ken Boyer at third, Lou Brock in left, Curt Flood in center, and St. Louis native Mike Shannon in right field. These were the underdogs in a David-versus-Goliath struggle. Villains, like Tommy Tresh and Joe

Pepitone, constantly expelling portions of chewing tobacco from the corner of their mouths, were aptly clad in pinstripes, looking like a kinder version of prison uniforms I'd seen on television. I found it difficult rooting against Yankee third baseman Clete Boyer because his brother played for the Cards. I could never despise Roger Maris or Mickey Mantle. Maris broke Babe Ruth's home run record with 61 in 1961. And Mantle was, in Dad's mind, among the finest "pure" hitters he ever saw.

I could have expounded on all of this if Sister Rose had only called on me when it came time to talk about the day's event. Instead she called on Paul, whose father took him to at least a dozen Cardinal games each season.

When he was finished reciting the lineups and statistics I didn't even know, I seethed with envy.

Michelle seemed to take delight in my jealous reaction.

"Of course, they weren't always called the Cardinals," stated Paul with didactic smugness.

"Is that so? What were they called?" said an engrossed Sister Rose.

"The Perfectos," uttered Paul.

"But that was only for the 1899 season. The owner changed the uniforms to a shade of red someone thought looked like a cardinal. The name stuck with fans and sportswriters, so the owners changed the name of the team to the St. Louis Cardinals."

"Oh, that's most interesting," said Sister Rose, visibly excited over such a revelation. "Very well done, Paul."

"This is going to be a very good class to teach," she beamed. "All of you have so much interesting information to share."

Just before he raised his hand, Paul leaned over to his friend Mike McCluskey, who whispered something that made them both brandish knowing grins. Mike was one of the best athletes in school and usually found a way to play against Matt's team. Mike's father was a good-enough baseball player to reach Class AAA before a back injury ended his career with the Chicago Cubs. I wondered if perhaps Paul benefitted from the information Mike whispered to him.

Eventually I got past that. I could take comfort in the fact that I now had real friends instead of imaginary ones, and Sister Rose was the best teacher I ever had.

Sister Rose inspired me to reach beyond the classroom for learning and achievement. When she announced that we could become altar boys if we memorized a series of Latin phrases, I did so with a fierce determination. For Sister Rose, I would have memorized the phrases in pig Latin. That I would have to get up early enough to serve the 6:00 a.m. Mass didn't deter my commitment to earn high praise. Mom saw this as a precursor to the priesthood. Perhaps Mom thought the sequestering period kept her son especially pure for the teachings of the Catholic church.

The first time I tried on the uniform altar boys were required to wear while serving Mass, it felt like something I'd wear for Halloween. The surplice, a wide-sleeved white smock with a plastic collar, was a vestment worn over a black cassock.

The vestments and sacred vessels, like cruets, were kept in the sacristy, a room adjoining the sanctuary.

To Ben Bernanski and Tom Costello, however, the sacristy often served as a staging area to test comedic material. When Ben said, "Hey, guys, check this out," you knew something funny was afoot. Ben seemed an average kid until he played the comic in his surplice and cassock. Then he demonstrated some athletic ability, pretending to walk unsteadily with an exaggerated pigeon-toed gait, flapping his arms like a crazed chicken. The altar boys who witnessed the scene burst into laughter, then covered their mouths upon remembering where they were.

I envied Ben's ability to capture an audience with his imagination so quickly and with such aplomb.

Tom, who was tall and lanky and had a neck that stretched like a periscope, served as lookout while his sidekick performed before other altar boys. If the church was a place for religious theater, the sacristy was Ben and Tom's backstage area. Just as Father Sullivan was making his way into the sacristy, Tom signaled for Ben to abruptly end his skit, and no one faced reprisal.

Father Sullivan must have caught on to the ruse, however, because he made sure Ben and Tom never served a wedding or funeral Mass together.

I became immersed in the rituals of serving Mass, like ringing the little bells during consecration and holding the gold plate during communion to catch any of the thin paper wafers dispensed during communion that might fall.

I didn't know the meaning of most of the Latin phrases I recited, but I enjoyed the sounds made when the words rolled off the priest's tongue.

"In nomine patris et spiritus sancti" was easy to figure out because it was recited while the priest made the sign of the cross. One of my favorite, both to listen to and for its meaning, was "agnes dei, qui tullis peccata mundi, misere nobis." The translation is "lamb of God who takes away the sins of the world."

I sensed I was becoming a part of something important and took pride in carrying out these assignments with the poise demonstrated by the older altar boys. I enjoyed serving wedding masses because there was usually a tip of a few bucks given by the best man or bride's father to each altar boy and a larger tip to the priest. During funerals, however, there was only one payment, and that was given solemnly to the priest.

My next funeral, I was paired with Tom Costello. When Tom was not with his sidekick Ben, he seemed like a different person. Instead of working a comedy routine, he was more likely to indulge his curiosity.

Tom focused on the polished brass vessel suspended by chains used to slowly swing over a casket. The holes in the vessel allow incense sprinkled over charcoal to shoot upward, giving the ceremony the necessary effect for a final prayer to the dearly departed on his or her way to heaven.

I will never forget Tom accidentally spilling lit incense in the back seat of the limousine as we were being transported to the grave site. He told me he wanted to know what it smelled like up close, so he lit the charcoal in the car and appeared panic-stricken as he searched frantically for the loose ember.

"I've done it now. Oh, I've done it now. We're in trouble," he whispered, his face strained with intense anguish.

Luckily, Tom quickly folded his handkerchief and scooped up the ember then deftly dropped it out of the window before it could burn a hole in the upholstery. It did leave a noticeable smell, however. It reminded me of burned wood.

When Father Sullivan asked on our way back from the funeral if we smelled "something funny" coming from the back seat, I feared he knew what happened.

"The incense did have a funny smell today," said Tom cautiously.

"Yes, I'd say it was a different kind of aroma," said Father Sullivan, who appeared to send a sly wink in my direction. "That reminds me. I need to clean out the fireplace before winter."

Moments like those seemed gift-wrapped in innocence and would have given me a story to tell. But Tom made me swear I'd never let another soul in on his embarrassing mishap, so I kept quiet to make good on my promise.

I continued to serve mass as well as funerals and weddings, picking up a few dollars for the effort. It wasn't the money as much as the thought that I was able to generate income on my own. What lingered, however, was the notion that someone could be so bold in one setting and so timid in another. I figured guys like Tom Costello needed an accomplice to pull off acts of daring.

Neither Tom Costello nor Tom Bernanski stood out at the server's picnic, however. That distinction went to Tony Campisi. It was a tradition for the church to treat its altar boys to a summer picnic and pool party at the seminary located a few miles from Presentation Church. A featured part of the year-end ritual was Tony demonstrating spectacular dives, all of which appeared skillful yet effortless.

Although he was studying to be a priest, Tony agreed to participate in the server's picnic as a lifeguard. I could see how his olive skin afforded him long hours in the sun, giving him the look of a bronze Olympian. When he stood motionless on the diving board, the well-defined muscles in his legs and back flexed slightly then glistened as if on cue.

The hushed respect that preceded each dive, like a golf audience reverently awaiting an important putt, was broken by a shout of "Did you see that?" or "Wow! He's amazing."

Even the sun seemed to pay its respects by poking out of thick clouds in time to cast an intense spotlight on the main event.

The dives were executed, from launch to entry, with the precision of a gifted athlete, causing a slight splash that sounded like cloth being quickly torn. I wondered why he would trade the priesthood for a more celebrated life in sports.

At first, I was reluctant to attend because I couldn't swim, but some of the altar boys said the pool was shallow enough to stand with your head above water, and I eagerly welcomed any chance to blend in.

Since this was a private pool, there was nothing to indicate how deep the water was. I assumed it was the same depth from one end to the other.

When I jumped in, however, I sank to the bottom like a rock.

When you're falling, uncertain of when you will touch a solid surface, panic takes over.

The brain doesn't function by taking sensory data and assessing how to proceed. This is unfamiliar territory.

The only chance you have is to follow the instinct to survive. The brain is saying oxygen. Got to get oxygen. Where is that? Where water isn't. But I'm not on solid ground yet.

Was I dreaming? When I finally landed on the bottom, I had the answer. I was confronting a reality I'd never known.

I couldn't scream at the arms, legs, torsos casually moving about not far from where I landed. They seemed unaware that I even existed. I saw someone bounce up and down and decided to do the same until I could launch myself toward the surface.

Each time I surfaced, I could see stretched-out faces that appeared to be laughing hysterically. The longer I tried to scream for help with unintelligible shrieks of "Glub," "Hallub," "Someblub," and "Ohmylubblub," the laughter grew more intense and my hope of survival diminished.

No one could hear any plea for help when I was underwater, but I did make a desperate request to the being I was told had a higher power than any of us.

The only human who understood that I wasn't fishing for laughs was Tony, who dove into the water and grabbed hold of my chest. As he was pulling me toward the surface, I was so disoriented, I began to flail my arms and push against him.

"Relax, I'm here to help you," I heard him say repeatedly.

Fortunately for me, he was strong enough to overpower my resistance and pull me to the shallow end of the pool. I was so embarrassed, the only thing I could think about was going home. Here was Pinky blushing in front of another crowd.

Before I could get up, Tony leaned over me and said, "You okay?" I nodded sheepishly and attempted to rise. My legs buckled, and I fell down. I expected more laughs but heard none. Tony extended his hand and helped me up. Before I could separate myself from the crowd, he said, "If you were searching for a way to heaven, you were going the wrong way."

The group of servers erupted into laughter. I could tell they were not laughing at me but appreciating the wit of my savior. I guess it was Tony's way of mitigating some of the shame I was feeling by sprinkling humor on it. The timing had the effect of lightening the weight of my despair.

I never said anything to my sisters or parents about the incident. However, I continued to think about the humor Tony spread over an incident I wanted desperately to get past. That was another skill I didn't know he had and helped explain why he reminded me of Father Sullivan. They both had a talent and genuine desire to help folks who couldn't fend for themselves. They knew how to deal with a troubled soul.

That night I thought about what it felt like to be at the bottom of the pool with muffled laughter hovering above the surface. It was like a liquid vault separating me from the outside world, threatening to take away my air supply. I thought I was waving goodbye to my family.

The vivid memory from that experience was strong enough to return in nightmares for years to come.

I didn't have a sense of what death was like or how close I came to dying. But the thought of that day without Tony Campisi scared the hell out of me.

Despite several attempts to learn how to swim as an adult, I never got over the fear of drowning.

When I drew the assignment of serving mass for Monsignor Marshner, I became confused about a ritual that was never explained during my training. Monsignor Marshner told me to pour wine from the cruet into his chalice until he lifted his little finger. This was the signal to stop pouring. I poured until the wine was at the brim before I saw his signal to stop. This left no room for the water in the other cruet.

He didn't just sip the wine like Father Sullivan. Monsignor Marshner guzzled the wine so quickly, his face flushed purple in seconds, the abrupt discoloration highlighting broken blood vessels around the cheeks.

My only reference to that was when Uncle Harry knocked back several drinks during a Christmas party at a relative's house. However, I never remember Uncle Harry's face turning a dark shade of purple.

Matt, who was my serving partner for this mass, had a troubled look.

For some reason, I was scheduled to serve several masses with Monsignor Marshner. After a 6:00 a.m. Mass, he seemed unsteady on his feet and welcomed the first chair he could find.

"I'm a little tired from reading scripture last night," he said. I discarded my cassock and surplice and was ready to leave when he stopped me and asked if I liked playing pool.

"Pool?" I said, instinctively searching for a way to mask my confusion.

"Yes, you're familiar with the game, aren't you?" he said, appearing annoyed.

"Oh sure," I said, searching for the right answer.

"Well, if you'd like to play Friday night, I could get the woman who works in the rectory to whip up some sandwiches for us."

"Oh sure, sounds great," I said.

"Fine, let's make it seven, and don't be late," he said with a stern look that suggested this would be anything but fun.

When I asked Matt if he thought anyone else had been invited, he appeared alarmed.

"Pool? Are you sure there's a pool table in the rectory?"

"Maybe he meant somewhere else," I said.

"Nah, that's a strange invitation if you ask me," he said. "I'll ask around, but I don't think anyone else was invited to something like that. If I were you, I'd find something else to do."

I wasn't sure how to handle this. I didn't want to make a mistake and ruin my chances of serving more weddings. On the other hand, I knew nothing about playing pool. The situation was resolved by yet another strange request.

Dad told me if I ever found myself trapped in a situation with an adult that was uncomfortable or confusing, I should get away, and he would back my decision.

When Monsignor Marshner told me to dress him before another Mass, I sensed this was not right. I never dressed my Dad; why should I do that for an able-bodied stranger? I left before he could berate me for being insubordinate toward a superior member of the Catholic church and never looked back.

The next day, Monsignor Marshner let everyone in attendance at the 6:00 a.m. Mass know that he was left without a server because "someone in this audience failed in his duties."

I left church and waited in the school yard until class began. I knew if there was ever going to be a note sent home, I had nothing to fear. When Mom asked why I quit, I simply said I got tired of it and wanted to do other things. When she pressed for an explanation of what the other things were, I said, "You know, things." She threw her hands into the air and said, "You try, but where does it get you?"

When I moved on to the eighth grade, my teacher was Mrs. Fant, a woman who wasn't nearly as interesting as Sister Rose. The only noteworthy event of the seventh grade was an essay I presented in front of the class. We were assigned to write about our summer vacation. Most kids penned stories about traveling to states in the

Midwest or beyond. I could only write about taking an excursion on the silver steamship called the SS *Admiral.* The trip, which included an hour up the Mississippi and an hour back, wasn't much to write about. I didn't want to admit that's all Dad could afford.

So I drew upon the creative skills I developed during my cloistered days in the backyard, forming a wild tale with characters and plots more suited for the comics page than the gray shades and jagged edges of life presented in novels. The comics page was my training ground, where larger-than-life characters came alive and spoke to me. They sometimes helped me forget that there were no real friends to talk to. These characters never judged me either. Through them I imagined that one day it would be different. To me, an imagination was as essential as a search light is to a miner.

Part of the assignment was to read the essay aloud.

I pretended my family embarked on an adventurous trip to Las Vegas, Missouri. When I could tell out of the corner of my eye that even Michelle was paying attention, I decided to go off script and sprinkle twists and turns to the plot the way a cook might add spices and herbs to enhance a meal.

Perhaps this would allow me to become more visible and liked beyond the friends I already had.

I was surprised at how easily I could hold their attention with a story that was concocted on the run. All I had to do was keep my eyes trained on the page instead of the audience, focusing on the creative trance radiating from within, and the words tumbled out like clowns rolling out of a compact circus car.

The angel that helped me remember Johnny Keane was granting me comic license.

There were so many students laughing that it took Mrs. Fant a few minutes to restore order. The next day, she summoned me at the end of class. I feared another note was imminent. With a blended look of exasperation and stinging resentment, she pulled out a map of Missouri and told me to point to the location of Las Vegas, Missouri.

"Oh, I guess I made the whole thing up," I confessed sheepishly. "Are you going to tell my parents?"

"No, but don't ever do anything like that again," she said with a trace of anger in her voice. "I was up all last night trying to find that city. If I wanted fiction, I would have asked for it. Next time write the truth. It may not be as spectacular as that story, but if it's real, it will have more meaning."

I was both relieved and surprised at her reaction. I never thought a story as crazy as the one I dreamed up would be mistaken for the truth. Several years would have to pass before I fully understood the best part of her message. The same could be said of how long it took to understand the full impact of backyard imprisonment served at the behest of my mother's unwarranted fears.

As comfortable as I was working with words, math problems were my nemesis. I would run home during lunch and ask Cynthia, who was a whiz at math, to help me solve the problem. Then I returned confident that I could prove I understood the lesson. When I failed to show the same aptitude during class, Mrs. Fant must have suspected someone was helping perpetrate a lie. She had a way of separating pseudostudents from the true learners.

At the end of each month, Mrs. Fant turned each row into relay teams assigned to solve the math problem on the blackboard. Our row would lag when it was my turn because I would use up valuable time struggling to solve the problem. If you couldn't do anything, you were urged to sit down and let the next student give it a whack. Mrs. Fant, perhaps getting even with me for the larceny I perpetrated during the essay assignment, changed the order of desk assignments, putting me last. Sitting across from me was Juanita Stirckland, who was equally inept at solving math problems. If you were dead last, there was no giving up because there was no one to hand the problem to. We struggled to finish the problem. With students screaming and Mrs. Fant casting a wary eye from the corner, I desperately searched for an escape route. My head throbbed, and I thought my heart was going to explode. I finally finished the problem when Matt mouthed out the numbers I needed to solve the problem. I felt like such a cripple that day.

My grades began to slide and stayed on a downward course the rest of the school year, causing Mom to fear the worst.

"Oh, you will rue the day you didn't take all of this more seriously," she chided, still burning over my decision to drop from the ranks of altar boys. I didn't want to know the full meaning of "all of this," so I remained silent while she uttered the familiar rant.

Dad, who assumed the role of good cop in this marriage, did his best to hold his tongue. Much later I learned what kind of childhood Dad had, living with a father who loved alcohol more than providing for a family.

I think Dad was concerned that I might slip back into my introverted ways because he took me aside and told me not to worry. "Enjoy your time as a kid," he said softly. "Think of it as a tall, sweet glass of lemonade on a scorching summer day. There will come a time when there's nothing sweet to take your mind off the punishing days of summer and beyond." He never had the luxury of being a full-time kid. Later, I came to an understanding of what that must have been like.

I rarely sipped from that tall, sweet glass of lemonade.

On the final day of the eighth-grade school year, my last hours spent at Presentation, a few of the rituals that I had grown accustomed to were replaced by Picture Day. The official photographer took many of our yearbook pictures earlier in the semester, but a wave of the flu hit our school hard in the final days of winter, and several students had to reschedule. Their final chance to make the 1967 yearbook was today.

That meant the king and queen, Barbie and Ken, Elvis and Ann Margret, would be unable to hold court in the play yard as celebrities because many of their loyal subjects were awaiting their turn to pose for the photographer.

Without an attentive audience to hang on their every word, the trio of Paul, Michelle, and Mike looked comically out of place, like a cluster of hairs springing up on an otherwise perfectly manicured scalp.

The longer they stood without an audience, the more perturbed they became. Paul repeatedly checked his expensive watch; his brow furrowed deeply as if he was being stood up by someone who agreed to meet him.

As irony would have it, the one person who was receiving any notable attention was Donna, who had befriended a new student named Sandy. Sandy transferred from St. William's Parish earlier in the school year.

Sandy was neither physically challenged like her new friend Donna nor lacking in the confidence it takes to blend into an unfamiliar environment. Although she wasn't pretty like Michelle, Sandy more than compensated with a zesty spirit and sophistication that came across as natural.

In addition to having an engaging personality, Sandy's intellect was such that she appeared to have no peer. Sandy's answers to questions posed by Mrs. Fant and Sister Celine, a visiting nun, were so impressive, they sounded as if she had done extensive research on the subject.

To the surprise of everyone, Sandy chose Donna as her confidant.

I noticed how relaxed Donna appeared talking to her new friend. When they laughed, it didn't appear fake, like the forced chuckles that emanated from the king and queen's circle.

Through Sandy's encouragement, Donna began showing how smart she was in subtle ways, and the two seemed to thrive on their mutual respect and enjoyment of one another.

Donna was now revealing a genuine personality that none of us knew existed. She even appeared to be growing.

The mistake everyone but Sandy made in assessing Donna was thinking that if the body stopped growing, the mind had to be equally underdeveloped.

On this final day of school, Donna was showing Sandy, in ungraceful fashion, a dance she witnessed from a television show called *Laugh-In*. The show featured short skits and one-liners aimed at a young audience. As the camera pulled away from a comic, another camera zoomed in on the background to give viewers a better look at twenty-something go-go girls jumping up and down and gyrating their hips wildly to the beat of a song. The show's dancers demonstrated a form of controlled mayhem, thrusting their arms into the air and jiggling their shapely bodies while inside a gilded cage hoisted above the stage.

Donna seemed to have shed all sense of self-consciousness and fear of ridicule as she appeared to be trying to put out a camp fire with exaggerated jumping and flailing of arms.

This elicited a hard stare from Paul, Michelle, and Mike. It was obvious they didn't appreciate an invisible stealing their thunder. The miffed trio closed into a tight circle and whispered to each other until it looked like someone said something amusing because they erupted into a paroxysm of laughter.

Then Paul slapped Mike on the back and said, "You know what would be funny as hell?" He then leaned back into the circle and whispered something that made Michelle squeal with delight. They walked over to where Donna and Sandy were standing, all three brandishing fake smiles. Mike proceeded to offer what sounded like a compliment.

Then Paul said something with a look of supreme confidence, as if he had made an offer Sandy couldn't possibly refuse.

By now Matt was back from having his yearbook picture taken and was witnessing this rare sight.

"What in the world . . .," said Matt with astonishment.

"Shhh, this is getting good," I whispered. When Donna shook her head and politely declined to give in to whatever request Mike just made, it looked like this might be the end to such an unlikely conversation.

But Paul joined in on the conversation to steer her back into his manipulative arena.

By now Donna looked confused, perhaps wondering why two of the most popular boys in the school would even utter her name in public. Sandy cast a wary glance at Paul, who reminded me of someone on television, trying to sell a product.

When the bell pealed, signaling class was back in session, Donna looked relieved.

The rest of the afternoon was rife with a rumor that quickly spread throughout the school. Through folded notes and ardent whispers, it was revealed that Donna was going to replicate the dance she performed at recess in front of the entire school.

Then another rumor surfaced, indicating that Donna was just kidding and had no intention of shaking her tiny frame before the student body.

Was she, or wasn't she? The buildup was so intense, students speculated with increasing excitement until the bell rang to signal school was officially out for the year.

When I saw Paul and Mike escorting Donna to the front of the church, I couldn't believe it. Sandy trailed them from close range, trying to intervene. However, Mike seemed to keep her from getting close enough to say something to Donna.

Paul and Mike kept Donna busy with praise for her willingness to "have some good, healthy fun shaking that tail feather."

They chose as their stage a buttress that flanked the steps leading to the front door. The concrete section, which usually held a tall stack of newspapers for sale to parishioners as they exited Sunday Mass, was about two feet in height and just wide enough for Donna to do her dance. What sort of story would be told after this was over?

Donna was so short, she had to be hoisted onto the makeshift pedestal. She started out slowly, awkwardly shaking her rear and shoulders the way she did at recess. What started out as a small cluster of curious students grew to a sparse crowd, and in just a few minutes, nearly everyone from the school was closing in on the scene as if it offered the spectacle of a lifetime.

I felt swept up by a surge of energy, like an underwater current that begins to tow you under. It feels too strong to fight, so you succumb to its will. Paul started the chant of *"Go, Donna, go, go, go."* Then it was Mike's turn with *"Go, Donna, go, go, go."* Matt stayed back and watched in detached silence.

By now there was a cacophony of laughing, chanting, and a deafening roar of encouragement from students pressed together so closely, it was hard to identify who was screaming what.

When Donna discovered this was an ugly ruse from the start, designed to humiliate her, she began to sob. A look of intense suffering quickly spread across her tear-stained face. When she tried to step off the pedestal, someone blocked her path.

"Give her room to step down," yelled Sandy, to no avail. "Someone please help her," she cried.

The look of acute pain on Donna's face turned to contorted, sustained anguish as she once again tried to exit the awful scene. She made repeated attempts to find a way out, but the crowd was now so deep and deafening, it created a state of disorientation.

Sister Celine, who was directed to the scene by Sandy, demanded with an intense scowl that we disperse.

"You should be ashamed of yourselves," shouted the nun, who was not much larger than Donna. When I looked around to see if any of the architects of this debacle were still there, none could be found. They fled with impunity.

Sister Celine eased Donna from the pedestal and shook her head when she saw how bewildered the eighth grader had become.

"This is a real person, not a puppet," scoffed Sister Celine in the direction of students who were already separating themselves from the scene. I couldn't get the image of a puppet show out of my mind. Did Michelle, Paul, and Mike really believe they were so superior to us that we were nothing more than puppets on strings they controlled? I walked home feeling ashamed of myself and more confused than ever. I wondered what the trio that instigated the cruel ruse felt. Anything?

When I had years to process what I was taking part in, I realized that there is something unsettling and inglorious about mob mentality. It can suspend inhibitions and any real sense of responsibility just long enough to allow you to take part in what you think is an innocent act.

You don't realize that you're no longer thinking as an individual. You're now thinking as a crowd, the loudest shouts directing the pace and severity of the passion play. It doesn't occur to you at the time that the pain and misery you are inflicting will leave lasting scars. Even though you were taught early on not to abuse an inanimate object, a piece of plastic, wood, or metal, as rudely as you're now treating a human being, you do it anyway. The whole thing is a roller coaster out of control, but you figure, if you're strapped in, you may as well ride this to its conclusion.

I had to come to terms with the fact that I was in the center of that mob ready to urge Donna on until I noticed Matt standing in the back with arms folded in detached silence.

I was no more certain who I was or where I was headed than when I started school there.

When I thought of the future, of what high school would bring, I was reminded of the daunting feeling the first time the Ferris wheel came to an abrupt stop. While the car slowly swayed back and forth from the apex of the metal contraption, my heart tightened, and a temporary feeling of paralysis swept over me. I could only think of what it would be like if the car became dislodged and hurtled to the ground.

Then I noticed Claire, who appeared not to notice my anxiety, leaning back and gazing dreamily at the moon. How could two people sitting just inches apart have such contrasting perspectives?

Life was becoming more complex, and I was having difficulty understanding it all.

As the summer unfolded, however, I still managed to cling to the notion that before long I could return to the happy-go-lucky state I once knew. Was I still innocent enough to warrant a sip or two from that tall glass of lemonade? Something told me those days had already passed me by.

In fact, the longer I had to process what we did to Donna that day, I was convinced we banded together to crush the spirit of an innocent. That meant none of us was a worthy representative of the fleur-de-lis.

I fully understood the meaning of the phrase "guilty as sin." And the image I couldn't erase from memory was the acute pain Donna suffered that day. It would always remind me of the Stations of the Cross and the irony that it would occur before the Our Lady of the Presentation Church.

The very day her personality and spirt rose to new heights was the same day they plummeted to new lows. I was glad that Jimmy Davidson didn't have to witness that humiliating spectacle. He never knew that someone thought enough of him to stand up to Paul and Mike.

Jimmy may have been deemed an invisible, but his character was still as spotless and true as anyone I had met in that school. His soul was far richer than the trio that crushed his spirit. His heart was purer than anyone who deemed him an inferior.

And the only one who stood up for Jimmy on the playground would pay for his courageous act. It wasn't until the following year that Matt told me he was jumped by two guys wearing hooded sweatshirts and ski masks.

"It was when I was coming home from a football game at Home Heights Field," said Matt. "I knew who they were."

"But how could you know when they were all covered up?"

"One of them was wearing a gold Bulova watch," said Matt. "They threw a five-dollar bill at me when I was lying on the ground and laughed, saying, "This should be enough for a new shirt. Clean yourself up. You're a mess."

3

The Art of Transformation in the Twenty-First Century

"Okay, I get the slow start and how the bullying made you more sensitive to the plight of others," said Tim. "That explains why you specialized in feature writing. I even get the origin of your penchant for fantasy over reality and why you improvised on your essay, but is that the full story?" he said with a look of disappointment.

"What about Danny's essay? Is there a title to it?"

"Yes, it's *Two for the Seesaw*," I said. "More about that later. We've only covered the twentieth century. I still need to get into the twenty-first century. And there will be some drifting back and forth, like a seesaw."

I paused then added, "Actually, I thought you would interrupt when I talked about the ledger versus open friendship."

"Yeah, well, I'm hoping that gets cleared up later," he said.

"Let me grab another beer and you can continue," he said. "I could use a beer."

"Bring two," I said.

When he returned, he said, "So that's the beginning of your taste for chicken salad."

"Yeah. So are you ready for the rest of the story?"

"Sure, keep the honey flowing."

Well, forty-five years later, I would have reveled in anyone's assessment that I was happy-go-lucky.

I was reminded of yet another grade school episode as I caught a glimpse of a storefront reflection. Our class was given the run of Holiday Hill. We were rewarded with a bus trip to the park for raising the most money in the school's March of Dimes charity drive.

We could walk free of charge through the Fun House, which contained strategically placed concave and convex carnival mirrors that distorted faces and stretched body sizes to an amusing degree.

The diversion brought such a rush of enjoyment and escape from reality, I wanted to go through a second and third time.

Part of the thrill was knowing that when I went outside, I could morph back into the dimensions that made me normal again. To my delight, this allowed me to invent new characters and mysterious escapades and have full control over the outcome.

The adult storefront reflection elicited a harsher truth, however, revealing a man with a florid complexion wearing a navy jumpsuit and blue baseball cap with a large red *C* stitched a few inches above the left front pocket.

Not exactly the stuff of happy, lucky, or anybody going anywhere interesting. That wasn't always the case. In fact, there were some experiences I wouldn't trade for a winning lottery ticket.

I'm still trying to distill the events leading to a descent not unlike that of a fighter pilot shot out of the sky. The difference between my demise and the fighter pilot's is that I unwittingly supplied the ammunition.

I wondered about this deep into the night. If I brought the character I'd seen in the storefront window into a bar called Smitty's, would the regulars turn it into *Evening at the Improv*?

"So, Doug, which correctional institution did you escape from?"

"Oh no, don't tell me, the Chicago Cubs have new uniforms this year."

Then another "Did the trash truck take off without you?"

And another "Couldn't you at least find something in the Dumpster that fit? Oh, wait, I guess it does fit."

Perhaps the one-liners would continue until I raised my hand to signify surrender.

In this daydream, Bob Haskins, a retired city cop, and Matt Moreland were the only two regulars who elected not to participate in the banter. Bob once told me of all the penalties he was guilty of as a high school and college football player, piling on was not one of them. I considered Matt my best friend, the one who reached out to rescue me from the despair that comes from loneliness.

I reached the pinnacle of success as a professional just a few years ago, as senior publications editor at a university in Ohio. Today I felt lucky to land the job I now held as a driver for the Colonial Bread Company. As much as I hated to admit it, Sister Gordiana's prophecy was dead on.

I couldn't get over losing what I thought would never elude my grasp.

Anna and the kids did their best to encourage me, telling me I could make a comeback, but I knew deep down there was no hope of that happening.

I was disheartened by the image of a once-proud journalist now reduced to bread-truck driver. But that was where I was, and I had to deal with it. I managed to soldier through the remainder of the route then headed to Smitty's.

My anxiety intensified upon seeing the check-engine light on the dashboard. I hoped Matt was at the bar. Perhaps he could ask his nephew Toby to figure out what was making the light come on.

There was nothing extraordinary about the neighborhood bar in terms of atmosphere.

A regular wasn't looking for that. What drew us in was knowing we could be free from the complex web of life for a few hours.

The mahogany section that separated bartender from patron suffered enough wear and broken-glass cuts to show its age and history. The mirror behind the bar looked like it hadn't been cleaned in years. Considering how we looked after pounding down a few beers, maybe that was a good thing.

Jerry Smith, the owner, said he had enough money to replace the tired wood, but then he'd be giving away all that character built up over the years.

"That alone makes it irreplaceable," he joked.

To avoid being the brunt of jokes at Smitty's, I wore a jacket over the jumpsuit. On an August day, the AC was always cranked up too high, so I would use this as an excuse for wearing the jacket.

Matt was sitting hunched over at the bar, his left elbow resting on the *Wall Street Journal*, a publication he trusted for sports features and stock market information. He rubbed his chin then thumb and forefinger. He picked up this habit when he was just sixteen, working at Holiday Hill. His boss, nicknamed Windy, had a habit of rubbing his chin, then thumb and forefinger before counting the money at the end of the work day.

When Matt repeated this ritual during our weekly poker game, it was a sign that his mind was not on the cards he was holding. Something was seriously wrong, either at home, at the insurance company he worked for, or both.

Matt and I got our first real job at Lambert's Farm when we were fourteen. The farm was a twenty-acre stretch of land situated about a mile from the airport. Our job was to pluck tomatoes from a long row of vines for fifty cents an hour. I learned the concept of serving as lookout or "having my back" when Matt covered for me while I was crouched down, taking a crap.

"What's he doin' over there?" queried Ron, the youngest of three strapping Lambert boys more interested in challenging us to a quick bout of "rasslin'" than helping us pick what he called maters. "Oh, looks like he's making sure he doesn't miss any of the low maters that are nice and ripe," offered Matt with a wry grin. "Well hell, then, looks like we've found a gen-u-wine mater picker in that one," shouted Ron. "Yeah, that's for damn sure."

Matt took our friendship to a new level with a noteworthy demonstration of loyalty. For the next few years, I tried to reciprocate but failed.

We played football at Mercy High School. As seniors, Matt was the best running back, and I was the starting left guard. It was Matt's dream to get a Division I football scholarship. He wanted to play for the University of Missouri, mindful of how faithfully his dad and uncle followed the Tigers on Saturday afternoons.

Matt was just 120 yards shy of the leading rusher in the Catholic Athletic Conference (CAC) going into the second to last game of the season.

DeAndres was our next opponent, the weakest team in the conference. Coach Tom Finan had designed a play specifically for Matt to move ahead of the CAC rushing leader, who was finished for the season with a hamstring injury.

The special play was called 47 bootleg sweep. We all knew the ball was going to Matt because 47 was his number.

My job was to block the defender for two seconds then kick out to the right sideline and clear the way for Matt to do his thing. I usually did the job well, but on this day, there was a defensive back who looked so scrawny, I thought I was looking at a scarecrow. My reluctance to overpower the defensive back allowed him to catch Matt's foot. This slowed Matt down enough to enable a linebacker to make the tackle.

Coach Finan pulled me from the game, and I was left to apologize to him and Matt in the locker room.

"No problem, buddy, I'll get it next week," assured Matt, who managed to rush for 90 yards against DeAndres. With just one game left and only needing 30 yards, it looked like Matt was going to realize his dream.

I watched from the sidelines as Matt turned the corner on 47 bootleg sweep. This time, instead of a thin defensive back, a standout linebacker was waiting for Matt.

He stood him up, and a safety went low to bring him down.

The force of the tackle caused Matt's knee to buckle, tearing the anterior cruciate ligament (ACL). Not only did Matt miss out on the rushing title, but the severity of the injury set him back long enough that scholarship offers were rescinded, and his football career was essentially over.

I failed again when I was best man in Matt's wedding. I planned to take the six-hour gap between the wedding and reception to work on my speech. I scribbled notes on index cards to have something to look at instead of staring at a crowd.

I wrote a line, drank a beer, and went back to add more. By the third hour, I became so drunk, I took a nap. When I woke, I went to work to add more lines. What I didn't realize is that with all the drinking and reminiscing with people in the wedding party, I lost track of the original story.

I tried to work on a different speech just an hour before we were due to leave for the reception hall, but everything became jumbled, and I wasn't sure exactly what I would say. The few notes that were legible didn't even make it to the reception hall. When I changed into the tuxedo, I forgot that the cards were in the pocket of a different jacket.

When I reached into the pocket for the cards, they were gone. As I took in the collection of happy faces frozen into heightened anticipation of something memorable about to take place, I felt lost and woefully unprepared. The stark emptiness that comes from witnessed failure is a self-truth you never forget.

I managed to utter something about how great a couple the bride and groom were then spotted Matt and his wife, Cindy, in the crowd. They appeared underwhelmed.

I let my best friend down on one of the biggest days of his life because I was too careless and immature to take the role as seriously as I should have.

I apologized profusely to Matt and Cindy. They did their best to deflect my horrific performance by saying it wasn't that big of a deal. There was no deflecting that look of utter disbelief and embarrassment etched on their faces.

There it was—another rite of passage gone horribly wrong.

It wasn't until I was a journalist that I finally made amends. I was friends with the office manager and found a way to get Matt an appointment to sell the publisher on a group life insurance policy for fifty-plus employees. Matt was so on that day, our publisher decided to let Matt's company insure employees from his entire string of newspapers, which totaled twelve.

"You really outdid yourself on that one, buddy," said Matt, who later told me he was having difficulty making his sales quota that year.

Today Matt seemed deep in thought, his face constricted and his drink untouched.

"I'd buy you a drink, but I don't think they sell alcohol on Planet Zebulon or wherever your mind is," I said, nodding to the bartender Alicia as she placed a beer in front of me.

"Huh, oh hey, Doug, what's going on?" said Matt with a worried look.

"You okay?" I said, hoping he would reveal what was bothering him.

"Oh, uh, sure. Why, don't I look okay?"

"Sure, just checking."

He steered the conversation toward sports, which meant whatever was bothering him could wait for another time.

When we reached a lull in the conversation, I took the opportunity to bring up the car problem.

"Matt, didn't you tell me your nephew Toby is going to school to become a mechanic?"

"Sure, the kid's a whiz already. Why, you got car problems?"

"Well, it's probably nothing major, but the check-engine light keeps coming on. I was wondering if he could look at it and let me know what it would cost to get it fixed."

"Not a problem. I'll give him a call and see when he's got time to do it," he said. "Look, Doug. I'd love to stay here and shoot the breeze, but I've got some things I have to do at home. I will give Toby a call."

"Oh hey, that would really help me out," I said. "Say hi to that wonderful wife of yours."

"Okay, take care," he said barely above a whisper, fishing some money out of his wallet to pay his tab.

Before he left the barstool, however, he pulled my jacket zipper halfway down and inspected the inside.

"I was wondering why you were wearing a jacket on a day as warm as this one," he said dryly. "Were you thinking we'd give you a tough time about that?"

I shook my head and looked down.

"We all know it's just a temporary gig. When you crank out that novel, all will be well, right?"

"Uh, sure. As far as the jokes go, I'm okay with that. I knew the AC would be set on freezing, so I just threw this on to keep from being uncomfortable," I said, reading disbelief.

"Yeah, well, I'll try to remember that's off-limits from now on. Take care, buddy."

I checked to see if any of the regulars I knew were in yet. It was still too early. I ordered another beer and a burger to go then paid my tab and headed to the library. Most times I picked up a magazine or walked through the fiction section to see if any of my favorite authors were on the shelf—anything to fill the time Anna was led to believe was being spent working on a novel.

When she asked about the story line, I said it's bad luck to talk about something before it's finished.

It was in the library that I noticed a mention of Michelle in the theater section of the *New York Times*. She was listed as the understudy in the role of Cassie for the Broadway musical *A Chorus Line*.

The article referred to her as Michelle Sanderson, but I knew that was her married name. She married a playwright who later tried his hand at writing screenplays that would become Hollywood movies. As far as I could tell, Michelle never made a name for herself on Broadway. She eventually settled for a brief role in a soap opera, but I never saw it because I was working when it aired.

I only went to one grade school reunion. There I learned what Donna was doing. She became a research scientist for Abbott Laboratories in Chicago. Paul went on to graduate from Harvard and had plans of getting into politics.

For some reason, that didn't work out. He later became involved in a Ponzi scheme and plea-bargained his way to a two-year prison sentence. Mike went to work for his father at the family sporting-goods store. He later took over the small chain when his dad died of a heart attack. But the business went belly-up during the recession of 2008, and Mike was last seen by Matt at an insurance convention in Tucson, Arizona.

Mike had no interest in striking up a conversation, mindful of what happened when Mercy met Bishop Dubourg High School in a key football game when we were juniors. Mike was the starting linebacker for DuBourg, leading the team in tackles. Despite the game being played in a heavy downpour, Matt managed to run for over 100 yards. One play stood out in Matt's mind because it was the only touchdown scored the entire game.

"Mike was chasing me and had the angle," recalled Matt with a wistful grin. "The defensive backs slipped, so it was just me and Mike. I slowed down then ran toward him instead of away. I did a stutter step to freeze him, and it worked. When he dove for my ankles, I jumped up to let him slide under me and jogged into the end zone. On my way back, I said, 'You need to clean yourself up. You're a mess.'"

As much as I would like to believe I accomplished something as a journalist, Donna and Sandy were the only two able to make the world a better place. Sandy earned a degree in political science from Stanford and joined the Peace Corps after graduation.

Perhaps Donna could find a way to cure a disease. Or Sandy could teach people in some remote region of the world to not only survive but thrive.

I tried more than once to find out about Jimmy. There were rumors he was killed in Vietnam, died of a drug overdose, or committed suicide. I couldn't confirm any of those. All I knew for sure was that his father finally got a better-paying job in Kansas City, and Jimmy earned his high school diploma there. The rest is left to speculation.

The haunting memory of Jimmy remains etched in my mind. The harsh treatment he endured in and out of the classroom at Presentation was unforgivable. If he had benefitted from honest friendship the way Donna and I did, perhaps he could have handled it better and moved on to make a better life. Even Sister Rose arrived too late to save Jimmy from his battered pride and crushed spirit. I fear one of the rumors was true. If so, it's a tragedy that didn't have to be.

When I had time to ponder Jimmy's fate, I was reminded of something Jimmy said while training to be an altar boy. It was the responsibility of the altar boys to extinguish the flame of each candle after Mass. This was accomplished with a small bell-shaped extension made of brass on the end of a pole. At the other end of the pole was a wick used to light the candles.

"You got the power to give light and take it away with the same stick," observed Jimmy.

"Whoever invented that must be a millionaire living in a mansion somewhere. I need to think of something like that. Everybody would be lookin' at me different. And I'd be tellin' them what to do instead of the other way around."

I also heard that Sister Rose left the convent several years after we graduated. I was unable to determine if this was just a rumor or fact. If true, I would have loved seeing the true outline of her body and texture of her hair. Where would she have lived? Was her reason for leaving connected to hormonal urges? Did she find a second calling more powerful than the first? I would always think of her as the first teacher to release me from that terrible vault that kept me so far behind the others.

4

A Past Revisited

I sat in the library parking lot, slowly munching on the burger and wondering when I was going to start on that mythic novel. There were no substantial ideas for a plot or title. That could come at any time. I had to keep thinking.

There were no *National Geographic* or *Smithsonian* magazines available that I had not already read, so I headed home, sucking on a few breath mints to offset the smell of alcohol.

With Anna and Danny on different schedules, we rarely shared a meal. When I was growing up, we always sat down together as a family. We didn't say much, but we kept the routine.

Anna was already asleep on the couch with an open book on her lap. I noticed the title, *Race Matters* by Cornel West. I recalled Anna telling me that West was a guest lecturer when she attended Southeast Missouri State.

I also remember Anna being the first to make diversity seem more a matter of logic than altruism.

"A variety of flowers can spark the imagination more readily than a bouquet of sameness," she reasoned. We compared our parents' approach to race.

"My parents feared the subject of race as if it were quicksand," she said with a trace of rancor. "For them, treading knee-deep into the truth about race was like sinking into a pit they couldn't crawl out of. Better to stay safe with lies they could live with."

No woman had come so close to my heart. I began to wonder if she was the one I'd hope to meet someday. She removed any doubt when we saw each other at a bonfire party.

Conversations filled the air for an hour or two. Then the intermittent chatter subsided, and we looked at each other in a way that seemed to diminish everything around us.

The flames from the center of the bonfire danced wildly before shooting straight up and then settling down as if answering the call from unattended hearts that needed warmth and a nudge.

Her cheeks flushed with a rose-colored brightness that put me in a trance. No poem, song, or sentence could have captured my attention the way her vibrant eyes did at that important moment. They were so alive with intelligence and fervor. I moved closer. She did the same, and before I knew it, we were talking, laughing, hugging.

When we slowly separated, I caught the wood-smoked scent of her hair.

That smell was so alluring, I gathered it in as if it were a waft of rare perfume. My lips moved cautiously toward her face, eager yet careful not to ruin a moment of intimacy the likes of which appeared to hold the promise of something extraordinary. A bittersweet tear found its way to the tip of my tongue. I didn't care what was going on around us. There was the fire. There was us. We were where we needed to be.

We leaned into each other with what felt like exhausted breaths. I was relieved that the lonely journey was not only over but about to be replaced by something exquisite. Parched souls were about to drink from the well of ardor. It was only a matter of time.

That was then. This was now.

I studied Anna's face as she slept, her hands firmly atop the book as if there was some need to protect it. The twitches and jerks of the head and body were signs of a bad dream.

"Honey," I said, nudging her until she woke.

"Oh, I drifted off again," she murmured, looking like she pushed herself too hard in the gym.

"Isn't the book very good?" I asked, helping her up.

"It's interesting. It's what I picked for the book club to read this month."

"I don't know if they'll like it, but it should spark some lively conversation. For now, I think I'd better get some sleep. I'd like to read it when you're done."

"Thought you might," she said, unable to stifle a yawn. "I've got to open the community center tomorrow."

After Anna retired from teaching, she became a volunteer at the community center a few days a week. She helped families with children who had difficulty reading.

Mindful of how much Anna hated the stale smell of alcohol on the pillows, I took time to brush my teeth and rinse twice with mouthwash before going to bed.

"I put the tax receipt on top of the fridge," she said.

"Oh yeah. Thanks."

I forgot about the notice for license renewal. I only had a few weeks to get the car inspected. It would fail if the check-engine light kept appearing. I didn't want to bother Anna with that problem as well as how much I was losing at the poker table lately. She had enough to deal with at work and home, now that she was making sure the bills were paid on time.

It occurred to me that since she was handling finances, she would notice withdrawals that didn't line up with the amount owed on bills. I had to tell her.

"Nothing to worry about, but the check-engine light came on today," I said, doing my best to sound casual. "Probably something minor."

"Just take it to Len's," she said.

"Yeah, I could do that, but Matt's nephew Toby is studying to be a mechanic," I noted. "I might want to let him have a crack at it. Could save us a lot of money."

Anna bunched her lips and said, "The last time you tried that, it ended up costing us twice as much. We're not rich, but we're doing okay. You deposited the bonus from the last paycheck, didn't you?"

"Oh, that reminds me, I'll do that today," I said, not knowing how I was going to deposit money I lost at the poker table. Maybe Matt could give me another loan.

I went back to the book she was reading to look at the dust jacket. This was the kind of book neither of us would have seen in our homes growing up in St. Louis. Our parents treated race the way one would avoid an embarrassing secret. The less said, the better. It wasn't that they had developed strong convictions through experience. Rather, the bigotry they knew was from their parents and the environment they grew up in. They lacked the inclination to openly question or object to racist comments uttered by family members.

Anna and I made it clear to our children that race was an important topic that could be brought up for discussion at any time. We talked at length about the latest tragic incident involving an unarmed black teenager and a white police officer.

That the eighteen-year-old would be left on the street for over four hours only exacerbated an already-tense situation.

The rioting and looting of property, much of which was owned by family-run businesses, gave St. Louis the reputation for being a racially torn city. I was for protest of a nonviolent nature because it brought about change in the '60s. It helped end the US involvement in the Vietnam War and led to civil rights legislation long overdue. But this was not the '60s. And Dr. Martin Luther King Jr. was no longer around to lead a movement.

Now we have Facebook, Twitter, the internet, and more cable channels than time to watch all of them. Some information is inaccurate, and that leads to confusion. With lazy fact-checking and a willingness to trust information from unreliable sources, folks are vulnerable to manipulation. I wonder each time I search for information on the last shooting or confrontation between civilian and cop. The question I ask each time is, Was death unavoidable? Or does this happen so fast that protocols can't be followed according to plan? I don't know. But I'd like to know. There is a demand for accountability from citizen and police. Perhaps body cameras will help, but I don't believe it will solve everything.

If there was ever a need for civil dialogue between law enforcement and civilian, it's now. If we can have town hall meetings to elect politicians, can't we use the same venue to have conversation devoid of screaming and finger-pointing but more about what's at stake for both parties? Just a thought that's been running around in my head for several months.

I wondered how long the hatred between locals and cops would last.

My understanding of race and where I stood on the issue took a long time to develop. I knew that Dad respected black athletes who played for the St. Louis Cardinals, stars like pitcher Bob Gibson and outfielder Curt Flood. When Gibson explained how home plate was something from which both the pitcher and hitter had to making a living, it made sense to Dad that the plate be divided in half.

However, when Gibson or Flood spoke out about injustices they endured or witnessed outside of the arena of sports, the public gave them labels like agitator, rabble rouser, or uppity. Flood was traded to Philadelphia but refused to report to the Phillies, thereby challenging baseball's reserve clause by calling it unconstitutional.

That was a decision that cost him a chance to demonstrate his uncommon skills for another team. Today's players are the beneficiaries of that challenge by way of free agency, which allows an athlete to offer up his services to the highest bidder.

I learned much later that Flood was an accomplished artist and had painted a portrait of Gussie Busch, his former Cardinal boss, and the Busch clan.

I had no interaction with blacks or anyone of color as a child because there were none at Presentation Grade School and only a handful at the Catholic high school I went to. It wasn't until I went backpacking throughout Europe that I realized how folks of color could not only be accepted as equals but be held in high esteem. I noticed a black man on a train in Germany talking to a man and woman sitting across from him.

The black man came across as educated and eloquent as he explained his take on what sounded like a political conversation. They spoke in English and a language I didn't recognize.

I decided then that if I ever had children, they would know about the courage of Harriett Tubman, Medgar Evers, Martin Luther King Jr., and Rosa Parks. They would have the benefit of a good education to follow the history of race and racism in America. They would know about King's directive: to judge people by the depth of their character rather than the color of their skin.

To that end, they would know that the Jimmy Davidsons and Donna Stearnses of this world were to be befriended, not shunned. They would learn that the fabric of America was strengthened and enriched by individuals who had plenty to contribute once their ideas and theories were discussed seriously. I would go out of my way to ensure my kids did not repeat my mistake of finding separation from invisibles and folks dismissed as outcasts. Didn't I learn that it was no more right to quarantine me for fear of disease than to force Jimmy and Donna into a social quarantine?

Anna's personal connection to race could be traced to Shirley, her best friend in high school. Anna didn't talk about her at great length. All she would say was that Shirley died in a car accident and that tragedy was too painful to elaborate on.

I thought that might be the best way to handle it.

Bob Haskins, one of the poker-game regulars, was a fifteen-year veteran of the police force. I thought about asking Bob what he thought of the confrontations between civilians and cops throughout the country but somehow never got around to it. I assumed he would have taken the side of the cop. Perhaps he would have shed some light on what went through their minds when they had to draw a weapon or decide in the blink of an eye.

I came across Bob's athletic exploits when I was working for the *Southeast Missouri Bulletin Journal* newspaper in Cape Girardeau, Missouri.

Bob played both ways as a running back and defensive back. One sportswriter called him a poor man's Gale Sayers because of his ability to elude tacklers while playing for a Division II school.

When Matt mentioned the shooting during a poker game, Bob seemed reluctant to talk about it. I wondered if his tight-lipped stance might have had something to do with the fact that I used to be a journalist.

Maybe he thought I was looking for a chance to get back into the game, and his opinion would stir another controversy. Even in retirement, you still think like a guy with a badge.

I knew some reporters who would do just about anything to get a scoop, but exploiting a friend was something I couldn't do. No story was worth that.

When I drove the Colonial truck downtown, the tension was palpable. If a black man or woman crossed the street in front of me, they took longer to reach the other side. It was, perhaps, a way to force me into the issue and to get me or anyone else to admit that this was a human being. From the tragic shooting came the phrase "Black lives matter."

Not every black person I encountered behaved this way, but it happened often enough that I grew to expect it. I hated the deep divide between protesters and cops, the problems caused by racial bias, and the lines drawn by those refusing to listen to an alternate point of view.

There was some dialogue about the shooting in Ferguson, but not enough to sustain a sincere effort to get at the root of the problem. Anna once said tension between folks who dislike one another will escalate into something ugly until someone realizes that dialogue and civility have healing powers.

There was a moment when I wanted to have a notepad and the credentials that showed I was a working journalist.

I was at a stoplight when a car blew through the light without slowing down. This occurred in front of a police car waiting for the light to change at the same intersection. The car that drove through the red light continued to the next light and stopped when it turned red.

I saw the cop lean toward his sleeve to say something into his radio. I expected to see flashing red lights at any moment. To my surprise, the cop turned slowly toward the car that ran the red light, stopped at the same intersection, and waited a few seconds before turning right before the light changed.

I had so many questions. Had the tension escalated to the extent that a traffic violation was not cause for a cop to risk a confrontation? Did it matter if the driver was black or white? Was the driver trying to force a confrontation by purposely blowing the red light? Or was I out of journalism so long, I was trying to read into something that wasn't there?

These questions needed answers, but I was not able to pose them to strangers.

I was left to observe like everyone else.

I could have asked Bob, but he seemed uncomfortable talking about police matters to someone unfamiliar with the day-to-day routine. The closest he came to weigh in on the subject was to say that he was glad retirement came when it did.

When I promised what was said to me or any of our friends would not leave the room, Bob assured me it wasn't about trust.

"It's hard to talk about this stuff," he said before closing out his poker hand and going home earlier than usual. "Don't take it personally."

Bob was not my only friend of color. When I was a journalist, I became friends with several individuals who happened to be brown or black.

I never had a negative confrontation with anyone of color as a journalist, but there were a few uncomfortable incidents during my time with Colonial Bread.

And yet the more I thought about them, the more I wondered if they had more to do with the raw anger from being pulled over all the time and finding it next to impossible to land a job. These were complex issues that wouldn't go away anytime soon and wouldn't be solved overnight.

5

A Scheme Is Hatched

I woke on my day off, determined to find a solution to the check-en-gine light for my car to pass inspection. I didn't want to wait until Matt called. If he took a week, that would leave me with just one week to get the car fixed. And there was no guarantee that Toby could take care of it.

I usually took my car to a local repair shop originally called Harry's and later changed to Lenny's. I went to high school with the owner and trusted him the way my father relied on the honesty of Len's father Harry.

In addition to being truthful with his customers, Harry loved to include them in a holiday tradition: a shot of whiskey at Christmas. I realized something about Dad when he tried to thank Harry for the gesture but declined the offer.

"Aw, c'mon, it's just a shot," I heard Harry urge in a hearty manner. Dad gave in and followed Harry to the back of the station. When Dad returned to the car, I detected a strong scent I had never smelled before. It piqued my curiosity the same way the thin curls of smoke from incense wafted into my consciousness when I attended a funeral Mass.

I thought about Anna's suggestion and figured it was worth a try to get an estimate from Len.

Len Schroeder took over his Dad's shop when he was twenty.

Harry, who had type 1 diabetes, had to have both legs ampu-tated after suffering blood clots and was no longer able to take care of the day-to-day operation. Len seemed up to the task of taking over, having worked with cars since he was a little kid. I remember visiting the place when my Dad had car trouble. The waiting area was small and sparse. There were no magazines or television to entertain the customers. Everyone just talked about the weather or cars or whatever was on their mind. There were other repair shops with cleaner waiting rooms, plenty of magazines, and usually a new television, but Dad avoided these places.

He said he expected the bill to be higher to cover all the amenities. Plus, he relied on Mr. Schroeder's honesty when it came to cite only repairs that were necessary.

Len envisioned handing the shop over to his son until Jessie announced he wanted to pursue a career in computer science.

Len took the news hard at first then considered what he might be handing his son. This was one of the few family-run repair shops left in the neighborhood. Durbins, which had more than thirty locations in St. Louis and fifty more scattered across the state of Missouri, had the resources and superior diagnostic equipment to take customers away from Len.

"Your family spends all that time building a business, you'd think it would be worth something in the end," he lamented one day with a forlorn expression. "It's not worth much of anything anymore."

I wondered: What would my children inherit when I was gone?

Len told me if I ever needed my car repaired, it wasn't necessary to make an appointment.

"Just bring it in and if I'm not busy I'll see what I can do," he stated.

It was a slow day, so Len had time to look at the car personally. After running it through a serious of diagnostic tests, he told me the problem was my catalytic converter.

"I can't give you any kind of deal on a part like that," he said. "It's gonna cost around $650 or $700."

"Wow, I'm going to have to think about this," I said, wondering how I could come up with that.

"What's to think about? You need to get the car passed, don't you?"

He noticed the expiration month on the license plate tag.

"Yeah, but I'm not sure I can pay for it today," I said, hoping he might find a way to give me time to pay it off.

"Doug, I'd let you slide for a few months if I could, but business has been slow, and I've got bills to pay," he said.

"Oh, I understand," I said. "I'll probably come back in a few days. Thanks."

I knew I couldn't put that much on the credit card. I was already maxed out with charges for school items Danny needed and my tab at Smitty's. There was also the $300 loan from Matt after I lost the big poker hand the other night. I decided I couldn't ask for more.

As I was driving away from Lenny's, I noticed the sign in front of McDonald's citing a special on Chicken McNuggets.

This triggered a memory of the place that once operated where McDonalds now stood. Claire called it the Chicken Factory. The gray building didn't have a professional sign in front, at least not one I can remember.

They slaughtered chickens in the back room then stripped the feathers by dipping them in a boiling vat that filled the room with steam. One day, Mom decided we were old enough to go to the back and asked the owner if we could see the business from start to finish. The owner sometimes allowed this if they weren't chopping heads off. The owner picked up the phone to answer a call, holding up his hand to signal he would get back to Mom and Dad with his answer.

Dad said he was against sending us back there, and Mom insisted this would be a learning experience. This sparked an argument.

While they were arguing, Claire slipped past the counter and was heading toward a door leading to the back room. She looked back to see if the folks were still arguing then flashed a mischievous grin. I took this as a cue to follow her.

I couldn't believe my eyes. A chicken was running around without its head, blood spurting out of its neck and onto a red-stained floor. I darted back through the door and never looked back. I had always wondered why the workers' black boots were stained in red and the small window in the door was clouded with steam. Then I knew. I expected Claire to make fun of me when we reached the car, but she simply stared out the window the entire ride home.

"They didn't need to see that," Dad fumed as he drove us home. This was one contentious moment Cynthia was powerless to referee.

6

The Scheme Lacks Vision

I was determined to find a solution to the check-engine problem.

"Hey, Matt, sorry to call so early," I said after he answered his cell phone.

"Lord, what time is it?" he groused.

"I wouldn't bother you like this so early, but I found out yesterday that my catalytic converter is bad and needs to be replaced. It's a $700 job. I was just wondering if . . . well, you know . . ."

"Oh yeah, I was supposed to ask Toby about that," he said, still sounding half-asleep.

"You know I wouldn't press you on this, but I can't afford what my regular mechanic is asking. With this and the money I've lost in gambling lately, I think it would really tick Anna off if she knew we're in serious debt."

"I understand. I'll give him a call this morning."

"Oh, I appreciate it."

"If there's a way to get this taken care of without the wife finding out the work is going outside Len's, I'd owe you big-time."

"Yeah? Like how?" When I didn't answer right away he added, "I mean in what way?"

"Well, I know how much you like baseball. I could get Cards versus Cubs tickets," I lied.

"Hmm, you do know my weaknesses."

I waited for Matt to call back. Two hours went by and still no call.

Finally, he called back and said Toby could replace the catalytic converter for the cost of the part.

"He said if you could get him tickets to the Cards game against the Cubs, he'd forget about labor costs. And uh, if the seats put him close to the field, he might even give you a break on the part."

"Oh, that's great," I said, somewhat relieved yet still not sure how I was going to get tickets to a series that I heard was already sold out.

"Yeah, he said they have some sort of service-learning program. He could pick up the car and do the work at a local shop. It's probably gonna cost about $175 for the part—unless you give him great seats."

"Matt, this would really help me out," I said, not sure where the $175 would come from. There seemed to be no end to the problems and the high price of solving them. As much as I was thankful to get the work done for a minimal amount of money, it was still more than I had. The only solution would be to find a way to get seats close to the field. I didn't know how I was going to swing that when I no longer had a connection with the Cardinals' public relations office.

I was so fraught with anxiety; it was difficult to concentrate. When I got like this, I would just run a few miles to calm down then devise a plan. But this wasn't a normal problem. I checked my cell phone for any messages. There were none. No texts or voice mails. Today was my day off from the bread company, so I had time to work off the tension at the gym.

I pulled into the gym parking lot with my hands shaking and my head feeling like it was going to explode. I found a treadmill, punched in my preferred weight and age—two hundred pounds and forty-five years instead of fifty-eight—then started off slowly.

I suspected I weighed more, but two hundred made me feel like I was making progress.

Gradually I worked up to a pace of a nine-minute mile. My heart felt strained, and my chest was beginning to tighten. I wondered if I was possibly setting myself up for a heart attack or a stroke.

I slowed the pace and felt more in control. I figured if I stayed on longer than usual, fatigue would set in, and I could take a nap and start on a strategy after I woke.

I took a shower at the gym, and when I reached my locker, my right eye felt tight, like it was being stretched. Then I saw a burst of black dots. A red shade came down over the eye. I wondered if the strenuous exercise caused a blood vessel to burst. I closed my eye and opened it quickly with the hope that the red would go away, but it only changed to gray then black.

I had to hold my right hand over my eye while driving home. Was I losing my eyesight? Panic closed in on me.

When I made it home, I found Anna in the kitchen.

"Anna there's something wrong with my right eye," I said, trying not to sound like it was an emergency.

"Wrong? What do you mean?" she said, her voice rising the way it always did when she sensed danger was imminent. "Oh, Doug, the eye is awfully red. What happened?"

"I don't know. I mean, I went to the gym and had a good workout. I guess I ran harder than usual, but that shouldn't make my eye turn bloodshot."

"I'm making an appointment with an eye doctor," she decided. When Anna explained to the nurse what I just told her, they said I should come in right away.

"Oh, I don't know. Maybe I made it sound worse than it really is," I protested.

"Doug, they don't make exceptions for patients unless it's an emergency. I'm taking you in and that's that," she insisted, grabbing her car keys. "Is your car behind mine?"

"Oh, uh, no, I put it in the garage," I said, mindful that I purposely parked it on the right side of the garage to make sure it wasn't driven until I could get it fixed.

When Anna focused on a goal, she had the ability to shut out all distractions until the mission was accomplished. I loved the look of sharp concentration and immense satisfaction when she taught her elementary students.

Her emerald eyes glistened appreciatively when a student demonstrated the determination to work until there was complete comprehension of the lesson. When she committed to learning about the true nature of a problem, she had this way of turning it into triage: solve the most difficult element first, then move on to the minor issues.

There was always a student who didn't understand what she was trying to relate, and for that person—if he or she was willing—there would be free tutoring on the weekend or sometimes after school.

It came as no surprise to me when she was informed that she would be honored as Teacher of the Year—this after just five years as a full-time instructor.

Those were idyllic years for us, moments so steeped in lyrical joy, only the most gifted gods of poetry could stuff it all into one stanza. While she was nurturing minds in the classroom, I was producing stories for the local newspaper. Some of them would eventually merit attention as award-winning work.

Anna was the first woman I trusted with information I never told anyone else. When I related how my first attempt at a kiss became a painful reminder of the damage braces can do to a girl's upper lip, she offered a knowing smile.

"I've got a story worse than that," she assured me, recounting an embarrassing episode of how her first boyfriend finally got enough nerve to move closer for that first peck. "I closed my eyes, puckered up, and proceeded to lose my balance," she recalled with a wry smile. "I gave him such a bad target, he fell forward and did a face-plant into the rose bushes."

I countered with a story about how I was so ignorant about the rules of spin the bottle that I wondered aloud, "So what happens when you win?"

We soon delighted in the discovery that we were both so lacking in carnal knowledge, we would forge our own path as curious explorers.

There would be awkward moments mixed with tenderness and reminders that we needed time to find our way. A guiding light came from Anna's emotional intelligence, something I was just beginning to understand.

We eventually enjoyed supreme moments of rapacious love-making and intimacy to the extent that communication wasn't limited to mere words. Anything that plunged us into a deeper realm of understanding of each other was valued like a rare element.

There were expressions that launched us into hysterical laughter or caresses that triggered thoughtful, lyrical phrases.

I was moved to such a state of bliss, I sent her a valentine message that no one else could have inspired.

"You are of some rare earth, a treasured footprint of goodness, sincerity, magnetic attraction, and oh, that thing that sends a tingle up the spine, through the heart and into the head," I wrote.

I feel the rich mud of your soul oozing through the naked toes of my imagination. I want to send so many messages to let you know how I'm learning about love in its most exquisite form. A shared kiss makes me morph into a kite, sending me up against the skin of a soft-blue sky. Your definition of freedom is my favorite flight. It is there that I'm completely serene with your precious essence. Oh god, I do love that place with you.

Happy Valentine's Day.

Love,
Doug

I thought those days would never end. They made me feel self-assured and sometimes too cocky for my own good. The sexual commingling was so intense at times, I imagined it might cause our hearts to burst. Anna had this way of letting her shoulder-length brown hair brush against my face then wrapping her arms around me, pulling me to the carpet, and landing these wet kisses that would make the most devout ascetic rip her clothes to shreds.

The only regret? That there were only two hands to get past the clothes as quickly as possible.

What followed was a feverish path to lovemaking that left us feeling like we were breathing rarefied air. The looks of contentment that were shared left us believing we had stolen an endless supply of Eros's secret potion.

How long ago was that?

Back then I was so cocky, I believed I was too good for a medium-sized newspaper and took a job in a larger city. I never gave Anna a chance to discuss such a move. However, I considered the possibility that she would grow to resent that if I failed.

Anna and Annette were to join me after we sold the house. However, it turned out that I couldn't have picked a worse time to make such a bold venture. With the housing bubble about to burst and the greed of bankers and so-called stock market experts climbing over each other to cash in on the financial windfall, it was probably inevitable that the economy would take a nosedive. I was one of the first to get laid off.

I took a job as senior publications editor at a university, but it wasn't the same as working for a newspaper. I went nearly a year without work after I left that job. I was awful to be around, always lashing out at anyone in my path.

How do you go from being an award-winning journalist to an unemployed has-been? I couldn't explain how it happened so fast.

Anna simply reverted to her German instincts, accepting the reality of what was in front of us. She decided to go back into teaching until I could get back on my feet. That meant she had to give up her volunteer work teaching impoverished families how to read.

I pledged to take the first job available so she could go back to the work she started.

As we pulled into the parking lot, I realized how much my sight deteriorated. I couldn't read the sign that said Overland Optical Center without Anna's help. I sensed something had gone horribly wrong. I might never find a way to reverse this.

Maybe I used up all my luck, and only gloom and doom awaited me.

I was surprised by how short of a wait I had before a nurse called my name. I was ushered into a small room with an eye chart and various instruments, including what looked like some sort of oversized microscope.

Every test the nurse gave me elicited a look of concern, followed by a "Hmmm."

When she took my blood pressure, she immediately wrote something down and said, "Kind of high. But don't worry. You're probably anxious about being here and having these tests," she said with an even tone.

When I was told to cover my left eye and read what was on the chart, I could only see a large E. Everything else was a blur.

When she told me to cover my right eye, I did much better, reading everything except the last two lines.

"Tell me. Did you experience a flash of light?" she said while looking down at the sheet she was using to document the tests.

"Flash of light?" I said, somewhat surprised. "I'm not so sure about the flash of light, but I definitely saw a lot of black stars."

"Oh," she said with a look of deep concern. "Well then, okay. We'll take some pictures to find out if what it looks like is actually your problem."

"What does it look like?" I asked, fearing this was serious.

"Well, it's not my place to speculate, but if I had to guess, I'd say you have a detached retina. But the doctor will be able to determine more when she sees the pictures we're going to take."

I was told to wait outside the small room with the other patients until the doctor was ready for me. I couldn't see much, but there was no mistaking what was on the television. There was a report of a hit-and-run accident. The reporter was interviewing a police spokeswoman who said that anyone who had information about this should call a 1-800 number immediately. I thought the first report indicated that there was an eyewitness.

I couldn't see the person who was being interviewed but could hear that the victim was in serious condition.

A couple sitting next to us in the waiting room were discussing what sounded like a condition the man had called macular degeneration.

"They said it's age related," explained the man, whose thick shock of white hair made him look like he was in his late sixties or early seventies. "Something about deteriorating cells that cause the retina to stop working like it should," he intoned sadly. "Well, we'll just do what the doctor says, and you'll get better," said the woman next to him.

"This is something that doesn't get better," he lamented. "There's no cure."

The woman looked at him with a confused look.

"Oh, you're always looking at things from a negative angle," she said, waving her hand as if dismissing what he just told her.

Detached retina today, maybe macular degeneration tomorrow, I feared.

I felt like the world was caving in on me.

"They told me it might be a detached retina," I said, searching her eyes for a reaction. Anna noticed the grave concern and grabbed my hand.

"We're going to get through this," she assured me.

"I know," I said, trying to sound like I wasn't in any kind of panic mode. "I know."

If only I knew what all of this was.

"Douglas Anderson," called the nurse in the direction of the waiting room. I had to strain to make out her face.

"Yes," I said, somewhat startled.

"Right this way," she said, motioning toward another small room that contained a computer, a chair, and another large camera.

"Hi, I'm Dr. Schultz," said a woman who appeared to be in her late forties or early fifties. "There's no question about what is wrong with your right eye," she said. "You have a detached retina, and you're going to need surgery immediately. The nurse will be able to schedule that for you. You do have cataract issues in both eyes, but that's something we can address later."

Dr. Schultz asked me if I experienced any head trauma recently.

"No, not recently. When I was 10, I fell down a flight of stairs, goofing around with my sisters. And in high school I got knocked out during a collision on the football field. But no, nothing recently," I explained. I wasn't sure if I should tell her that, in each case of trauma, I experienced blurred vision the next day.

She asked me about alcohol consumption.

"Oh, you know, a few a week. I'm mostly just a social drinker," I lied, mindful of the nights I drank the universe into oblivion.

Dr. Schultz didn't react to my replies. She merely jotted something down on a sheet attached to a clipboard and wished me luck with the surgery.

"Tell me. Where is the retina?" I said, hoping to get a sense of where the damage was.

"The retina is light-sensitive tissue at the back of the eyeball," she explained. "It contains cells that are sensitive to light and trigger nerve impulses that pass by way of the optic nerve to the brain," she added in monotone fashion, sounding as if this were something memorized and recited hundreds, maybe thousands, of times. "Without the retina, you wouldn't get a visual image of what you're looking at. Its function is not unlike the camera capturing an image."

"Okay, so what went wrong?" I desperately wanted to know.

"The middle of the eye is filled with a clear gel called vitreous, which is attached to the retina. When the vitreous breaks away, the retina becomes detached. Sometimes the vitreous only partially detaches, revealing small dots called floaters."

"Even if I can get the retina attached again, will I have to worry about macular degeneration down the road?"

"Anything is possible, but for now I think we should concentrate on getting the retina attached and go from there," she said.

"You mentioned cataract issues," I said, desperately needing to get as much information as possible to know where I stood.

"Yes, well, the cataract problem will get worse when you have retina surgery, but it will be cleared up when you are healthy enough for that type of surgery," she said.

"Okay, well how do you get cataracts?"

"They're caused from proteins blocking and distorting light to the retina," she said. "The proteins form a shield that keeps you from seeing clearly."

Just like that, I was facing a surgeon's knife.

"Will surgery be able to give me back the vision I had before this happened?"

"Well, there's no guarantee that the first surgery will work. Sometimes there's a need for a second surgery. But the surgeons from the Retina Institute here are very good. You will be in good hands," assured Dr. Schultz.

"What if I don't have the surgery now?" I said.

"You *will* go blind if you don't take care of this right now," she responded solemnly.

When I told Anna what I was facing, she simply repeated what she said earlier.

"We will face this as a family," she said with an assurance that reminded me of her strength.

I wondered about the consequences of a less-than-satisfactory outcome. What would I have to give up if I was blind in one eye?

The nurse placed a call to the Retina Institute and informed me that I would need to be at Belvedere Hospital at 5:30 a.m.

"Call this number in a few hours, and they will be able to give you more details about what you need to bring with you and how long you need to fast the night before," she added.

I couldn't help thinking that I was on the verge of becoming a helpless individual if the surgery didn't work. I was reminded of what Mom looked like when we cared for her the last nine months of her life.

When the doctor told us she had Alzheimer's, Anna and I decided she should move in with us. My sisters lived out of town, so it made the most sense.

There were instances when I felt like I was caring for a mischievous puppy. I would clean soiled clothes, only to find that they were soiled a few hours later. Bad girl. Bad, bad, girl! It was difficult to sustain any kind of anger, however, because the helpless look that defined her condition made the sour mood dissipate in a matter of seconds.

The rate of her deterioration could be measured by bizarre statements like, "Is your mother still alive? Do you know my son, Doug?"

When I reminded Mom that I was her son, Doug, she laughed and patted me on the arm.

"You can make me laugh," she said shaking her head.

I might have reminded her that during my preschool years I seldom laughed. That's because I had to stay quarantined in the yard. Mom repeated the phrase "Children are meant to be seen, not heard."

I cringed when I heard that phrase. I remember when I was too young for school, sitting in a room with Mom while she ironed her blouses and Dad's shirts. While she ironed, she stole quick glances at a small black-and-white television to keep track of the latest episode of her favorite soap opera. The inchoate sense of resentment grew stronger the longer I had to remain still and mute. She would blame burned edges of a shirt collar on me.

"You shouldn't have distracted me," she chided.

The memory that stirs the most angst is of a gray November day in front of the St. Louis Zoo. A stranger remarked that I was so still, it looked like I stopped breathing.

"Isn't he just the most wonderful, well-behaved kid?" bragged Mom, oblivious to the stranger's sense of peril.

Much later I realized Mom was intent on maintaining complete control. What she didn't realize, however, was that she planted a seed of resentment. I could relate to the animals peering sadly out of bars and slowly pacing back and forth to keep from losing what was left of their sanity. That look of hopelessness and the sullen foot drag were difficult to witness.

From the firmly rooted resentment and hatred grew a search for escape. I could see that words and the imagination that propelled them would bring me the freedom I so desperately needed.

To keep sane during the quarantine period, I pretended to have conversations with cartoon characters I discovered in the Sunday comics page. I looked for *Peanuts, Popeye, Mr. Peabody and Sherman,*

Pepé Le Pew, *Beetle Bailey*, and Wimpy saying he'd gladly "pay you Tuesday for a hamburger today."

Although I didn't realize it at the time, my imaginary world became more real with each character and conversation.

While my mother's intentions may have been good as far as keeping me physically healthy, the isolation rendered me socially inept. When I did start school, I was so painfully shy, it took years to get comfortable interacting with kids my age. Matt was one of the first to start the unburdening process by befriending me. Then, because Matt was popular, others offered their friendship, and I bridged the gap from darkness to incandescent streams of light.

I finally let go of the bitterness and focused on helping her in the last stage of her life.

I had to remind myself that this wasn't about me. It was about compensating for inadequacies and providing dignity to what once seemed like a hopeless situation.

I found that if I stayed calm and open-minded about this, there could be rewarding moments—like when I cooked breakfast for the first time for the person who cooked countless meals for me.

It was simply a matter of scrambling eggs. But Mom looked at the plate as if I had just handed her a rare jewel.

"That looks good. You are good to me," she said with a grateful smile. I knew this was coming from someone who didn't know I was her son, but I wanted to believe, somewhere in her heart, she knew of some connection.

Regardless, it reached inside of me and stroked something that had been unattended for a while. I didn't care if she knew exactly who I was. She knew someone was helping her, and that very truth touched my soul with rich tenderness.

Oddly enough, when she was at her weakest state, I was reminded of a time when she demonstrated her strength. Claire came home sobbing, relating bits and pieces of a harrowing tale that had all the makings of abuse by a nun named Sister Hermana. Whether Claire said the wrong thing or not, she didn't deserve to be shoved so hard against the blackboard to temporarily lose consciousness.

Mom stormed into the administrator's office and let them know that if they ever tried anything like that again, she would have those responsible arrested.

That was a time when people didn't sue as readily as they do today. Jail was enough of a deterrent.

Now I had to be strong for her.

When I came home, she sometimes gathered herself and struggled to get off the couch and make her way into the kitchen. She had to rock back and forth to gather momentum to stand then lean on a four-pronged cane to keep her balance. When she was erect, her spine was acutely curved, forcing her to stare at the ground as she inched forward.

There is so much effort into movement when you're ninety-six years old. It often pained me to stand there and bear witness, mindful I couldn't make it much better.

I remember watching a helicopter hovering over a target and thinking that it wasn't much different from Mom navigating her rear into the seat of a chair without falling to the floor.

When we had dinner together, I sensed Danny was uncomfortable. Both Danny and Anna did their best to make Mom feel at home, but there seemed to be something preventing them from drawing closer and becoming friends.

Mom couldn't hear much and struggled with her speech the way stroke victims fight to arrange words in intelligible order.

When you find yourself in this situation, eventually you realize that there are other ways to communicate. I realized the power of a smile or simple act of kindness.

I became proficient in the art of improvisation and pantomime. Instead of asking Mom if she was hungry, I pretended to hold up an imaginary eating utensil and mimic the act of feeding.

At first, she just stared at me like a dumb animal. Then she realized what I was trying to relate and nodded her assent. There were moments of dumb-luck humor. When Mom tried to turn on the light next to the La-Z-Boy recliner, she lost her balance and made one of her patented crash landings onto something that made her scream.

When the chair lifted her legs, the upheaval spread a look of fright across her face.

"Make it stop. Oh, oh, what is this thing doing to me?" she yelled, looking like an unwitting player in a raucous comedy skit. I discovered that she accidentally sat on the remote button that automatically raises the bottom to the level you wish to keep your feet elevated.

When I showed her what happened, we shared a hearty laugh. The longer I was around her, the more I saw that each day was likely to offer up an interesting surprise. Thus, I never really expected anything but the unexpected. I just went about the day, knowing I would be called upon to use my improvisational skills.

One such surprise came in the form of a small tomato patch Anna started. She planted the tomatoes just outside the kitchen door so Mom could chart size and color. When I noticed that there were several tomatoes growing to a substantial size, I showed Mom and made sure she knew it was Anna who started the garden. Slowly shaking her head from side to side, Mom insisted I deserved full credit, reacting as if someone had just given her access to Eden.

"They are beautiful," she exclaimed, extending her crooked index finger. "I'd like to get closer."

I reminded her that it was over ninety degrees and would be too hot for her to tolerate.

"When the weather cools some, then," she said with a look of disappointment.

7

Warning Signs

A sense of dread pulled me into a dark abyss.

Was this the kind of life I was headed for if the surgery didn't work? Would I need to develop a new set of improvisational skills? I wondered.

I decided to take a nap and do my best to concentrate on a successful surgery. Once I was under anesthesia, I was in the hands of skilled professionals.

When I woke, I heard voices. It sounded like Anna talking softly to Danny.

"But what if . . .," said Danny.

"No, sweetie, let's not go down that road," whispered Anna. "Let's just have positive thoughts. I'll tell you what I told your father. It's going to be okay. And it will."

"What's that you're reading?" queried Danny.

"I found an old *National Geographic* and thought it might be good to go over an interesting article," she said.

"Article about what?"

He wanted to know what Anna was trying to conceal.

"Nothing, just an article," she replied with what sounded like anger creeping into her voice.

If I had to bet, I would say it was an article about the retina. I remember an issue last year about diseases that caused blindness and the hope for a cure. For some reason, I skipped that one.

True to her nature as a consummate teacher, Anna was constantly looking for ways to stay informed about as many subjects as possible. This would give her incentive to start digging.

I made sure they could hear that I was up before I entered the living room.

"Danny, I guess your mom explained my situation," I said. "I just remembered that we were supposed to go to the Scouts tomorrow night. I may not be able to make that meeting."

"Hey, don't worry, Dad," he assured. "It's actually the meeting just for Scouts. We're supposed to come up with ideas on an essay that we need to write. Remember? The essay that will be read by the scoutmaster at the end of the year."

"Oh yeah. They're going to pick one essay that stands out and read it to everyone during the Christmas party. As I recall, the topic this year is friends and family. Well, once I get over this problem with my eye, I can help you if you like. I mean, I can't write it for you or anything, but I could give you a few pointers."

"Thanks, Dad, but actually, they want us to do this entirely on our own. I think I'll just write about an important experience and see what they think."

"Fine, but the offer still stands if you have trouble getting started."

"Thanks, Dad, and hey, good luck with the surgery tomorrow."

"I may need some luck tomorrow, thanks."

I loved Danny as much as Annette, but there was no getting around the fact that we were never going to have the close relationship I had with my father. When my Dad took me to my first major league baseball game, I was transformed from a boy who was connected to a family by blood to one who understood what it was to bond with a parent.

When we pored over the newspapers for information about the Cardinals, checking the box scores for vital statistics that only we could decipher, it felt special. We knew a code neither my sisters nor mother understood.

Danny would never love sports the way I did, but that was fine with me if he continued to mature. I saw a kindness and tenderness in him that had to come from Anna.

Annette was more like me, willing to take risks, always restless to find another challenge.

When I told her it's no sin to reach for something seemingly beyond your grasp, her blue eyes shone with a sharp awareness of what I was trying to tell her.

That's why she was pursuing a doctorate in psychology.

When she was a child, it didn't look like she would be someone who would be going to college.

Her grade school teachers said she didn't seem like a very good candidate for the academic world.

The same was true in high school until she became a junior. Something or someone managed to help her find a way to get better grades. From that point on, she was determined to succeed, thereby gaining more respect from her teachers.

When I asked her why she chose psychology as her major, her response surprised me.

"Do you remember when I used to have those terrible dreams?" she said.

"Sure, you woke everybody up with those screams," I reminded her.

"Yeah, well, I used to have this recurring dream . . . well, more like a nightmare. I never said anything because I thought it would pass, but it never did."

"What was the nightmare?"

"I wake up to find the family gone with a note on the table detailing how to reach the new city. But for some reason I can't figure out how to get there," she said. "It's called separation anxiety."

"I'm so sorry," I said, mindful that I was the source of her bad dreams. "I didn't know I was doing this to you."

"I didn't tell you that to make you feel bad," she said. "I used to have bad dreams when you and Mom got into arguments."

"I'm sorry about that too."

89

She paused then added, "I'm not saying this to make you feel guilty. I'm just trying to explain. Anyway, all these dreams made me curious about the conscious mind and the subconscious when we go to sleep," she said.

"When I told you that when I lay my head on the pillow I'm terrified of the unknown, you said there was nothing to worry about because there will always be a family to stand watch over you, to support and protect you. You said you'd always do your best to keep me safe. That worked when I was little, but the older I got, the more I realized that there are too many aspects of life that are beyond our control."

Unexplained fear gave way to relentless curiosity. From that point on, she wanted to know more about what goes on during that strange time when our conscious mind goes to sleep but the subconscious portion of our brain stays awake.

I think she said she was fascinated by the role that subliminal messages play on our conscious minds.

"I feel terrible that I never asked you about this until now," I said.

"Don't feel terrible. I still love you and Mom and Danny. I'm just sensitive to much of what I see and hear. All I can do is try to understand that, deal with it, and move on."

"Well, I'll try to remember that. And as far as the moving is concerned, that's not going to happen anytime soon. Your mother and I have signed a peace treaty, so don't expect any heated arguments."

Annette's serious demeanor softened into a smile.

After we hugged, I left her room with plenty to think about.

Annette's greatest strength was her indomitable will to overcome whatever obstacles stood between her and the goals she set out to accomplish. I admired that. It was the same approach I took when I became a journalist.

8

No Surgical Cure for Myopia

I thought of Annette when I couldn't find sleep the night before surgery. I spent most of the time tossing back and forth, fighting off the weight of some very bad dreams. How long before this burden overwhelmed me?

Since we had to be at Belvedere by 5:30 a.m., the time to get ready was set for 4:00 a.m. We were on the road by 4:45 a.m.

"I talked to the nurse at the hospital, and she said they want you to take a few tests before you go into surgery," said Anna. "When did you talk to the nurse?"

"When you were taking a nap. Don't worry. It's normal procedure. The surgeon wants to meet you and go over all the risks and that sort of thing," she said. "Nothing to get upset over."

While Anna was filling out papers, I was escorted into a room to have my blood pressure checked. Then a cardiologist checked my heart. I was told to take off my shirt so they could place several sticky tabs on my chest for an EKG.

There were so many questions to answer and papers to fill out, I wondered if I was ever going to reach the operating room before the end of the day.

The surgeon, whose nameplate indicated he was Dr. Phillip Graham, informed me that he would be unable to operate because my blood pressure was too high.

"It's 195 over 98, which is too high," he said, giving me the impression I screwed everything up.

"Are you serious?" I complained.

"No anesthesiologist would consider taking that kind of risk," he stated grimly. "In fact, he would just walk out of the operating room."

With that he said I needed to take a higher dosage of blood pressure medicine. The prescription could be filled out in his office.

"If it goes down to a normal number, we can do surgery the next day," he said and left the room.

I walked back to the waiting room and gave Anna the unwelcome news.

"Okay, well, we'll just have to regroup and do this all over again tomorrow," she said resolutely. When she saw how down I was, she grabbed me and said, "Hey, it's not the end of the world. At least it's something that can be fixed."

"Yeah, I know. I can't expect you to drop everything you normally do to take care of this," I said.

"I was supposed to report to the volunteer center for my next assignment with a new family, but that will just have to wait. It's not a big deal, Doug," she assured me.

"I don't deserve someone as good as you. I'm a lucky man," I gushed. "Have I ever told you how much you mean to me?"

"About a thousand times when we were first married, but I don't recall hearing it lately," she said wistfully. "Thanks."

We drove to the pharmacy to pick up my prescription, which included some eye drops that cost over $100. When we returned home, I went to bed. My nap was interrupted several times by phone calls. One was from Annette. Then I could hear Anna telling someone at Colonial that I wouldn't be in for several days.

"Okay, I'll have him call you to let you know when he can come back," she said. When Anna said I was unable to come to the phone, I jumped up and raced into the kitchen to make sure she didn't hang up. "If that's Matt, I need to tell him something," I said.

"Hey, Matt, it looks like the poker game will be at your house for the next few weeks," I said. I explained what happened and why I wouldn't be able to join him and the others for a few weeks.

He assured me it wasn't a big deal.

"So hey, this sounds serious," he said.

"It's just a little corrective eye surgery," I said in a dismissive tone. "The doc said it's something he's done a thousand times. Not a big deal. A walk in the park is the way he put it."

"Oh, okay. I've never really known anybody who had that. Well, good luck," he said. Matt was about to hang up when I realized this was an opportunity to take care of the check-engine light for a price I could afford.

I moved to the bedroom so Anna couldn't hear and asked Matt if his nephew could take care of it.

"Uh, well, actually, I think he can because he said they're not having class for another week. He can take care of it on his free time."

"Great. I'll tell Anna I'm taking it to Len's Automotive, and it should work out just fine. We can work out how much to pay him later, if that's okay,"

"Um, yeah sure," he said, sounding confused.

"Oh, you're wondering why I have to tell her about going to Len's," I guessed.

"Yeah."

"It's a long story. Basically, she's worry your nephew isn't experienced enough to handle a project like this. I'm sure he is, right?"

"Well yeah, I mean he's got skills," said Matt, sounding irritated.

"Okay, didn't mean to insult you," I said.

"So it's a go?"

"Well, I thought it was decided that the whole thing could be taken care of if you come up with tickets to a Cards-Cubs game."

"Yeah, I know. I'm still working on that. I've placed a few calls, and I'm waiting to hear back. It's just a matter of who comes through."

How could I tell him such an outrageous lie? I had no clue how I was going to come through with tickets to that series.

"If, for some reason, it doesn't work out with the tickets, he'll still do it for the $175, right?"

"Hmm. I really think you should do your best to get the tickets first," he said. "Toby believes you still have connections. I mean you do, don't you?"

"Oh yeah. Like I said, it's probably going to happen. It's just a matter of who comes through for me. Just make sure he picks up the car before I come back from the hospital."

I still had a few days to come up with the tickets.

We arranged for Toby to pick up the car when Anna was at the volunteer center later that day.

Since the car was in the garage, Anna wouldn't know it was missing until we returned from the hospital because her car would be in front of the house.

I tried to go back to sleep but couldn't relax enough to drift off. On any other day, I would read until my eyes became too tired, and that would send me back to slumber land. Since I couldn't see anything out of my right eye, how was I supposed to focus on anything?

I fashioned an eye patch out of gauze so that only my left eye would be used.

It worked. I fished through some old stories I wrote after leaving the newspaper. I found one about my father. It was titled "My Favorite Warrior."

It is a natural tendency of the brain to herd chaotic thoughts into relevant explanations. Perhaps that is what I was doing when I interpreted the simultaneous departure of my father and the swift descent of a flower petal as a significant confluence.

I didn't identify this as a corollary event at the hospital. Rather, it seemed the mind could not understand what the eye saw. So the mind's eye replayed this over and over in waking hours as well as in dreams until some sense could be made of it. I asked my sisters and mother if they noticed the flower petal tumbling to the floor the second Dad took his final breath. They said they did not.

I was left to figure this out on my own. I had several unanswered questions. The last breath chased the flower's petal to the ground. Gust of grief? No. Well, yes. A lament of things never said. Handshakes that should have been hugs. Creative souls never running wild together. But there's more. The mind says, "Look again." The petal died, but the flower stayed alive. Was this a symbolic way to understand my father's passing? Did this mean that because there were family survivors and the flower remained alive, life goes on?

Or was there a more profound interpretation? Was this telling me that since I was the only one who noticed the two seemingly related acts, there was a message meant just for me?

The days and hours leading up to my father's death brought even more questions. I was twenty-one years old and not sure which direction my life would take. I completed my degree in English and knew deep down I wanted to find work that would enable me to spend what talent I had on the printed word.

I just didn't know I was willing to go broke trying. The obvious choice was to try my hand at journalism. I knew the pay was terrible, yet I also knew that if I could prove myself, perhaps winning an award or two along the way, the money would get better.

At the time, I was working out of Lambert Airport, delivering lost luggage for an independent company. The airlines handed the work to the company, and the group I hired on with subcontracted the work to self-employed drivers. This is the only time I was self-employed.

I made more money than I expected, but it became abundantly clear during midnight runs that this was not a job for the future. In fact, I considered this job something of an ironic allegory. Wasn't I about as lost as the luggage I was returning?

Misdirected baggage that needed to be rerouted. I was drifting, and it didn't feel right to do that.

My dad never told me about his father. I found out years later that his dad was a drunk. Dad had to quit high school to pay the bills. And yet without a high school diploma or college degree, he still managed to become a publisher of a magazine.

That all changed, however, when he joined the Navy during World War II. During his time in the military, he must have decided that he wanted to start a family. That meant finding jobs that were not as unstable as the publishing business. It wasn't until much later that I realized he sacrificed his passion for the printed word, taking the pedestrian jobs of payroll master and real estate salesman to make sure his family had uninterrupted food, clothes, and shelter.

I learned how unselfish and dedicated a father I had when I volunteered to accompany him to host an open house on a cold

November Sunday afternoon. The sky was shaded in gunmetal darkness, the lawns browned out from winter's frigid breath. A quiet stillness descended on the area as a gentle breeze sent leaves scattering across the pavement.

Since he only worked part-time as a real estate salesman, Dad's weekends were often spent waiting for prospective buyers to show up and inquire about price, details of the house, and financing.

I immediately felt like an intruder when we entered the house. The fresh paint reminded me we were in someone else's house. The smell of Sunday roast being overcooked in the oven was absent, the rooms devoid of furniture. Our voices sounded loud bouncing off the walls. I unfolded the lawn chair we brought and tuned the radio to the football game.

After a few hours of no-shows, I realized that the transistor radio and space heater were essentials to get us through the five hours the house was expected to be open to the public.

The radio would break the boredom because we could listen to the St. Louis Football Cardinals game against the Cleveland Browns. The space heater would keep us from freezing. Since the house had been vacant for some time, there were no utilities turned on, and we had to make the best of an inconvenient situation.

I asked Dad, whose uniform consisted of a mustard-colored sports jacket, why he volunteered to host this open house when he knew from experience that only a few people would show.

He explained that as a part-time salesman, he had to hold an open house in the fall and winter to have an opportunity to sell the same house in the spring and summer. It had to do with getting a listing on a house. Full-time salesmen got the most coveted listings and the pick of prime real estate because they worked the phones during the week. It didn't take long to realize that without the football game to listen to, this could become a lonely stretch of time.

I also realized that selling a house was a slow process that required some luck and plenty of patience.

I imagined what it must have been like when he did this by himself, with no one to talk to. He was willing to put up with this to provide for his family.

I asked Dad why he was so loyal to a team that never made the playoffs and seemed destined to repeat the same losing scenario year after year.

"It's like staying loyal to a friend," he explained. "If your friend is having a difficult day, a lousy month, or even a tough year, you don't stop calling him a friend. You don't abandon that person when times are tough. Well, the Cardinals are my friend, through thick and thin."

As we listened to the game, Dad talked about how much he admired Cardinal safety Larry Wilson. I expected him to talk about how tough number 8 was. Instead he listed Wilson's unwillingness to give up no matter the score.

The rare week Wilson was listed as doubtful was when he had two broken hands. Wilson indicated in a pregame interview that he would play if the doctors cleared him before game time.

I asked Dad if he expected Wilson to play with broken hands.

"We'll see," was his response. "A man's word is an important thing, so I don't think he would be leading anyone on, only to look like a fool later."

True to his word, Wilson not only played with his hands in soft casts, but he also intercepted a pass.

I understood much later that Dad was using sports and players he admired to teach me something about life. Dad's father was an alcoholic who made plenty of empty promises. Dad's word was gold. He never quit on us once. How could I ever measure up to that?

When I was delivering lost luggage, I found myself inside Wilson's home on a bitterly frigid day in December. The ticket read L. Wilson, so I thought nothing of it until I noticed several NFL footballs propped on the mantle.

When I realized whose house I was in, I wanted to examine the writing on each football. Wilson was out of town at the time, but I learned something of his family from a woman who seemed to be taking care of the youngest son.

The boy appeared to have special needs.

"Mr. Wilson loves that boy way more than any football or award that's on that mantle," declared the woman with conviction.

When I tried to clear the icy path leading to the main road, the tires on my pickup truck spun long enough that another of Wilson's sons told me to wait inside the house until he could hook a chain from his truck to me to pull me out. My appreciation was greeted with a wave of the hand, as if it were nothing more than what any of their neighbors would have done.

This was a man who raised his sons to keep their feet planted firmly on the ground. That meant something to me.

The hospital my father stayed at was shorthanded, especially on the late shift. So we agreed, as a family, to take turns sitting with him. Two nights before he died, it was my turn. The bone marrow cancer ravaged his body with such rapacious force, he couldn't lift his head. Thus, without the aid of a nurse, it was up to a family member to comfort him.

On this evening, I came home earlier than usual because it wasn't that busy at the airport. There was a phone message for me to get to the hospital as soon as possible because it looked as though this was one of those bad nights. On more than one occasion, he pulled the intravenous tube out of his arm. This was the first time in his life he had an extensive stay in the hospital, and his instincts were to fight the ordeal. I quietly applauded his protest of what must have seemed an exercise in futility. During one of our father-son sessions, laughin' with our shirttails out and just gettin' philosophical, we proclaimed to each other and the world that our individuality was precious cargo and not to be kicked around.

Much to my delight, I discovered that he not only had the strength to lift his head, but he was also lucid enough to remember the days we enjoyed taking in baseball, hockey, and football games.

We reminisced about Cardinal baseball games in old Sportsman's Park and the newer Busch Stadium. I reminded him of our first game together. It was a day slathered in pungent aromas, raucous cheering sections, and kaleidoscopic snapshots, all serving as potent stimulants for the imagination.

Dad told me to pick out a player who looked exciting—someone who eats, sleeps, breathes baseball. I focused on a player who behaved as if this were the seventh game of the World Series. His name was Ted Savage, an outfielder with the St. Louis Cardinals.

Since I was only twelve at the time, I focused on Savage as a larger-than-life character who seemed to bend and reshape life at will. His behavior during batting practice was so spirited, I was mesmerized by his every move. Dad bought a scorecard and noticed that Savage was going to start. Dad taught me how to signify a strikeout with a capital *K*. He showed me how to reverse the *K* if it was a called third strike.

Then it was on to identifying players by position: pitcher was number one, catcher two, first baseman three, second baseman four, and so on. If the player at that position figured in the out, got a hit, or made an error, I was instructed to enter it accordingly.

As I learned how to enter the assigned codes into the small boxes in the scorecard, I lamented that there was nothing special to pencil in for Savage's performance thus far. Then there was a screaming line drive directed at Savage. Undaunted, he rode the horsehide meteor into the wall, snared it, and collapsed. And yet he never let the white speck fall out of his leather glove.

A funereal hush descended on the stadium crowd. When a stretcher was rolled out, I asked Dad with beseeching eyes if Savage was going to die. I must have thought Dad had the power of a Roman emperor. I wanted so much for him to signal thumbs up to guarantee Savage's fate.

"Did I do wrong by picking him?" I asked. Dad shook his head vigorously and pillowed my shoulders into his soft hands.

"Don't worry," said Dad. "He will live for another day. Ted Savage is a warrior."

From that experience as a boy came an embellished yet poignant observation as an adult: I titled it "Warriors Revisited":

> Sometimes time and memory distill a rite of passage in ways worth revisiting.
> The hot dogs were slathered in digestible mayhem.
> Peanuts perfumed the air with brash benediction

Bleachers gloved us into a raucous, Rockwellian pack.

The grass gleamed like an emerald isle sainted by Patrick, Mark, Luke, and John.

My ephemeral world was resplendent with brilliant Cardinals in cotton and cleats.

Cigar smoke laid its calling card at the doorstep of my virgin nostrils.

I opened the door for more.

Pennants flapped of their own will.

Beer was mother's milk to fathers who forgot where mother was. And Dad forgot how bone-weary he was.

Was it the look I had? Christmas in June? Whatever, he seemed to grab a cup of coffee from my enthusiasm.

Dad said pick out a player who excites you, someone who looks like he eats, sleeps, breathes baseball.

I focus on Savage, the man who seems larger than life,

a spirited character who ushers me to the altar of his professional passion.

He treats a start in the outfield like a wish come true.

He rides a horsehide meteor into the wall and collapses.

A funereal hush fogs up my Rockwellian glasses.

I lay down the glasses to get a better look.

I ask Dad with beseeching eyes,

"What's that stretcher for?

Will he die?

Did I do wrong by picking him?

Don't let him die, Dad!"

Our eyes are riveted on the crumpled figure.

Savage's pipes instinctively fight for more wind like a weathered but proud accordion.

Dad says Savage will live for another day.

"He's a warrior," says Dad.

Years later I went back to that scene.

I had questions that needed answers.

Would Savage attain warrior status if he couldn't play ball?

Is a black man with athletic skills more noble than one who lives a pedestrian life?

How do you measure talent? Human worth?

Is aptitude in anything still important if nobody notices?

What if your gift, your calling card, draws no applause?

No matter.

I still say I know two warriors who could do more than eat, sleep, breathe baseball.

And I would never again see baseball with Rockwellian glasses.

Dad told me, with halting breath on his hospital bed, that I demonstrated a measure of courage as a boy. I didn't understand what he meant.

"How?" I blurted.

"Remember when you had to take your first booster shot?" he whispered, his voice barely audible. "You didn't even cry," he said, slowly nodding his head as if reliving the feeling that swept over him. A few minutes later, he fell silent.

He lowered his emaciated face and slowly receded wraithlike into a dim form I no longer recognized. We never exchanged another word again. My immediate lament was that I never took the opportunity to tell him how much I loved him. I was the only one benefitting from his final lucid moments, and I let that rare pearl elude my grasp.

Over time I've learned that I couldn't mature fast enough to appreciate all of what my father was made of. He had as many layers as an onion. Some were there to make you laugh, to forget the temporary pain, but the ones closest to the core, the ones he kept hidden, those are the ones I wish I reached before time expired. Those were part of his pain left unattended.

I acted on the descent of the flower petal, however. I wrote sports articles for the local journal on a freelance basis with hopes of getting someone to hire me full-time. I was convinced Dad told me that I should answer the call of my heart and pursue a career in writing before it was too late. Don't let one petal of your passion for the printed word die out. I also believed that I would see things that others might not. Isn't this part of what it means to be a writer? The task of herding images, thoughts, and observations into a story for an audience was the perfect fit for my creative soul. I didn't have to face the audience until the work was complete. I could have control of the beginning, middle, and end of that story, a luxury not afforded in the day-to-day struggles of life. And when I captured the essence of something noteworthy, it would be preserved in print.

I finally landed my first full-time job as a sports editor in Cape Girardeau, Missouri. When I learned that I could get paid for something I would have done for free, I felt a blaze of satisfaction. Life's haze was beginning to clear. If ever there was a profession I could deem my calling, this was it.

The possibilities seemed limitless. I stayed in that town for several years, winning over a dozen awards, three of which merited national honors. I was also lucky enough to meet Anna in Cape Girardeau while she was embarking on her teaching career.

I went on to meet some extraordinary individuals and received letters that rank among the most moving I've ever received.

I later moved to Ohio to become a senior publications editor and then came back to St. Louis to work as a public relations director. Although I was no longer in journalism and didn't have the instant power to publish, I still had a desire to push the creative pen. I couldn't conceive of a time when I wouldn't write. But in what capacity? Fiction? It's something to talk about writing a novel, but to get started and accomplish this is quite another. I wrote some short stories to get started and then pounded out two manuscripts that continue to gather dust somewhere in a box in the basement.

Oddly enough I received a poster with names of authors from Missouri in stylish font. Incredibly, my name was on this poster. I thought it was a joke my friends cooked up. When I confronted each of them, however, they adamantly denied being a part of such a scheme. Upon investigating further, I realized that the poster was legitimate. To this day, I don't know how my name got on that poster. Perhaps a harbinger of things to come?

Probably not. But I can still take comfort in the fact that I acted on a dream. I have witnessed feats from more than one extraordinary warrior. Yet only one continues to give me the courage to press on at critical junctures.

When I finished reading, my good eye felt tired. Still, I was glad that I picked it up and went over it again.

I was now at another critical juncture. I was facing the loss of sight in one eye and the ability to support my family. I was also wrestling with financial difficulty at a time when I was virtually powerless to do much about it.

I needed to find a sense of inner peace on the eve of surgery. I struggled to find sleep. Most people welcome sleep, but I dread it because it's the movie with all the wrong characters and a plot in which I only survive but never triumph.

I have this recurring nightmare in which I am presented with a challenge. Sometimes it involves getting someone to the hospital in time to save his or her life. Other times I'm told that the captain of the ship I am on has taken ill, and his last request was for me to take the helm.

But when I begin to steer, the ship doesn't obey my commands. Instead of speeding up, it slows down. When I want to make a sharp turn, it insists on keeping the course it was on when the captain was at the helm. I usually wake up before we crash into something or everybody drowns, but there is this feeling of helplessness and utter futility that I failed the people who counted on me.

In another dream, I can get back into the newspaper business if I'm able to pass a brief test. I am told to cover a simple assignment and write the story within an hour, something I did hundreds of times.

Yet on this occasion, I'm having difficulty getting to the interview. There's an unusually high volume of traffic, I'm moving in slow motion, and I can't seem to find the person I'm supposed to interview.

I pored over all of the problems that seemed to weigh on me before finally drifting off into a fragmented sleep pattern.

10

Anna's New Career

After I shut off the alarm, Anna went through a check list of everything I would need to get through the presurgery routine.

"They mentioned yesterday that you will need your insurance card, some identification, I guess a driver's license, and a list of any medication you're on," she noted. I noticed that she looked as if she hadn't slept.

"You didn't get much sleep last night, did you?"

"Oh, I get enough sleep as it is," she replied with a wave of her hand. "One day isn't going make much of a difference one way or another. You were pretty restless yourself."

As we headed toward the hospital, I was struck by how calm and still everything seemed at four thirty in the morning.

"Nervous?" said Anna, staring straight ahead, both hands on the steering wheel. "No, not really. I'm concerned about the blood pressure issue. I mean this won't happen if the numbers don't pass muster with the anesthesiologist. But other than that, I have no control over what happens, so I don't see any reason to worry about it."

When we entered the hospital, there were only a few medical personnel walking the halls.

I presented my insurance card and ID, and we were escorted to a room on the first floor. I was told to stand on a scale so they could record my weight for the anesthesiologist. I couldn't believe it when they told me I weighed 237 pounds. I was only 5'11".

"I thought I was around 200," I moaned.

"Maybe a few years ago, but not now," she said, maintaining a professional demeanor.

I was told to sit on a table while my blood pressure was taken. I was surprised when they told me it was 132 over 79. The medicine worked.

I changed out of my street clothes into the hospital open-back gown and slippers then filled out various forms. I was surprised by one form that listed the amount I would owe following surgery.

I was about to enter the operating room with my eyesight on the line, and here they were essentially giving me the bill. This struck me as so inappropriate and poorly timed, I wondered how this disturbance would affect my blood pressure on the next reading.

I could see getting an estimate from a plumber before the work was done, but getting a presurgery estimate just before I was wheeled into the operating room seemed ridiculous. Did they really want me worrying about how I was going to pay for the surgery just before I went under the knife?

Anna raised her left eyebrow when she saw the red circle around the total I would owe following surgery. I could just see the wheels in her head spinning, trying to calculate how we would be able to pay this off.

She didn't know the full extent of our indebtedness.

We decided early in our marriage to set up a rainy-day fund for emergencies like this, but it could only be used after we exhausted every option.

The last time I checked, it was up to $1,200. Each time we thought about using it for Annette's tuition or dental work that Danny needed, we found a source that kept us from dipping into the fund. Perhaps this was one time when the fund had to be used.

After an hour or two, I was transported via wheelchair to an area outside the operating room and introduced to the anesthesiologist.

"Hello, I'm Dr. Yokohomo," said the woman clad head to toe in white scrubs.

"Oh, hi, Doc. Say, I loved all of your husband's albums," I joked. Either she didn't get the gag or was insulted because she simply looked away and proceeded to cite the drugs I would be given to knock me out.

I was presently taken to a temporary holding station with curtains on both sides until they were ready to send me into the operating room. It looked like an assembly line of sheep waiting to be sheared in one form or another.

There was a legion of nurses and technicians who asked me to state my name and date of birth. I assumed this was a standard procedure to make certain I was aware of where I was as well as the purpose of my visit.

The next thing I remember was waking up in the recovery room. I looked at the clock that showed 3:30 p.m. That meant I was in the operating room for nearly four hours. The patch over my right eye created an itch. I was told this was normal.

When I looked at Anna, she appeared exhausted.

"How do you feel?" she queried, trying to manage a smile.

"Not bad, how about you?"

"You're the one who had surgery, remember?" she replied.

"I know, but you've done all the presurgery work, talking to the insurance company and taking care of things I usually handle. You look a little tired," I noted.

"I didn't get much sleep," she admitted "Anyway, I talked to the doctor, and he seemed pleased with the way the surgery went," she said, allowing a smile to work its way into the corners of her mouth.

"Oh, well, that's encouraging,"

"The doctor wrote a prescription for something to help with the pain," she noted. "We can pick it up on the way home."

"I don't know. I mean, I don't feel any pain right now," I objected.

"You might feel some pain later. Let's just get the medicine, and you can decide later whether you want to take it," she suggested, looking somewhat annoyed.

"Okay, makes sense. What would I do without you?"

"You'd probably find a way to survive," she said with a hint of sarcasm.

When we reached the parking lot of the pharmacy, I cringed. Mary Henderson was walking into the store. Mary's son Sean was in the same grade as Danny. That's when Anna and Mary first met. They also did some fund-raising for the school two years ago.

Mary was going through a tough time with her husband, and I was having problems in my marriage, so we began to correspond via email. I knew this was reckless and selfish, but it seemed to pull me out of a depressed state. To keep anyone from identifying her, she signed the emails MH. The email address she used was from a coworker.

What started out as an innocent correspondence began to escalate into something more serious. Hugs turned into kisses, and I knew it was only a matter of time before we slept together.

Over a few drinks, we talked about taking a yoga class together. I tried to remember to delete the emails each day, but there were a few she said she sent I couldn't account for.

When Mary asked why I stopped writing, I feared Anna knew what I was up to and started deleting them. I told Mary to stop sending messages, and that was the end of it.

"Hey, instead of going in, let's just use the drive-through," I suggested.

"Why?" objected Anna, looking more annoyed.

"Oh, I don't know. Maybe the store manager will get suspicious when he sees this eye patch. He might think I'm a terrorist or something."

"Whatever," she said with an exasperated look.

We headed home in silence. I wondered if something was weighing on her mind.

"Anna, you look like you're deep in thought," I said, hoping conversation would allow her to reveal what she was thinking and ease the tension. "Care to share?"

"Well, actually, while you were in surgery, I started talking to a woman who was waiting for her son. He also had some problem with his eye. Anyway, she told me about grant writing. It pays well, and it seems like something I could do."

I knew where this was headed.

"Anna, I'm not finished as far as working goes," I said.

"Oh, I know that, but the way the doctor described the recovery period, it looks like you might not be able to drive for a little bit. Look, Doug. I've added up the medical bills we're going to face in the next several months. They're going to be significant, even with the insurance coverage you have from work. We're going to need more income to get over this. Maybe I could try to do some grant writing to get us over the hump."

I had a bad feeling about this.

"Is this something you need to do right away? I mean, we haven't even seen the first bill yet," I countered. "Sometimes the hospital will give you a break if you can't afford to pay the entire amount. That's what happened to Matt a few years ago. Maybe we'll get the same kind of break."

"That was more than a few years ago," she noted. "If I had to put a number on it, I'd say it was at least six or seven years ago. The health care situation has changed dramatically since then. There's all of this in-network, out-of-network stuff, and what looks like your deductible really isn't because they find ways to tack on this charge and that cost. So I'm not holding out hope that we'll get any kind of break. What do you have against me working again? It's not like I'm going to do this for a long time."

"I know, but you wouldn't have thought about something like this if it weren't for my eye,"

"Okay, I'll give you that, but what if this kills two birds with one stone?" she offered. "I mean, it could give us some extra income and help me do my part for causes I believe in. It would be like doing volunteer work, only now I'll get paid."

She must have noticed the frustration I was feeling because she immediately changed the subject.

"Oh, I almost forgot. While you were sleeping, I got a call from Annette," she said.

"I thought we were still discussing the grant-writing thing," I replied, feeling anger building up inside.

"We can go over it later," she said with a decisive tone. "Don't you want to hear about your daughter?"

She had me there.

"Okay, so how is Annette?"

"Well, she's been wanting to take a break from working on her dissertation proposal, so she's coming home for a few weeks," she added, staring straight ahead.

"I thought since you're not going to be able to drive, she could use your car while she's home. Her car isn't running very well, and she didn't want to trust it on the highway, at least not until she can get someone to look at it. One of her roommates is coming back to St. Louis this weekend, so it should work out just fine."

I felt trapped. How could I tell her the car wouldn't be available?

"Uh, yeah, it's great she's coming home for a few days, but my car won't be available,"

"Why not?" said Anna with a surprised look.

"Well, I took it to Len's, just like you suggested, and he seemed really busy. I need to take care of this to pass inspection in time, so I thought about Matt's nephew Toby."

Before Anna could object, I said, "Toby goes to trade school, and he's been telling me that they get credit if they can do a project that helps someone in the community," I explained. "So I told him about the check-engine problem, and he said that with a qualified mechanic's supervision, he could fix it. I arranged for him to pick the car up while you were at the volunteer center."

Anna was livid.

"You're telling me Len was too busy, so you found a cheaper solution," she said, folding her arms with a look of disdain.

I needed something to diffuse her anger.

"Look. I'd think, as an educator, you would be for something like this," I said, desperate for leverage.

"Don't patronize me with this kind of crap," she fumed. "Give me credit for having a brain."

She turned to me with a scowl.

"Doug, why did you do something like that without at least running it by me? I thought we agreed just last week that the lack of communication was one of the reasons we were drifting apart. And now you do something like this."

She had me in the guilt vise.

"I'm sorry. I didn't think it was that big of a deal," I squirmed.

I was drowning, searching for a floating device.

"Since we're talking about lack of communication, why didn't you tell me that Annette was thinking of coming home?"

Without hesitating, she replied, "Because I didn't know until she called while you were sleeping."

I was trapped like a rat in a corner, and we both knew it. I didn't know how I was going to get out of this one. Maybe I wasn't.

It was one thing to deteriorate physically, but now my status as husband, father, and breadwinner was eroding.

Perhaps she was tired of living in the creative shadows of her husband. Maybe she was looking for an opportunity to see what she could accomplish in an area that was new to her.

Some of the poems she showed me when we were dating were excellent. I remember how she described rain as liquid poetry—and how strongly she felt about the destructive nature of guns in the hands of folks who had no business owning them.

I recall her phrase "instruments capable of creating a lifetime of sorrow in an instant of senseless fury." Then the line about the selling of the Iraq War to the American public. I believe the phrase was "launching weapons of crass seduction."

And her line about her woeful relationship with her mother, calling them "familiar strangers stuck in the same cabin on the same voyage that goes nowhere."

Her eloquence seemed sharpest when she could not restrain her anger over something that cut to the core of her being.

"Here's a bulletin for you, Douglas Anderson," she once told me after I was so sure I had written the best article of anyone in the newsroom that year.

"Don't become so bedazzled with your accomplishments that you lose sight of why you became a journalist in the first place," she warned. She understood the power and purpose of humility.

Another time she tempered my gloating grin with "Oh, so now you own the patent on style and substance, the one and only man of letters worth reading? Huh, let's go over that column again." I needed that and told her so.

When we shared stories of past experiences, it became evident that both of us had been through some difficult trials.

How could I forget the story about her complicated friendship with Shirley?

Anna's mother and all those people Anna believed to be close friends were telling her what to do when she knew deep down it wasn't right. It was all so confusing to her at the time. Then it wasn't so confusing when the accident's aftermath left Anna with something so troubling, she refused to discuss it in detail.

It had something to do with why Anna was so dedicated when she entered the teaching profession. Perhaps that would also explain why she wanted to spend time as a volunteer with those who needed help but couldn't afford to pay for it.

For me writing was as necessary as getting up every day and having a sense of purpose. For Anna it was more of a catharsis.

Interestingly, her pull toward writing ceased when she began her teaching career. With the birth of Annette and then Danny, she probably didn't have much time to record her thoughts.

She needed my support, and I would be a complete jerk not to give that. It wasn't often that she pushed so hard for something like this.

She knew she had the talent to write. Perhaps she assumed it will always be there, like a face, an arm, or a leg. But faces change with age. Arms and legs can atrophy from lack of exercise. If you don't use what's left, a precious gift will have been wasted, gone forever.

When we reached home, she slammed the car door and walked briskly into the house. She took heavy strides into the bedroom and closed the door. I knew she didn't want to be bothered. She needed some space, and that was about the only thing I could afford to give her.

One way to pull her out of this funk was to start dinner. I struggled to find the pots and pans I would need. Then I felt a throbbing pain in my head. I felt so useless, an utter failure in just about every way imaginable.

I opted for a nap. I took a few pills to kill the pain and headed to the couch. Before I could lay my head down, however, I thought this would only tip off Danny that Mom and Dad were fighting, so I headed for the basement. We put a cot down there to accommodate a party guest who had too much to drink or was too tired to drive home.

I noticed the plaques that were sticking out of a box in the corner of the room next to some old Christmas ornaments. I didn't need two good eyes to see what was written on the plaques. I memorized the shapes and sizes of the awards and their order of importance. There were first-place awards for investigative journalism, feature writing, enterprise reporting, and even a second-place award for spot reporting.

There was also the framed newspaper advertisement promoting me as a "sportswriter who believed everyone has a story to tell."

I turned that facedown. It had collected a considerable amount of dust.

The applause I received when my name was called brought a flood of memories of activity in the newsroom: Tim Brown's face glowing after following through on a tip that led to a scoop and accolades he richly deserved. The nervous pacing of Jamie, the night editor trying to produce a catchy headline. It was a close-knit fraternity, and we sometimes shared thoughts and insights that sparked conversations deep into the night. The final stages of production, waves of editing, headline writing, a careful search for errors enabled us to bond the way I imagine cops and firefighters do.

Being honored for something I loved gave me an immense feeling of satisfaction. Finally, all the long hours and dedication to the craft were being noticed by judges from cities I never visited. I had taken a bold step away from the shadows of self-doubt and mediocrity. No more "Woe is me" crap.

I recalled a phrase my French teacher used: *raison d'être*, the most important reason for being.

It was a tradition that the entire staff would gather in the main meeting room and lightly applaud each contest winner as their name was announced. I remember wondering if the same feeling of aplomb swept over athletes and entertainers when they pleased an audience after an extraordinary performance.

What made this better than the glittered backdrop bestowed upon well-known celebrities, however, is that it came with a naked truth of what the work was about.

One could take pride in telling what needed to be told with as much skill and accuracy as talent would allow, all the quiet praise echoing within the inner sanctum of who we were and what we could become. It meant something to hear praise echo from the outside world, but more so when it came from peers. The players know more about what it takes to hit a home run than those who witness the feat.

I now know no other job could have provided such a complete sense of contentment. It was better than money.

Back then my mind was moving too fast to appreciate such wisdom. I was not geographically committed like some reporters, photographers, and advertising staff I felt lucky to work with.

I was determined to advance beyond this newsroom, this city, this region. To foment the drive for richer pastures, I had to separate myself from the flock I grew to love.

Many with the talent to work for a larger paper didn't think about that. They were happy with what they had because that sense of place was the stuff that would nurture the roots of family homes, weddings, funerals, and yes, an occasional scandal.

I envied them for that. But fierce ambition, I would eventually learn, has its price.

As I fingered away dust from the edge of one of the plaques, it struck me that these awards were about as relevant to my life today as the holiday ornaments that would probably never adorn another tree.

Just when you think you have acquired something eternally golden, an accomplishment that will sustain you for the rest of your days, vicissitudes of life have a way of rendering it transitory.

I noticed some clippings that were in another box next to the awards. There were also some things I wrote when I knew how deeply I loved Anna.

One poem caught my eye. It was titled "She Brings Me Sunshine."

I discovered a shard of her sunshine.
Was this something good for body and soul?
Or maybe something to be isolated and rejected?

I had to find out.
But to know her in the present, I needed to find out about her past.

How else could I trust her current words and motives?
Was there a touchstone to tell me if this was something other than fool's gold?

"Not so fast," she said.
"I'll give you time for your scientific assay, but only if you walk and talk with me.
Here, down this lane. The place where I learned of truth plain and simple.
If you move aside those countless hurdles, those tests of character,

I'll show you something truly precious.

I'll find a way to surgeon away the scar tissue on your heart and soul
if you feel the honest brush stroke of this artful kiss
and see your way to a faith beyond flesh.

You will know me now and again."

And then maybe, just maybe, your unique sun will shine upon me.

I felt her intensity in hot patches of touch and
search and embrace.

All this quilting her personality, imagination, and
affection in a way I had never known.
That's some will, I thought.

The way she persisted until the moon traded
places with the sun,

suddenly I didn't care about the details.
All I knew was that there was finally a *we*.

I discovered a new way to be whole.

Next to this, I found another piece written to document her
wondrous effect on me.

She introduced herself as my soon-to-be email-
pal sunshine.

"Fine," I said, "but who are you? Surely not some
LOL wink wink robotic computer user."

"No, I'm your sunshine, sunshine," she said.

"Yes, that's nice, but who are you?" I repeated.

She realized I needed stories, shades of her past to
handle all of this sunshine.

Then I could understand her present and see her
future.

"I'm the girl who had an epiphany at the tender
age of serendipity," she said.

I laughed. She didn't. That's because the epiphany was not funny but sad.

When Anna and her classmates were herded into the boiler room to escape nature's nasty roar, she was struck by a poignant realization.

If this was to be her last day on earth, Anna would not know what it was like to tell her family—yes, even her mother—she loved them.

Nature's roar subsided into a nasty cough. And Anna knew she had an announcement to make

She told her story with such passion, her family was transformed overnight. From that point forward, Anna's declaration of love would be the family crest and a chain of hugs never to be broken.

That said, Anna still found it difficult to cast her natural ray of sunlight on her friends. Years after her epiphany, during a school reunion, they asked who that girl was in the middle of the room.

Yes, the one with the white dress and glasses, the one with the average-looking brown hair.
Then Anna had another epiphany. Why not let her exterior reflect her interior and then the whole world would know what she knew? Her joy from inside only blossomed when her sunshine could be felt by others.

So she let her hair burst forth with sunlight. and her smile followed suit, with ray upon ray of love.

When I realized this, I knew that I needed Anna's sunshine—to make my eyes moist then dry again.

Then I knew I needed her sunshine to renew my sense of hope and love in an epiphany that felt like serendipity.

I hoped this would be our own crest and a chain never to be broken.

I felt a tear rolling down my cheek. God, I hated it when things were fractured between the two of us. There had to be a way to get things back to where they were.

All this reading brought a heaviness to my eyes, sending me into a deep sleep. When you surrender yourself to sleep, you have no idea where your subconscious will take you. This time it was Johnny Miller's backyard.

He was something of an anomaly in that he had no use for sports in a neighborhood that thrived on games.

Since this was before I met Matt and the others at school, I was only a spectator to the games the neighbor kids played. I was more than happy to become his friend.

Johnny was the only kid on the block who knew what it was like to live with a divorced mother.

I can trace one of my first sexual arousals to the time I witnessed Johnny's Mom in her underwear. She was doing the laundry in the basement, and I happened to walk by one of the basement windows when she was sorting the clothes.

Since I was on the outside, looking in, her back to me the whole time, she was unaware I was eyeing her.

I was mesmerized by the fullness of her breasts, resting yet somehow threatening to leap out of that immaculate white bra and causing my rapidly beating heart to explode. The contrast of tanned skin against the white bra put an electric charge into my entire body.

Perhaps the fact that this was a part of the female anatomy I had never seen before could explain why it left an indelible impression on my mind and an erection that seemed to last forever.

I was drawn to Johnny mostly out of curiosity. He seemed not to care that being different—declaring that science was more important than sports gave him rebel status. I didn't care that the other kids just thought this qualified him as nerd of the neighborhood.

Johnny's mind was sharp as a razor, more educated than most of us. He was a fountain of information on just about anything but athletics.

He showed me how to burn a hole through a leaf by holding a magnifying glass over it during a sunny day. When he demonstrated the myriad ways to use his Swiss Army knife, I became his most prized pupil.

Because I was about the only friend he had in the entire neighborhood, Johnny said he would lend the knife to me.

"But you must bring it back in a day or so," he insisted with a look so serious, I felt like I was looking at an adult rather than a kid.

I couldn't wait to pull out all the blades and test the myriad uses of this knife at home. I pulled out the longest blade and threw the knife against an old oak tree in our backyard.

To my dismay, the tree rejected the knife, causing the blade to bend upon impact. When I tried to put the blade back into the body of the knife, it wouldn't fit. So I worked vigorously to straighten it out. This only made it more crooked. I anguished over what to do.

I couldn't take it to my sisters, Cynthia or Claire, because they would just tell me that I really screwed up and that the best thing to do would be to buy Johnny a new knife.

At the tender age of nine, I didn't have any money to speak of— at least not enough to buy something as unique as this.

I imagined that I misplaced the knife. When I told Johnny what transpired, he became so angry, he insisted our friendship would cease if I didn't produce the knife. Johnny said he would be forced to tell his mother what happened if I didn't come up with the knife before the end of the week.

"Either way you need to take care of this before my mother goes to your mother and tells her what a bad kid you've been," he threatened, causing me to feel like this was a parent-to-child confrontation.

I realized then and there that bullying didn't necessarily involve physical strength.

Eventually my parents found out about it and told me if I couldn't find the knife, they would have to buy a new one, and I would have to work it off by doing extra chores. There would also be no TV for a month.

I retraced steps to the buried knife and showed Johnny what really happened. To my surprise, he just laughed and told me he knew how to fix the crooked blade.

"All you had to do was tell the truth in the first place," he said, shrinking back to the kid I wanted to hang out with.

There was no getting around the fact that I was more interested in saving my hide than being honest about what happened to the knife.

"Dad, Dad, are you sleeping?" came a voice that sounded like Danny.

"Huh?"

I tried to focus on the face in front of me, but the only eye that functioned offered a hazy picture.

"Oh, Danny," I said, still trying to focus on his face. "Say, Danny, have you ever worked with a Swiss Army knife? I mean in the Scouts?"

"What? What made you think of that?"

"I don't know, just wondering," I said.

"No, can't say that I have ever worked with a Swiss Army knife," said Danny, appearing perplexed.

"Oh, okay, forget that I said anything. Just one of those things that pops into the old man's head."

"Well, Mom wanted me to tell you that dinner's ready."

As I made my way up the stairs, the house felt cold and remote, like an uninhabited baseball stadium in winter. There was an eerie stillness to the place, like the sudden noncommerce quiet that envelops a community on Christmas.

11

Echoes of a Family Adrift

The dinner table was once a communal setting, a place to come together as a family and recover from whatever wounds were inflicted on us by the outside world. There were occasions when it became a setting of celebration, like the time Annette announced that she scored a 34 on the ACT test. We all knew this gave her scholarship leverage and increased the number of schools interested in her.

Then there was the time Danny won top prize at his school's science fair.

Now it was a telling reminder of how far apart we were. The silence reminded me of the meals we shared when my mother was alive and struggling with Alzheimer's. I hated the sound of her fork tapping the plate, like a metronome with a loose spring. I watched her palsied hands attempting to steady her fork long enough to gather food.

After witnessing several failed attempts, the sound of the fork tapping out what could only be interpreted as a death knell, I realized I would have to feed her from this point on.

"So when does the patch come off?" said Danny, mercifully breaking the uncomfortable silence.

"Oh, that reminds me," said Anna, showing no outward signs of anger. "You have a follow-up appointment with the Retina Institute tomorrow. I believe they said they would take the patch off then."

"Okay, what time is that?" I said, noticing that Danny hadn't touched much of the food on his plate.

"I'll have to check what I wrote down, but I think it's for nine thirty," she said.

"So, Danny, what's going on at school? Anything interesting?" I said, trying to get him thinking about something other than my medical issues.

"Nah, not really. I'm still trying to come up with an idea for the essay," he said. "I know Christmas is several months from now, but I'd still like to get something going on that."

"What do you have so far?" said Anna, the lines fanning out just below her eyes, showing fatigue.

"Nothing, I can't even settle on something from the title they gave us," he said with a shrug.

"Whenever I had difficulty coming up with an idea for a column, I usually just focused on something that had a profound effect on me," I said. "It might have been an experience that changed my thinking on a particular subject. Or maybe something that led to a realization about life."

"Yeah? Like what?" said Danny, looking somewhat perplexed.

"Well, like the time I covered the flood in Cape Girardeau, when I went to the Red Cross shelter and interviewed the woman who lost her house and all her possessions. You would think she would be depressed, yet there she was, trying to tell jokes to her children and the family next to them. How could someone tell jokes at a time like this? I wondered. I think she just felt blessed that she still had the most important thing in her life: the love of her children and the life they were still able to share."

For some reason, this seemed to lift Anna out of her sour mood.

"That's an inspiring story," she said with enthusiasm. "I remember the column you wrote about that. It was one of your best." She beamed.

"Well, thank you."

"Danny, have you ever read your father's columns?"

"Huh?" muttered Danny. "Have I what?"

"Columns," barked Anna, sounding as if she were addressing a distracted student. "Have you looked at any of your father's columns?"

"Not all of them. I've seen a few. Those were mostly about sports," he said with a frown.

"You should look at them. They might spark an idea or two," encouraged Anna.

"Maybe I will," he said, staring at his plate. "That's a . . . important story about the Red Cross shelter. I didn't know about that."

His eyes swept downward as he said this, appearing to search for something that fell off the table. His mind was focused on something, but I could tell it had nothing to do with the Red Cross story.

After dinner, I waited for Danny to retreat to his room and brought up the matter of Anna going back to work as a writer of grant proposals.

"Anna, I don't know why I said what I did, but the more I think about it, it seems like a wonderful idea," I encouraged.

"Oh, I don't know. I mean, I haven't even investigated what is involved," she said with a look of self-doubt. "I don't know if I'd be any good at it."

"There's only one way to find out," I said, doing my best to show support.

. "I'll get more information," she promised.

"When you focus hard on something, you usually find a way to be successful at it," I reminded her. "I don't see why this would be any different."

That was enough to put me back in the bedroom.

The next day, the eye patch was removed, and I was given a few tests to measure the status of my right eye. I couldn't make out much of anything except the largest letter at the top of the chart.

I asked why only half of the eye was functional, the other half covered in black. It was if someone pulled a shade halfway down. "You have what is called a gas bubble," said the doctor. "It's there to stabilize the retina. It will go away over time, probably in a week or so."

"A week? You mean I can't go back to work for at least a week?"

"Oh no, you're not even legal to get behind the wheel right now," he cautioned. "If you have a job that requires driving, I'm afraid you'll have to be off for several days. We'll know more in the next visit. Sometimes the healing process goes faster with one person than another."

When Anna learned of my situation, she made the decision to go back to work full-time.

"I guess I'm going to find out if I can get work as a writer of grant proposals," she said. I noticed a change in her demeanor. Her confidence in focusing on a problem and finding a solution was as strong as ever.

Now all I had to do was find a way to get my car back in time for Annette's visit.

When I called Matt to find out how long it would be, he sounded distracted.

"Toby told me it would be done in a few days, so it shouldn't take very long," he said. "As far as payment goes, Toby said more than once that a few tickets to the Cubs-Cards series would do just fine."

"Did you come up with the tickets?"

"Uh, oh yeah, I need to make sure they'll be sent to me in time. Thanks for reminding me," I said, still not sure how I was going to swing this. "I appreciate you doing this for Toby," said Matt.

"Never hurts to keep your connections with the Cardinals, right?"

"Yeah, right."

"Okay, I'll give you the details when I have them."

I didn't want to ask a favor from a former colleague, but I was desperate. I called Tim, the reporter with whom I shared fond memories of the *Southeast Missouri Bulletin Journal* newspaper in Cape Girardeau.

***

"You worked the police beat but spent time in the sports department when you were hired over twenty years ago."

Tim registered a look of disappointment.

"I'm sure you remember the conversation," I said.

"Yeah," he replied with disdain.

***

"Hey, Tim, it's Doug," I said when the woman at the front desk transferred the call.

"Hey, Doug, what the hell. What are you doing? You still writing? I'll bet you're working on the great American novel."

"Um, well, it's not really going that well right now. I tried my hand at fiction, and it tried my patience. I'm not sure I'm any good at that," I confessed.

"You were always good at feature articles," he said. "In fact, if you had any kind of fault, it was that you tended to embellish."

"Yeah, what was it John Ramsey used to say? I could find a way to turn chicken shit into chicken salad," I recalled.

"Yeah. Old John had a knack for sayings like that," he said.

"How's John doing?" I ventured, feeling a wave of nostalgia.

"Um, John's having a bit of difficulty in his marriage," he confided. "Too complicated to go into right now."

"Hmm. Okay, fair enough," I said, wondering why one of the best headline writers I ever worked with couldn't boil it down into a few sentences.

"Well, how are things at the paper?"

After a slight pause, he said, "Things have changed drastically in the last year. Rumor has it we're going to be working for a new publisher soon. The paper is being sold. Some of the good reporters have already left."

"Really. Like who?"

"You remember Scott Reid?" he said.

"Yeah, the young guy with the wire-rimmed glasses and ambition to make it to the major leagues of journalism," I recalled.

"Yeah, well, you made quite an impression on him because when he gave a tribute to some of the editors and reporters who helped him become an award-winning journalist, you got the highest praise."

"No, you're kidding," I said, astonished Scott would even say something like that.

"I'm not kidding," he said. "Remember when you told him about how you were able to get better quotes than the competition?"

"Um, was it something about following your nose and gut, even at the risk of running into a dead end?" I said.

"Yeah, that's part of it," he said. "The gist of it is that you told him you interviewed a tiny woman who was putting sand into bags after the 1993 flood with a shovel that was taller than her," he added.

"Oh yeah, I told him that sometimes the quote that gives real life to a story comes from a source some might dismiss as irrelevant," I said. "I remember telling Scott about how I approached janitors, lowly assistants, and people who were considered invisibles for information. They were so delighted that someone was taking them seriously that they gave me more than I needed. And it was usually information that was gold."

"Exactly," he said. "Scott advanced past Triple A and is now in the majors with a great gig in Kansas City. He's working for the *Star* as a feature writer."

"Oh, that's great," I said, feeling a sense of deep satisfaction welling up from within. "You know, Tim, you're good enough to play in the majors," I reminded him.

"Yeah, yeah. Well, I think my chance at that is gone," he said in a dismissive tone.

When I tried to reassure him, he seemed agitated.

"Look, Doug, it's great to hear from you, but . . . don't . . . Let's just not go there."

"Oh, okay," I said, disappointed he was still unwilling to admit to how much talent he had.

After a few awkward seconds of silence, he said, "Oh well, keep working on the novel. You always did magnificent work here. I know it will eventually come through for you."

"But . . . now I haven't heard about what you're . . .," he said nervously.

"I'm picking up writing gigs here and there," I lied, hoping he wouldn't pry too much into my current job status.

Before he could ask about the writing jobs, I quickly added, "Look, the reason I'm calling is I need a favor."

"Oh, sure. Name it."

"I need a couple of press passes to the Cards-Cubs series," I said. "My wife was always nagging me to show her what the press box at Busch Stadium is like, and I need to make up for a mistake that put me in the doghouse, if you know what I mean."

"Yeah sure. Well, I'm not in sports anymore, as you know, but I can probably get that. The guys in sports are busy with local stuff, so they couldn't use the passes anyway. Okay, I'll give you a call to let you know for sure, but it seems like a done deal at this point. Let me look at the schedule here. Oh, there's a series between the Cubs and Cards next weekend. Should I try for that?"

"Man, that would be great," I said, relieved that I had a genuine plan in place. I could get my car back in time to pass inspection, and everything would be back to normal.

He called the next day to confirm that the passes would be available and ready to be picked up the day of the game.

"All I ask is that you and your wife enjoy the game without drawing any undue attention. I mean if they suspect that you don't work for the *Southeast Missouri Bulletin Journal* anymore, we could lose our press credentials for a long time, or for good," he warned.

"Hey, I used to be in the business, remember? I think I know how to act in the press box."

That's when he quickly apologized and told me to enjoy the game.

"Okay, Tim, I owe you big-time for this," I said, not really thinking that I'd ever come through with a return favor.

It's what we used to say to each other all the time when I lived there.

"Hey, if you're planning to come down sometime, give me a buzz and I'll set up a great weekend," he said.

"Oh, I'd love that. Sounds great."

***

Tim signaled he needed to take a break.

"Didn't really want to relieve that moment, but I guess it does explain where you were coming from," said Tim. "You were clinging to a once-proud image, and it was hard to let go. It doesn't excuse what you did, but I have a better handle on where you were at."

"I know," I said. "Do you want me to stop?"

He thought for a few seconds then replied, "No, I need to hear the whole thing."

"It's not easy, but keep going."

***

12

Pressing My Luck

I called Matt to let him know that Toby would be experiencing a rare treat.

"How's the press box sound?" I declared.

"Oh, sweet," he shouted. "I knew you had great connections."

"Yeah, well, listen, Matt. I want to make sure Toby knows how things work in the press box," I stressed.

"Oh yeah, so what does he need to do?'

"The passes are under my name and Anna's, so Toby needs to find a date for the game. Was he planning on taking a girlfriend?"

"Oh yeah, he told me there was some hot gal he's been wanting to ask out but was looking for the right time. She's a big Cardinal fan so this would be perfect."

"Okay, well, just remember to tell them that they need to act like they're Doug and Anna Anderson. If they're asked to show some type of ID, they need to say that my wife and I couldn't make it due to some family emergency and that they were going to cover the game in our place. Make sure he knows that it's a press box full of reporters working the game. They can enjoy themselves but not to excess, if you get my drift."

"Oh sure, I'll let him know," said Matt. "The check-engine light doesn't show. He brought the car by my house, and we took it out on the highway to make sure. I'll swing by later today."

"Okay, I appreciate all of this," I said.

"Hey, I appreciate what you're doing for my nephew," he said. "He's been kind of drifting for a while. Maybe having a girlfriend will make him grow up a little. This helps everybody out, right?"

"Yeah, I guess it docs."

I had nothing left to do but recover so I could go back to work.

It seemed like my time dragged while everyone else in the house was busy with various projects. Danny was involved with the essay, Anna was working feverishly to learn the nuances of writing grant proposals, and Annette was about to inhabit our home for a few weeks.

Since it was difficult to do crossword puzzles or read anything longer than a few lines in the comics section of the newspaper, I decided to watch television. I found a station that played reruns of old westerns like *Gunssmoke*, *The Rifleman*, and *Bonanza*.

I tried to count how often Pa and Mark were uttered on *The Rifleman*. I lost count. I didn't know much about guns, but it seemed like Lucas McCain fired off more bullets than a rifle could hold.

The only time I spent with Anna was doctor visits.

I grew weary of watching television, so I walked around the house looking for projects that could eat up some idle time until I was ready to return to work.

Staying sober for several days brought positive changes. There was more clarity and sensitivity to people and places. I noticed that the front door needed to be sanded down and refinished. The sun had beaten down on it for so many years, the wood was rendered dry and on the verge of being warped. That would be a good project when I was cleared for strenuous activity.

There was an antique table in the basement that Anna and I found when we explored old abandoned houses in the country. When I cleared off the thick layer of dust, I saw how it was in dire need of refinishing. The table reminded me of the time we invited Anna's parents to dinner to announce that she was pregnant with Annette.

Her father, who was a prominent trial attorney, seemed to be thinking about a case he was working on because he barely changed his expression. Her mother was also lost in thought. I knew they didn't approve of me.

"How much do journalists make these days?" said her father with a disarming stare. "Enough to support a family?"

The dinner became such a disappointment, we didn't have them over again for a few years.

While I pondered how I would be able to accomplish these projects, Annette arrived. She seemed to enliven the house by simply showing up. Their tight, natural embrace at the front door reminded me how much they missed each other's company.

It reminded me of the relationship I had with my father.

When Annette learned that Danny was going to write an essay for the Scouts, she vowed to help him if he wanted her input.

She announced that she had a new boyfriend. When I asked her who he was and what he did, all the things a father wants to know, she said she would provide all the details later.

Annette quickly changed the subject, electing to address my medical condition.

"So the operation was a success?" she asked with a hopeful look.

"Sure, I was in the hands of the best," I said.

"Good to hear," she said. "Now, you didn't say the best what."

We had a good laugh over that. Annette had the same comedic timing my Dad had. You couldn't teach that. It was either inside of you or it wasn't.

13

Warning Signs

It was nice to see the whole family together for our evening meal. Anna prepared lasagna, everyone's favorite, with soup, salad, and fresh bread.

"So tell us about your boyfriend," I said, passing the salad bowl to Annette.

"Well, he's someone I met at the library. We were both doing research and noticed that we kept the same schedule. We met for a cup of coffee, and then one thing led to another and we became friends then roommates," she said, searching our eyes for approbation. We gave no indication that there was a problem.

She continued.

"He's a really nice guy, very smart. He's from the East. He tells me his family isn't rich but lives comfortably. I didn't care how much money they have. He's in medical school right now. He's not sure what he wants to get into, maybe research instead of a traditional practice. He tells me the malpractice insurance is a lot cheaper when you're in a lab instead of the operating room. Mice and rats can't afford to retain an attorney."

"Oh yeah, funny," Anna said. "Well, I'm glad you found someone who makes you happy. Does he have a name?"

"Oh, sorry, his name is Alex," said Annette, appearing cautious about what information she wished to share about her new boyfriend.

"It's not real serious or anything," she said then looked down at her plate.

"But it could be," I said.

"Oh, now, don't go pushing her into anything," cautioned Anna.

"I'm not," I replied. "I'm just hoping one day we'll be taking pictures of the clan with the grandchildren."

This caused Annette to clear her throat and get busy eating. I noticed that her face looked fuller, and she seemed to be putting on more weight. That was a good thing because she was always too skinny in high school.

"Does Alex like to cook?" I ventured, trying to find something to break the silence.

"He's okay. We're both so busy lately, we just get a bite when we find the time," she said, tugging nervously at her piece of bread.

"Hey, are we going to keep talking about me, or does Danny get a word in once?" protested Annette, seemingly uncomfortable about something said or unsaid.

"What's going on in your world?" she added, looking in the direction of Danny.

"Not much," he shrugged. "I'm struggling to get started on an essay for the Scouts, and I joined a chess club, but other than that, not a whole lot going on."

"Chess club, I'm impressed, little brother. I was awful at that game the first time I tried it, and I'm still terrible. It's just one of those games that you either have it or you don't. You have it."

Danny looked pleasantly surprised.

"Yeah, I guess this qualifies me as the family nerd." He shrugged.

"Nerd? Nah," said Annette. "Not even close. So tell me about this essay," she enthused.

"The topic is family and friends. I have a few ideas, but it's mostly just putting them down," he said. "My problem is I'm just not as creative as you guys," he complained.

"Maybe we're better at language, but if you've got a good story, it doesn't matter," insisted Annette.

"How do I tell it, though?" he said. "That seems to be the hard part, organizing all of that."

"I'd be happy to help out when I can get the time," she added.

"Okay," he said, looking down.

"No, really, I'd like to help," said Annette. "I'm going to be somewhat busy on something I hope will lead to material for my dissertation. I'm going to talk to the director of the Juvenile Detention Center tomorrow. He said I could start out as an observer, and then maybe if it appealed to me, I could be a regular volunteer. It would really give me insight into all the problems a teenager has when he or she makes bad choices."

"That sounds interesting," I said. "I bet that would give you some good material. But you should be careful. Some of those kids could be violent if they've got drug problems."

"Oh, I think I can take care of myself," she assured us. "Besides, they have people to handle that sort of thing."

"So how did you decide you wanted to help teenagers?" I said.

"Well, I think you already know about my interest in the conscious and subconscious mind and the role that subliminal messages play. Parents get mad at their children and call them lazy, stupid, or the kind that never amounts to much. You hear that enough and you start to believe it. So you figure you're destined to become a loser. Forget about school, what's that ever going to do for you? And a job? If Dad can't get one, how am I ever going to land one? Teens are going to make some bad choices; I'm just interested in limiting the number and the severity. Instead of a teen saying 'No way,' I want them to say 'Why not?' I want them to know that if they're willing to mine their talents, to know the power of knowledge, they can combat systematic injustice.

"But to dream big, you must develop a plan that can work.

"You need to know that arguments designed to bring you down contain all sorts of fallacies.

"They need to know about hasty generalization, omissions, distortions, and thought-terminating cliché. These poisonous substances can creep into your subconscious and play a nasty role in race and gender bias. The same holds true with self-esteem. That's where you deserve high praise," she said, casting an appreciative glance at Anna.

"Instead of stressing the negative, you accentuated the positive. Mom, I remember when you told me that the best lessons come from failure, not success. That's true. When I fell, you showed me how to pick myself up. I was thinking about this the other day. It all turned around when we had that talk about undoing all the nots. Remember?"

"Yes," said Anna with a look of quiet satisfaction. "I tried that with some of my students, but it didn't make the same impression."

"Oh, it turned my world around," stated Annette with conviction. I was confused.

"Are you talking about knots in your stomach?" I said, feeling left out of the loop. "Help me out here. I don't remember that."

Annette and Anna burst into simultaneous laughter.

"No, not K-N-O-T," said Anna. "It's N-O-T. As in, I'm not pretty, not smart enough, not athletic enough."

Annette's face flushed with excitement.

"Yeah," she said. "Once I worked on the negative force that was keeping me from getting good grades or making new friends, I felt unburdened."

"I'm constantly wrestling with this nurture-versus-nature thing. Are we just products of our environment, or does nurturing change things in our favor?" she said, her eyes enlivened and blinking as she spoke at a brisk pace.

"You nursed an underdeveloped mind with spoonfuls of encouragement and, when the time was right, ushered in a series of challenges. You enabled me to develop a sense of self that wasn't imitative of magazine art, literature, or movie characters. Imagine going from fear of trying to having the confidence to take on just about anything no matter the odds of success or failure. I was so lucky to benefit from such skillful nurturing."

She continued, "And now I know, a kid living in Wellston doesn't have the same advantages as a kid living in Ladue or Chesterfield. But they need to know they're not doomed. I think I can show them how they can make a difference on their family and the world."

Anna's face beamed from a look of pride. It reflected what I was feeling.

"Your mother is getting into something new as well," I said.

"Oh yeah, what's that, Mom?"

"I'm just thinking about it right now," said Anna. "I'm kicking around the idea of writing grant proposals."

"You'd be good at that," said Annette with a rush of enthusiasm. "Especially if you wrote proposals for grants that go toward education."

This sparked an idea.

"You know, I was thinking the same thing," said Anna with zest. "I'm not sure how I would go about it, but yes, that's something I could bring up when I send in my proposal."

When it was time to go to bed, I noticed that Anna was deep in thought.

"Are you thinking about what you're going to say tomorrow?" I said, studying the pensive look.

"Oh, uh, no, actually, I was thinking about what Danny said at the dinner table," she said.

"What? You mean about being a nerd? He should know better than that. I thought I told him about the kid I knew in grade school," I said, trying to remember if I meant to tell him or if I actually did.

"You mean the kid who was bullied," said Anna.

"Yeah, Jimmy."

"If you told him about that, I wasn't there," she said, pulling the covers up. I began to doubt that we had that talk.

Anna leaned back into the pillow then popped back up. Danny's comment was still on her mind.

"I don't know. It struck me that I'd never heard him talk like that before," she said. "At first I thought it was because Annette was here. It seems he's always been in awe of her accomplishments. I do remember him saying something about how many friends she has," she added. "I just think self-deprecation, especially in someone as young as him, is a sign that we should pay more attention to his wants and needs."

"Oh, I don't know. I've always thought self-deprecation was overrated."

Anna's face quickly flushed.

"There you go with the jokes. It seems like every time I try to talk seriously about one of the children, you try to make light of it with humor. Not everything is a joke," she said sullenly.

"Honey, I know that," I said, attempting to appease. "Like I said, it's probably nothing more than a phase that he'll get over before you know it."

"I'm more bothered by what Annette said earlier," I confided. "The thing about undoing the nots. That's the first I heard of that. Where was I when that lesson was going on?"

"Oh, you were probably working on a story at the newspaper," she said. "It's not a big deal."

"No? This is the one thing that turned her life around, and I didn't even know about it," I protested. "She only looked at you when she mentioned how much a part you played in nurturing her."

Anna turned away and shook her head.

"She meant both of us. It just looked like she was talking to me."

I wasn't convinced.

"I don't know. She'd be right in giving the praise to you. I was always away when she needed help with something."

Anna dismissed the notion with a wave of her hand. That usually meant she was done talking about it.

"I've got to get some sleep," she insisted. "I'll need to be sharp for tomorrow."

That was code for no sex tonight. I was hoping with the entire family here, she'd warm up to some lovemaking. We always had sex when the family was in harmony. I thought tonight would be one of those nights. I figured wrong.

The next day, everyone flew out of the house—Danny to school, Annette to talk to the director of the Juvenile Detention Center, and Anna to her interview for what she hoped would lead to a new job at a university.

I padded around the house, looking for something to occupy my time. I went through the TV channels but found nothing interesting.

From time to time, I closed my good eye to see if there was any improvement in the right eye. The progress was so slow, I wondered if my sight would ever be completely restored.

I searched for crossword puzzles, magazines, anything to make time pass. When I was looking through a stack of magazines on the bed stand, I found the *National Geographic* article Anna was reading titled "A Cure in Sight."

One paragraph caught my attention. It read, "Roughly one in every 200 people on Earth—39 million of us—can't see. Another 246 million have reduced vision."

There was a chart showing the effects of glaucoma, cataracts, refractive errors, and age-related macular degeneration.

I found the information so depressing, I decided to go back to watching television.

There was a commercial for a convection oven that got my attention. The woman pitching the product looked a little like Claire. It reminded me that I hadn't talked to her or Cynthia in several months.

Claire and her husband moved to Chicago when he was promoted to sales manager of the Midwest region. Cynthia was living in San Francisco. Her husband was some sort of software engineer and needed to be close to Silicon Valley, so off they went ten years ago.

I decided to call Claire and see what was going on in her life. I left a message, telling her it wasn't an emergency but I wanted to catch up on what she and her family were doing.

When I was trying to insert the eye drops into my right eye, I heard the phone ring.

"Oh, Claire, hi. Thanks for calling back," I said.

"Well, I thought maybe something was wrong, but then you didn't sound like it," she said. "Anyway, it's good to hear from you. What's going on there?"

I told her about the detached retina and what Anna and the kids were doing.

"What about you?"

"Rob works long hours, so I really only see him over the weekend," she said. "The kids are pretty much trying different jobs to find out what they want to be when they grow up. You know, typical early-twenty-something stuff. That's great about Anna. I'm thinking about going back to work myself. I mean we don't need the money so much as I need to get out of the house before I go crazy. You know?"

"Oh, do I. I can't go back to work until this eye heals," I lamented. "I've been going nuts just trying to find things to do. I can't drive, and everybody is so busy, I don't feel right about asking for a ride, even if it's to the grocery store."

"Oh gosh, I wish I could help," she said. "You'll be ready to go back to work before you know it."

"Yeah, you're right. It's not a big deal. Speaking of crazy, remember those red blazers Mom made for us? I couldn't believe she expected me to wear that thing to school."

Claire was laughing as I spoke.

"Oh, that was so funny the way you stomped on that thing on the way home from grade school," she mused. "You were so mad, I thought your eyes were going to jump out of your head. Hey, maybe that's the reason you had problems with the retina. You pushed it too hard."

"Yeah, right," I said. "Funny."

"Seriously, what made you so mad, I mean other than the fact that you hated wearing that thing?"

"I was supposed to play the organ at school the very day she made me wear that thing," I recalled. "Mom was so proud of what she made for me, she felt certain this was the perfect attire for a recital in front of my peers. It's not a recital, I reminded her. I was just playing a few notes on the organ.

"On my way home from school, some of the kids from the sixth grade made fun of me. I believe they yelled, 'Hey, Liberace, you got any more of those jackets at home?'"

"Oh my god, so what did you do?"

"My face turned as red as the jacket. I was so mad, I just pulled the jacket off and stomped on it until it was a crumpled mess. I remember what you and Cynthia told me later," I recalled.

"What was that?"

"You told me that Dad shouted to Mom that he didn't want her turning me into a pantywaist."

"Oh, that's right," she said. "Gosh, we could go on and on. It's nice to reminisce like this."

"It sure is. Hey, you know what, you guys should come here for the holidays, if not Thanksgiving then Christmas," I suggested.

"That's funny you should say that because we were thinking that we haven't had an old-fashioned Christmas in a long time. I mean with you and Cynthia. Maybe I could give her a call and see if she's up for it. You know how awful those Christmases were with Mom getting all depressed on us."

"Yeah, it went from being my favorite time of the year to my least favorite," I said. "So we should make up for it starting this year."

We talked for a little while longer, and she promised to get back to me on whether they would be coming to St. Louis for Thanksgiving or Christmas. After I hung up, I thought of the time Claire showed me how to get free candy out of a machine. We were taking piano lessons at the St. Louis Institute of Music and knew this was something Dad couldn't afford. So we did our best to show Mom that we were woefully inept. We thought that would make her realize we should stop taking lessons.

It didn't work. When Mom was set on something, you couldn't change her mind. As I made my way out of the lessons, anguishing over the notion that I was likely the worst student my teacher had, Claire found a way to lift me out of my despair. She showed me how to smack the side of the candy machine then quickly jerk the lever in such a way that the candy just fell down the chute without any payment.

She even went so far as to show me how we were lucky.

"Hey, you've still got your hearing, don't you?" she noted. I didn't understand how this was an advantage. "Beethoven was a genius, but he didn't even get to hear half of what he created. So consider yourself lucky." The laugh we shared felt therapeutic.

14

Family Matters

I remembered what it was like on Christmas. We were in a house rather than a home. One year the holiday season lost its luster. The silver Christmas tree seemed like a discarded object from a remote planet taking up space in the living room. Lights blinked dutifully, sending reflections off haphazard tinsel and strategically placed ornaments.

The color wheel labored to turn a fake, anemic tree into something dazzling. The opposite occurred. The wheel functioned like a cheap, overused toy that was determined to run its batteries down so it could finally go to sleep. The routine of a Sunday pot roast ceased being because nothing was on schedule anymore. And Mom was retreating to the bedroom with that monumental headache.

When I left for Cape Girardeau, I tried to restore my interest in the holidays by clearing the slate and starting over. I went to the basement and found something I penned to rekindle the spirit of Christmas.

One was titled "Christmas Eve":

> It has that curious look and feel
> A fragile whisper that could become a pronounced promise
> White flakes circling the air like wounded helicopters
> Then some serious stuff

An army of poetic rain rendered splendidly
retarded
Soft slanted sheets of holiday livery laying down
low
To blanket
America's woes and foes? Oh no!
Tonight it's nature's wintry linen offering a fresh
start
The wondrous hush is formidable
No ethnic rancor
No natural disaster
No global beast armed with nuclear rhetoric
No Homeland Security hue to watch
No talk of corporate scandal
No steroid-enhanced athletic feat to challenge
No abuse-begets-abuse incident
A lottery winner?
Tonight I don't care who gets the instant cash
It's Christmas Eve
I've got precious sustenance
Food, books, movies, family, friends, honesty,
hope . . .
And well, the restless push for peace
Let it rain!

I received a call from Cynthia a day later.

"Doug, are you blind or something?" chortled Cynthia.

"Yeah, got a tin cup I can use?" I countered.

"Gosh, you must be in a bad way," she replied in mock seriousness. "You can't even come up with a tin cup? I guess I'll have to get
back there and make things right."

When we were done joking, she asked me about Anna and the
kids.

"Claire tells me she might make it there during the holidays."

"Yes, she did mention that," I said. "You interested in joining
us?"

"I'd love to. I just need to get with Brad and see what his schedule is like. After talking with Claire, it seems like we haven't done anything like this in more years than I realized."

"It sure has. We'd love to have you guys here. I know the kids would get a big kick out of it too."

I knew the conversation would eventually get around to what I was doing with myself these days.

"You're in between journalism gigs?" she said.

"Well, the way it looks, I might be out of the profession for good," I lamented.

"Oh no, not my award-winning little brother," she said. "Seriously, Doug, I have never seen you so happy as when you were writing for the newspaper. Writing pulled you out of that horrible shyness you went through as a kid. Maybe sitting behind a computer screen gives you the buffer you need. Anyway, I think you should exhaust every avenue before you wave the white flag."

"I know. I'm just saying I'm not holding out hope that it will happen. If the right thing comes along, I'll think about it."

"Oh no, Doug, you have to get aggressive when it comes to things like this," she insisted. "Paying lip service isn't going to get it done. I thought my days as an artist were over, then Brad suggested that I put together my own show with paintings I thought best represented who I was and what I cared about. Do you believe I made very little money in sales that weekend? But once again I felt the fire in my belly. I'm still painting. I think I might have a show at one of the studios in Oakland."

"Oh, that's great," I said. "I know what you mean about the fire in your belly. There was a day when I thought it would never go out. Now, I don't know."

"You've got to decide whether you want to keep writing on a regular basis then go from there," she advised. "The will has to be there, or it won't happen."

"Yeah, I know. Right now, I'm working on getting my sight back in my right eye, but I think I might start a journal and see where it goes from there," I said, the thought just popping into my head.

"Sounds like a good plan," she encouraged.

Cynthia pulled me out of an embarrassing moment I will never forget. I was trying to earn money selling cookware the company advertised as unbreakable.

Cynthia said I could make a presentation to some of her friends.

"But first you should practice," she advised. "Show me your presentation, and I'll tell you if it needs work."

I brought all the plates, pots, and pans out and started my presentation. When I got to the plates, I accidently lost control of one of the knives. It landed blade first into the middle of the plate, shattering product and confidence in one fell swoop. I was crestfallen. In her inimitable way of picking up the pieces, Cynthia immediately suggested that we go out.

"Let's take a road trip," she suggested. "I think you could use a break."

She drove to Babler State Park, situated on the outskirts of St. Louis. She talked about how she discovered the depth of her keen interest in art. I'll never forget how she held her hand up to the wooded expanse and slowly moved it to the right. It was as if she were tracing the tree line, recording the brilliant colors of fall foliage, then relying on memory to transfer the panorama to paper or canvas.

"I wanted to see if I could draw or paint what stood out," she explained with rhapsodic fervor. "When I realized that what I was putting on paper or canvas was something different yet relevant, I knew there was an artistic desire that needed to be fed if it was going to grow.

"Anyway, I believe you have that same kind of desire, not with a piece of charcoal or brush but with a pen. I hope you don't take this the wrong way, little brother, but I hope your heart isn't set on becoming a salesman."

I knew she was referring not just to the recent catastrophe with the plates but to the time Mom devised a plan to help pay for our piano lessons. She made dish rags out of nylon netting and sent us out at the tender ages of twelve, thirteen, and fourteen to peddle them door to door for fifty cents apiece. When we sold out of the batch she made, she sent us out with a second batch. Then those sold out, and she raised the price to one dollar. The new price seemed too steep for housewives trying to make ends meet, so Mom decided we should say we were selling them on behalf of the Boy Scouts and Girl Scouts. This caused Dad, who had to drive us from one block to the next, to wage a fierce protest.

"They would be doing something illegal," he reminded Mom.

"Oh, legal schmegal, it's all in good fun," she countered in a tone that suggested she was in one of her manic moods. When someone asked me what troop I belonged to, I mumbled something unintelligible, and the fraudulent venture was essentially over.

The laugh we shared over the memory of another one of Mom's schemes gone bad felt warm and overdue.

She was right about the appetite for art. I sensed something was growing inside, but it wasn't until Cynthia recognized it that I found the courage to put observations and thoughts on paper. Before that I was just fantasizing over what I could do with all that stuff running around in my head.

15

Sights and Sounds That Humble the Soul

There was something about reconnecting with family that always made me feel more empowered when it came to addressing problems.

For the first time since I started the job as a driver, I sensed not all creativity was lost. There were observations I was making every day while driving around that I could record and edit when I had the time.

I developed friendships along the route. One of them was with James, a chef at one of the restaurants on my route. When I saw James in something other than his kitchen whites, I noticed how impeccably dressed he was, even in casual attire. There was never a wrinkle in his shirt or slacks. If James showed up for work in pajamas, there wouldn't be a single flaw. He could wear anything with distinction.

When I told him how impressed I was with the way he carried himself—he merely tilted his head and, with mock seriousness, said, "You trying to get a free meal or something?"

We usually kept the conversation light, talking about sports or a movie. One day I noticed that he was fidgety. He told me he was concerned with the medical dilemma his fourteen-year-old daughter faced.

"She had cancer and needed to have a kidney removed four years ago," he stated solemnly. "We're worried about the other kidney."

When he said this, the taut features in his face revealed a concern he must have held for some time. I told him I hoped that it worked out for the best.

"Thank you, I appreciate that, brother," he said, peering at me longer than usual. I realized this was the first time a black man referred to me as brother. I took that as a compliment. I wondered if he called any other white man *brother*. If I had to bet, I'd say it was more about character than race.

I remember watching an elfin figure struggling to cross Tucker Boulevard, one of the widest streets in St. Louis that reminded me of the Champs-Élysées in Paris. When he planted his feet, his legs were so weak, they immediately buckled, forcing him to rely on a walker to maintain his balance.

He didn't appear to be more than four feet tall and couldn't have weighed more than eighty or ninety pounds. A series of convulsions caused his head to snap back repeatedly. Undeterred, he continued to push forward.

I realized that amid the powerful current of physical setbacks stood a mighty will to wage such a dramatic battle. An intense feeling of admiration welled up inside as I watched him fight to make it across the street before the traffic light changed.

There were times when I wished I still functioned as a reporter, feverishly recording sights and sounds along with rich quotes from interesting subjects.

Watching the diminutive individual struggle to cross the street, I couldn't help but think of Mom and her struggle to overcome her physical limitations. Also, it put into perspective how lucky I was to still have the kind of health I enjoyed.

I liked watching steam rise from the manholes. I enjoyed hearing car horns bouncing off skyscrapers. The sound could not be duplicated in the county. There was an air of importance to the sounds of the city, a reminder that folks were busy in their role of daily commerce. Folks were providing for their families, and that was a good thing.

During a route throughout Illinois, I was struck by an iridescent white ball shining through a thick cluster of leafless trees, an impromptu look at the earth manifesting itself as art.

Rising above it all was the Gateway Arch, a powerful, sublime stainless steel structure designed by Finnish American architect Eero Saarinen.

The Arch is the centerpiece, the crown jewel, of the Jefferson National Expansion Memorial. Complementing Saarinen's visionary work is the $380 million CityArchRiver project. An article published by the *St. Louis Post-Dispatch* provided a detailed account of a $176 million renovation of the Gateway Arch's Museum of Westward Expansion, which is scheduled to open for Fair St. Louis in July 2018.

"The 46,000-square-foot underground addition, which will include interactive story galleries, video walls, a fountain, a café and—if you can't take a tram ride—a replica of the 'keystone' piece of the Arch, with windows that reveal a live webcam view from the top, 630 feet up," wrote Valerie Schremp Hahn of the *Post-Dispatch*.

If you look at it enough times, from various angles, you see legs coming out of the base then arms that shoot into the sky and connect at the top like clasping hands morphing triumphantly into what appears to be a parabola.

It's not a parabola. The more you probe, the more interesting the monument becomes, offering insight into its creator.

The monument of Saarinen's architectural genius is a catenary arch. Catenary comes from the Latin term *cantaria*, which means "chain." If you allow a chain to hang freely from two supported ends, you will see the shape of a catenary arch. Turn it upside down, and you get the inverted-U shape of an arch.

This magnificent blend of art and architecture is the result of an individual's daring to push the envelope on his creative skills. Saarinen made the width the same distance as the height, 630 feet, to achieve uniformity in the structure.

This is what allows him to redirect forces of gravity so that the arch's curve is the sturdiest portion of the monument. He has managed to use gravity as a source of strength so that the St. Louis Arch can support its own weight and won't succumb to the forces of an earthquake. A fifty-mile-per-hour wind would only cause the structure to sway a mere one and a half inches. The Arch has the capacity to sway as much as eighteen inches.

It is the tallest man-made monument in the US and the highest accessible building in Missouri.

The Arch was completed in 1965, four years after Saarinen died at age fifty-one. What an injustice. The very person who dreamed up such a lasting monument never lived long enough to see it stand taller than another building in the St. Louis sky.

Then again perhaps he didn't need to see the physical manifestation of what he envisioned in his mind's eye. The knowledge that all that arduous work, which started in 1947, would reach completion may have been enough.

The $13 million price tag to build the Arch in the mid-'60s is equivalent to $195 million in 2016. Although that is a hefty sum of money, it's still less than the thirteen-year, $325 million contract New York Yankees slugger Giancarlo Stanton signed in 2014 when he was with the Miami Marlins.

No matter which direction I went, I could find a portion of this magnificent edifice poking its head up and around office buildings. There were times when it would cast giant shadows then catch a splash of the afternoon sun and shimmer, showing off before a cluster of tourists. Traveling from the Illinois side of the Mississippi back to St. Louis, I was struck by a poetic sunset, the Arch appearing to sweet-talk the skyline into a salmon pink blush.

When I had time to distill the mesmerizing scene, I marveled at the collision of nature and architecture, launching the imagination into a phantasmagoric journey. I see Saarinen's architectural accomplishment as an allegory: an individual's quest to make something unique that would stand tall and proud long after he withered and went away.

Pondering the significant achievement of Saarinen and the projects undertaken to enhance such a work, I saw how vision, commitment, and will can accomplish almost anything. What if that same kind of vision, commitment, and will were spent on ways to address and alleviate civil unrest and poverty in the U.S.

The Arch and its surroundings stood for more than just architectural elegance and a man's quest for artistic endurance. A documentary on PBS recounted the men who braved fierce winds, bitter winter temperatures, and countless risks to build a lasting symbol of westward expansion in America. The pride that spread across the faces as they spoke of that time was awe inspiring.

The brief time spent inside the Arch exposed phobias developed from childhood. Attempting to mimic Claire as she easily ascended the old sycamore tree in our backyard, I found, halfway up, that I didn't much like rising to any height that might result in a fall. Claire appealed to my sense of logic.

Logic would say that if the branches were strong enough to support my weight on the way up, they would be equally sturdy for the descent, she reasoned. And if the bark was tough enough to bend Johnny Miller's knife, it wouldn't fail me so long as I was able to maintain a tight grip on the branches. But I didn't live by the laws of logic because I didn't trust myself trespassing into the unknown. I had plenty of time to ponder the nether regions during my sequestered period.

To Claire each step represented a step toward an adventurous journey. To me it meant a chance to place myself in serious peril.

I can still recall the paralytic terror as I imagined how easily one slip could send me plummeting to the ground, causing severe bodily harm. Also, during a hide-and-seek episode, the closet I hid in felt suffocating instead of protective. Making matters worse was a slight hissing sound discovered when I crouched down into a fetal position. The ominous sound gave the impression air was being sucked out of the closet.

So I dashed out of the confining quarters and was quickly found, thereby eliminated from contention.

When Claire discovered that the hissing sound was coming from the deflated football I was leaning on, she erupted into screeching laughter, giving me reason to feel ashamed.

"Shouldn't have been leaning on the bogeyman," she howled. When she could see that this information didn't alter the fear written on my face, she added, "Oh, grow up. You can't be a baby your whole life."

I didn't want to reveal my fears to Anna, Annette, or Danny as tram cars slowly pulled us to the top of the Arch, so I suppressed them, masking the internal strife with a stoic demeanor.

When we reached the top, I watched visitors eagerly striding to one of the thirty-two windows to take in the expansive view. I knew this would be somewhat tricky since I feared looking down from a tree limb. I took a few deep breaths, moved as close to the window as I could tolerate, and took brief glimpses before retreating to a safe distance. Anna viewed my timid behavior with an arched eyebrow. She knew but didn't say anything to the kids. I was thankful for that.

There were times when I would be sent across the river into small towns in Illinois for deliveries to restaurants or hospitals. One day I decided to go through Smithville, a town known for its highly productive steel mill. Once a booming blue-collar community, it showed signs of gradual deterioration. Steep, undulating mounds of coal and an elaborate configuration of rusted metal pipes that hovered over the mill seemed sadly forsaken. So, too, rusted-out rail cars that appeared to be serving out life sentences in inertia.

The leafless row of trees on the side of the road were bent in helpless patterns of disarray, like old skeletal frames too frail and malnourished to put up much of a fight against a strong wind.

Most of the jobs were sent overseas, and there was nothing to replace what kept the city alive. The promises of a new president that things would change back to the thriving days of yesteryear appeared to be nothing more than talk. As the smoke emanated from one tall cylinder still in use and pushed itself against the sky, I instinctively rolled my window up the way one would protect himself from secondhand smoke. There was something depressing about the acrid smell and helpless look of a once vibrant town left to slowly deteriorate. The houses appeared neat yet somehow the same for too many years. Too much tired wood. Like people, you need youth standing next to old age to get a sense of completed family trees. There was no sign of a city in flux, with new construction and projects designed to head toward a more promising future. Everything looked as it likely did twenty or thirty years ago and perhaps would remain twenty years from now. Traversing these streets was like going through a time machine, watching what once was turn into rust. My life, like the aging houses and factories of this town, showed no signs of getting back to what once was.

I asked for a new assignment so I would never have to take the same route that brought me to this city again.

Making observations elsewhere became an enjoyable habit. But throughout the day, there were several reminders that I was tethered and under constant scrutiny by corporate devices like the GPS app on the company smartphone assigned to each driver. Our every move and minute were tracked and monitored. From the second we slowly waved the time card over the keypad on the time clock to mark the start of a shift, we were company property, and there were numerous ways for the corporate cameras to track our every move from beginning to end. There were random drug tests at least once a year.

I understood the reason for all of this. I was driving a vehicle worth as much as I paid for my house. The company had every right to ensure that I was doing everything in my power to protect its investment. All the myriad rules and regulations were designed to make sure an accident was an anomaly, not a routine occurrence.

I also realized that I signed on to perform a job that ran counter to my creative soul. Instead of dreaming up story ideas, I was locked into robotic tasks such as check left mirror, then rearview, then right, then repeat until the neck feels like it's on a swivel and the brain is on hiatus. My day from start to finish was so heavily scripted, there was no room for spontaneity. Any deviation from the script could result in a verbal or written reprimand. To keep my record clean, I learned to keep to the script the way an actor would dutifully follow each line. It worked for a while. Then I began to feel like an impostor. I had that fenced-in, restless feeling all over again. Only this time I wasn't naive to what was going on. This time I had a question to answer. How long could I feed the stomach yet neglect the soul?

Like many of my peers, I was willing to abide by the myriad rules and intense scrutiny because benefits like health insurance and a matching 401K made my financial situation less dire.

And yet amid all the measures of accountability and role-playing, I still managed to relax enough to mentally record images and experiences that, hopefully, would one day fill the pages of a journal.

One image struck a chord. It was of a man wearing tattered jeans and a black hoodie. The hoodie covered enough of his head and face to nearly render him anonymous, a threadbare silhouette against a gray sky. His right hand was cupped over his right ear, the left hand pressed against his stomach as he did a slow dance. He appeared to be locked into a trance, oblivious to the outside world. Perhaps he was reminding himself that his dignity was still intact. No one could foreclose on that. At least that's how I interpreted the dance.

I tried to find ways to separate those who were truly homeless from folks just looking for a handout. I learned you can try to present desperation, but only a very good actor could pull off the fake. A vacant stare is hard to project. There was one guy who was asking for help at a stop light close to a university. He walked with a limp and was hunched over like someone suffering from curvature of the spine. His face looked too healthy to pass for homelessness. I wondered if he was practicing for the lead role in *The Hunchback of Notre Dame*. When I saw him limping his way up and down the narrow median in a driving rain storm, I wasn't so sure.

One guy walked in front of the bread truck and signaled for me to roll the window down.

"I need your help," he said, revealing only a few teeth left in his head. "Me and my sister ran out of gas. I really need some money to get some more gas," he said with a look that appeared more theatrical than desperate. I remembered this very scam from a few years ago. I felt like telling him to devise a plot that sounded more original. Instead I said I was on a strict schedule and didn't have time to stop.

There were others who appeared to be the real thing. One scene that haunted me was a woman with a sign that read "Pregnant, traveling, broke."

She had such a forlorn, defeated posture. The ghostly stare and dark eyes grabbed me by the throat and wouldn't let go. I felt engulfed by the tragic implications.

She refused to make eye contact when my truck moved closer. She was wearing a heavy denim jacket and weather-beaten jeans. She had a round, doughy face that looked as if it were carved from a pumpkin then bleached ghostly white. Upon further inspection, I noticed that her face was puffy and looked as if it had been smacked more than once. I couldn't wait for the light to change. There was nothing I could do for her, given the time constraints of my job. But I did manage to find a five-dollar bill to give her. It felt like guilt money.

"Thank you, sir," she whispered, still staring at the ground.

I was grateful I had a routine that gave me an excuse to move along.

That scene haunted me.

I couldn't imagine Annette reaching such a state of desperation that she would resort to something like that. Where was this woman's family? Did she feel so abandoned that this was her only real choice?

I knew if I dwelled on that scene, I would be depressed the rest of the day. There were plenty of positive images to summon from memory.

I thought of the woman who is a custodian at one of the grocery stores. She taught me about the power of politeness. When she held the door for me one day, I was both surprised and somewhat suspicious. The next time I had the chance to return the favor, I did. She thanked me with a warm smile and went on her way.

One day it was raining so hard, I wondered how I would be able to transport the bread from the truck to a dry area of the dock without ruining the product that was my livelihood.

The female custodian turned a few plastic trash bags into protective covers and threw them over the sheets of bread as I moved the trays into a safe, dry area. I couldn't believe she went out of her way to help me like that. You don't forget such a kind gesture.

"That was a considerate thing you did for me the other day," I reminded her the next time I saw her.

"You'd do it for me, wouldn't you?" she queried. "Well then, what's the big deal?"

As beautiful as that moment was, there were others that were not so innocent or altruistic. When I maneuvered the truck into a dock for a delivery one day, I noticed a guy who drove for an office-products company was shouting in my direction. I asked if he was talking to me.

"Yeah, I'm talkin' to you muthahfuckah," he bellowed. Mindful that there was a security guard in a shack adjacent to the dock watching this, I assumed that if this reached the point of a physical struggle, the guard would intervene.

To my surprise, the guard just stood by and watched as the guy in the office-products truck continued to call me every name he could think of.

His argument was so muddled, I had a tough time figuring out what it was that was making him so angry. I finally realized that he was telling me that his truck belonged in the spot I was trying to park in.

"What, is your name on this?" I shouted sarcastically, reverting to a schoolyard tactic.

"You stupid muthahfuckah," he screamed. "Don't you know nuthin'?"

I was becoming so infuriated, I sensed this could easily escalate into a fistfight. I couldn't afford to get into a scuffle while on the job, so I decide to just ignore him and go about my business.

When I looked for the guard, he was nowhere to be seen. The next time I showed up at this dock, I asked the guard about the guy screaming at me.

"I was watching and planned to move in if it got too bad, but then you seemed to end it before it got out of hand, so I just stayed put," he explained. The guard was black. The guy who was screaming at me was black. I wondered if this incident had to do with a black guy who was tired of being screwed over by a white man. Maybe he needed a tale to tell in which he emerged as the most powerful figure.

When I talked to some of the workers inside the building, however, they said the guy was having some personal problems. Anger dominated my thoughts as I steered the truck out of the dock area.

I was so easily baited into that argument, I wondered if it had to do with racial bias or a normal reaction to an aggressor.

I once shouted racial epithets growing up, but that was simply to mimic those around me. When I began to think for myself, I realized this was not who I wanted to be and evolved into a different person.

It made me rethink the belief that being cool around folks of color during a hostile situation was enough to show that I was on their side.

Deeply rooted hatred just didn't go away because someone proved he or she wasn't a bigot. This stuff took years to develop and wouldn't change with a cleverly arranged phrase or a nice gesture.

Each time I pulled into the lot to enter the dock area, I wondered if the office truck driver would be there, waiting for me to start this all over again. I only saw him briefly two more times and then never after that.

I asked the guard if he said anything to him.

"I told him if he has a complaint, he'd better say it to a guard and not you," he explained. That restored my faith in the professional relationship I felt we had from the beginning.

16

Race Matters

The shouting match weighed heavily on my mind in the ensuing weeks. I managed to talk to a few black guys I worked with about what it was like when they were growing up. I realized that to me a cop was someone to go to if I was in trouble.

To them a cop meant a person who had the power to arrest them.

I was never a victim of racial profiling, so I couldn't say I understood what that felt like.

One of the drivers I befriended was nicknamed Country because he grew up in a rural area in North Carolina. His real name was Corey. It seemed everyone wanted to share a story or just chat with Corey.

His laugh was warm, robust, and spontaneous, breaking down barriers. It made me feel like I could tell him just about anything without being judged.

I asked Country if he was ever pulled over for a minor traffic violation.

"Man, I was with my girl on the way to the prom," he recalled, shaking his head. "I'm wearin' a tux, you know. I had to save up for more than a month to rent this thing. My girl's wearin' this satin dress. You know, that cop didn't have any reason for pullin' us over. When I kept askin' him to tell me what I was doin' wrong, he got more and more pissed off and finally made me lie facedown on the street. He humiliated me in front of the girl I was supposed to take to the biggest dance of my life."

I told Corey I understood why he would feel the way he did toward cops. But from the look on his face, I wasn't so sure he believed me.

I thought of a story I could tell Corey that would demonstrate my understanding of what it's like to be manipulated by someone in a more powerful position.

When I was unemployed, I decided to take a freelance job with a fitness magazine. Although the editor never promised the assignments I took would lead to a full-time gig, I wanted to believe that if he liked my work, it would happen.

One of my assignments was to cover a talk given by a former pro athlete at a high school. After his speech, I asked him if I could have a brief interview. When the interview was over, I thanked him and prepared to leave.

"Hey, I was wondering," he said, giving me reason to pause. "Do you write any material on the side? I mean for pay, of course."

I was so broke, I didn't hesitate at the chance to make more money.

"Sure, what do you need?"

"Well, I don't have a publicist. I mean I fired the one I had because he didn't really do what I wanted him to do," he explained. "All I really need is for someone to work up a little bit of information on who I am and what I've done as an athlete. You know, something I can send to prospective companies who want to hire a motivational speaker."

I told him that would be very easy to do.

"I could work something up for you," I assured him.

"How long would something like that take?" he asked with increasing interest.

"Oh, an hour or so," I blurted, not really knowing how long it would take because I'd never been asked to do something like that.

"How much do you charge per hour?"

Since I was so desperate for cash, I said, "I could do it for, say, $20 or so."

This prompted him to give me his card.

"Call me and we'll get it done," he said.

I called him and got the necessary information and told him I'd call back when it was done.

It only took a little more than an hour, so I figured it was still worth the effort at $20. When I called him, however, he seemed to want to add more information. When I called to tell him I added that information, he had more facts to add. Each time he added information, I wondered if he knew this was driving up the price. I didn't say anything because I figured an ex-pro athlete was probably used to paying top dollar for services rendered. And he did ask how much I charged per hour.

During our phone conversations, he asked me about the magazine. I told him I was just working on a freelance basis but hoped to get hired permanently in the near future. He asked what it would take to get hired full-time.

"If they like my work enough, they'll offer a full-time gig," I said.

I finally put the bio together and agreed to meet him at his hotel room. On the way to the hotel, I realized that my gas tank was on empty. My wallet contained just a few dollars, certainly not enough to buy a gallon. I really needed the money that was waiting for me at the hotel.

He read over the material I put together and seemed pleased with the results

"Okay, well, I thank you, my brother," he said, handing me a $20 bill.

"Um, it took me about six or seven hours to put this together," I said, feeling embarrassed to point this out.

"Oh, well, we agreed on $20," he insisted. "I mean, if the price was to change, shouldn't you have told me that?"

He was taking advantage of my reticence, and I deeply resented that. A blind sense of rage consumed my thoughts. When I sent a story to the *Boston Globe*, I was paid $150. And that was for something that only took a few hours. This took six or seven hours, so I was making less than $3 an hour. How could I let this person devalue my work? I immediately thought that because he was black and I was white, it was his way of getting one over on a member of a race that likely had him at a disadvantage for a good portion of his life.

I was tempted to wad up the $20 bill and throw it back in his face. But I needed the damn money to put gas in my car, so I could make it home. I felt like telling him I had standards and skills that couldn't be cheapened like this, but instead I swallowed my pride and left with my tail between my legs. I should have at least protested, but I feared any kind of argument might result in a complaint to the magazine, and I couldn't afford to take a chance on that. I wasn't sure if his motivation was to humiliate me because I was white or merely to get work done for next to nothing.

I wanted to tell Corey this story, but I was afraid he might take it the wrong way. I didn't think we knew each other well enough.

But I did have a sense of what it's like to feel powerless even though you are smart enough to know someone is taking advantage.

I saw something in Tim's demeanor that piqued my curiosity.

"You're thinking of something," I said.

"Just wondering," he replied with a pensive look. "If you would have said something to Corey, what would have been his reaction?"

"He might have said, 'Welcome to my world.'"

Once again, I learned something from my mentor.

"Okay, back to the story," urged Tim.

When Corey learned I was once a journalist, he seemed intrigued, saying, "I bet you ran into some interesting folks." I told him about the series of stories on gangs. There was a quote that spoke volumes about some distorted impressions. A convenience store owner told me some people in that town looked at nine white kids with bats and saw a baseball team. If they saw nine black kids with bats, they recognized a gang.

Corey looked down with a sad expression and seemed to retreat into a thought or memory he didn't care to share with me. We finally broke the silence by moving on to other stories I covered both in sports and news.

I valued the interactions with workers like Corey because they were honest with me and gave me more insight into what I was just guessing at before I met them.

The older black drivers were easy to approach. However, the younger guys weren't nearly as friendly. It was as if they assumed I was no different than many white men they encountered as they were growing up.

I wasn't interested in gaining their friendship just to change their minds. I would simply be myself, and if they accepted me, fine. If not, there was nothing I could do about it.

Rasheed, who was a new driver, seemed like the other young black guys at first. Then I noticed that he didn't go out of his way to speak. He would respond to a question in short sentences but rarely elaborated. I never saw him initiate a conversation.

He had a powerful build yet was not intimidating. The eyes appeared kind yet unsure what to make of the new landscape. One day I noticed that Rasheed was in the lane next to me as we were making our way back to Colonial. He signaled that he wanted to enter my lane, so I held back to allow him to ease into the lane.

We ended up at the dock area at the same time. As we were unloading our trucks, Rasheed looked up and said, "Doug, you let me in. Thanks!"

Without hesitating I said, "Well yeah, it would have been shitty to not let you in. We are on the same team, you know."

His face relaxed some, and I detected a slight smile. He was genuinely surprised I would do what I considered a common courtesy. I saw that as unnecessary distance.

The gap seemed to disappear once we talked about sports and music.

"There's this festival in Austin, Texas," he said with enthusiasm. "One week it showcases films, the next music. I try to go every year."

I told him I heard bands I liked in bars downtown. I asked him if he frequented any of them.

"I went into a place a few blocks from here with my girlfriend," he said with a pensive demeanor. "Before I could get comfortable, the bartender says he needs a credit card to start a tab. Now maybe that's the rule for everybody, but it made me feel like he didn't trust us. I didn't make a big stink. We just decided to leave and find a place that didn't ask for that. And we found a place a few blocks away. We had a few drinks, listened to some cool music, had a nice, relaxing time."

There was another conversation that brought me closer to an understanding about how Rasheed saw his role as father. We rode together so he could teach me his route. I asked about his five-year-old daughter. An expansive smile replaced his stoic demeanor.

"We went to the zoo the other day," he said. "She asked me to buy her this thing and that. I wasn't going to let her trick me into spoiling her when I knew I needed to spend money on things she really needed, things for school. I read to her at night. She likes that."

Then we came to a moment I will never forget. He said she was watching a cartoon involving a cop chasing a bank robber.

"She said, 'Cops are bad, aren't they?'" recalled Rasheed.

"I said, 'Oh no, sweetie, cops aren't bad. Don't think that.'"

I saw an alternate trace of sadness and a glint of hope in his eyes. He wanted her to keep an open mind, to judge for herself. We exchanged knowing glances, and that was that.

There was another worker at Colonial who intrigued me. He was a tall, lanky guy named Butch and was deaf. I assumed he was also mute because I never heard him speak.

His eyes appeared to be on constant alert. Darren Smith was the only one who knew sign language, and when he left for another job, Butch was left to play charades with anyone up to the challenge. Few seemed to have the time necessary to interpret his message.

I couldn't help noticing how often he drifted into a sullen posture, pulling his black stocking cap down a few inches above his eyebrows.

His job was mostly custodial, keeping the floors clean and trash cans empty.

When Butch started hanging out in the parking lot after 6:00 p.m., watching drivers when they returned from their route, a few became suspicious. We developed a habit of lingering for a few minutes after returning to unload our trucks. It was a way to relax, swap stories, and develop a sense of camaraderie.

Someone suggested that Butch notified management we were milking the clock because it soon became a rule that we were to time out immediately after unloading the truck.

Butch might have become the company pariah were it not for Corey's intervention.

"There's cameras to pick that up," noted Corey. "C'mon, guys, get serious."

From that point on, Butch summoned the courage to communicate via flailing gestures, grunts, and shrieks, answering with some hand signal or abbreviated verbal reply. Corey did his best to understand Butch's meaning, but sometimes he had to tell him to start over.

"I just told him if I look confused, just slow down and start over," explained Corey.

When I asked Corey why he was willing to stand up for Butch, Corey dismissed it as something anyone would do.

"Guy's gotta have friends same as us, you know, dog? His day is always gonna be harder than ours."

That was all I needed to hear. I never believed the rumor that Butch was the one who betrayed us, especially with his severely limited communications skills.

Also, he seemed to suffer from abject loneliness, keeping his head bent downward to avoid eye contact when he understood that drivers blamed him for the end of our post-route social gathering.

When I considered what I knew about the damage isolation can cause, I should have understood Butch's plight better than anyone.

Seeing him in a different light brought me closer to a measure of his wit.

He greeted one of the drivers named Tom with arms raised and outstretched, perhaps a way of saying "How's it going?"

Tom had a habit of approaching Butch with index and middle finger forming a V, universally known as the peace sign. Butch quickly offered a look of mock disappointment, followed by a "back at you" peace sign. I realized he was trying to convey that he wanted more than a peace-be-with-you salutation from Tom. It was as if he was saying, "Is that all you got? C'mon, man, talk to me."

Butch must have read something in my smile because I noticed a glint of appreciation. It was like watching a comedian who knows he connected with an audience and felt encouragement to continue.

There was also a guy whose friendship I valued who went by the nickname Big City. His real name was Andrew. Both Country and Big City sounded like a couple of tough guys, but they were actually two of the kindest, most congenial men I've ever met.

They both loved sports, so there was never a time when I felt like we had nothing to talk about.

One time I got into a conversation with Country about basketball players. We were talking about the era before the three-point shot.

"One guy who always stood out for the way he could shoot was Pistol Pete Maravich," marveled Country. This took me by surprise because there were other players from the '60s and '70s with championship resumes. Guys like Oscar Robertson, Jo Jo White, Clyde Frazier. Why Pistol Pete?

I asked Country why he was so enamored with Maravich.

"Oh man, he could light it up from anywhere on the court. I'm convinced he was a white man in a brother's body," he said with a look of admiration.

The longer I got to know Country, the more I came to understand and appreciate the origin of his soul.

"Back in North Carolina, we didn't have much, but there was this understanding that if anyone came to your house, you would share with them what you had," he explained, letting his large hands expand.

"My parents didn't live very long, but what they were able to teach me still stays with me today," he added with a tone of reverence. "Family and solid friends are more important than material possessions. You can *try* huggin' a brand-new car, but it won't *try* huggin' ya back."

Corey's parents died when he was still in grade school.

"I kinda knew that the trip to St. Louis wasn't for sightseeing, if you know what I mean," he said solemnly. "It was to put me in a home with relatives until I could get out of high school. It was kinda lonely at first because I didn't know anybody. I remember I had to walk out of the way of these three guys who looked like they were sizing me up. I was used to buttoning my shirt. That's how I wore it back in North Carolina," he said, pulling his hands up to his neck. "I'm sure they looked at that and said he's not one of us. But you know once I got to play sports, it all changed. Pretty soon everybody wanted to pick me to be on their team." He beamed with pride. "I was *in*."

Corey offered newspaper clippings that revealed he was a better-than-average basketball player and a good-enough hurdler and football player to get an athletic scholarship to Lincoln University in Jefferson City, Missouri.

"I remember trying to hurdle a guy who dropped down and was waiting to tackle me," he recalled, his eyes focusing intently on the memory. "As I tried to hurdle him, he reached out and caught just a portion of my foot. That slowed me down enough that another defender was able to bring me down. The coach shouted out, 'This isn't no track meet out here!'"

This caused Country to erupt into that wonderful spontaneous laugh of his.

"Those were good days, just the way we played 'em."

Corey's football story triggered a reflection of my woeful attempt at blocking the seemingly helpless DeAndres defender. Why couldn't I laugh about my experience the same way Corey did about his?

Learning about the lives of Country and Big City helped me see how many stereotypes they refuted. They both worked at Colonial for over thirty years, they were with their kids from birth until they went on to college or marriage, and as far as I could tell, never spent a day in prison.

They wouldn't have survived the company's exhaustive background check if they had any kind of arrest record.

I wondered how I measured up as a father compared to these two. Did they keep secrets from their kids the way I did? I guess everybody goes to the grave with at least one big secret, but maybe none as haunting as mine.

Would I ever summon the courage to reveal what really happened in Ohio? Maybe not.

17

Work Busies the Soul

I finally received permission from my eye surgeon to return to work. I had become so weary of the old Western reruns on television, I welcomed the chance to get back into a routine that would enable me to be a financial contributor.

I was greeted by my boss, Justin, who told me I should reassure Country that I was okay.

"I don't know how he got so confused, but when I told him you had a detached retina, he thought I said detached rectum," said Justin with a wry smile. "Country said, 'Oh dog, that's gotta hurt.'" That was Justin's way of saying welcome back.

I was somewhat eager to get back on the road after such a long absence.

To keep calm, I searched for a radio station that offered soothing music. I settled on a jazz station and another that provided classical selections.

I became enamored with songs like *Scheherazade* by Nikolai Rimsky-Korsakov.

The plaintive, soulful, compelling strain of violins reminded me of the time I spent sitting along the banks of the Mississippi when I lived in Cape Girardeau, Missouri.

I took Anna to the spot along the Mississippi that helped me through some tough decisions.

How could I forget the night a fiddler unwittingly became part of an impromptu ruse? He managed to settle us into silence as he filled the dense summer air with a tune that had a mesmerizing effect. The combination of the player's closed eyes, rapturous expression, and feverish bow strokes pulled us in like it was part of the Mississippi current.

When he was done, he leaned back and bowed in our direction as if acknowledging an attentive audience.

"I hope you enjoyed that," I whispered into her ear.

"Oh, it was magnificent," she exclaimed with contentment. "Did you? I mean . . . you didn't," she wondered aloud.

"Oh yes, it cost a few dollars, but what's that compared to watching your face glow like that," I said, hardly believing I was pulling this off. When the fiddler left, I admitted that it was just a stroke of luck that he began playing as we sat down to watch the river traffic.

"Well, I have to admit it did seem a little too good to be true," she said with a hearty laugh. When we saw the fiddler as we headed back to my apartment, we asked him why he chose the soulful melody.

"It's not really a song or anything," he stated softly. "It's just something that came to me as I stared into the river. That happens sometimes."

Later on she told me that was the night she was sure she was in love with me.

The river had a way of taming the discordant rhythms of my life. It had a serene, sometimes hypnotic effect that put things in slow motion so that even the most complicated problem could be simplified and broken down into something that could be solved.

That it washed away the inner struggle and brought me to the very root of my problems made me want to return again and again. When I left, I had a better outlook on life. I realized then and there that my shrink, for better or worse, was the mighty Mississippi.

The classical station offered information about the composers and musicians whose artistry filled me with inner calm.

The scenery that I drove past while listening to this music seemed to drift by lazily, the way clouds appear when you're looking out the window of an airplane.

I had two new stops added to my route. One took me by a community college. I noticed an individual at a bus stop. He was in a wheelchair tilted back. His head was at a ninety-degree angle, soaking up the sun on a beautiful autumn afternoon.

A blanket covered his legs, which appeared to be strapped to the wheelchair. I was moved by this scene because it made me realize that this individual was taking every advantage of what was available—a bright, salubrious sun on an unusually warm October afternoon.

And he was taking the public bus rather than one designated solely for disabled passengers.

I don't think he considered himself disabled. At least that's the feeling I got as I drove past. After I made my delivery, I drove by the bus stop and noticed he was entering the vehicle via a step lowered for disabled passengers. He did not look as if this was an imposition. Rather, it was just the way things were.

Could I summon the inner strength and take the same positive attitude if I had similar circumstances to deal with? I knew I needed my eyes to get back what I already had, but Butch needed his eyes to connect with the outside world. He appeared to function with a stoic resolve I could only envy.

18

A House Divided

Anna was busy with her new job as a writer of grant proposals. She seemed to have found a renewed vigor despite the demands the job put on her time. Annette was hard at work at the Juvenile Detention Center, taking notes and making observations that would help her put together a dissertation worthy of a PhD.

And Danny spent much of his time after school with the chess club.

In a strange way, even though we were all situated in the same house, it was rare to find everybody together for a family meal.

Annette's phone calls from her boyfriend quickly escalated into arguments I couldn't help but overhear. I didn't catch all the words, but it seemed to have something to do with how long she intended to stay. There were other intense conversations she elected to take outside the house.

Either she sensed someone was listening in, or it was information she wasn't ready to share.

When I brought this up to Anna, she sighed and had this knowing look that usually meant there was something she was keeping to herself.

"Is there something I should know about?"

I had to find out.

"Well, she hasn't come out and said this, but I think she might be pregnant," she said with a look of concern.

I was stunned.

"Why do you think that?"

"She's been waking up with what seems to be morning sickness," said Anna. "Don't say anything yet because it's just a guess. I want her to come to us with something like that."

"You're just guessing," I said, unable to hold back my anger. "How could she be pregnant? She barely knows the guy," I fumed.

"Keep your voice down," she whispered. "I really don't know anything yet," she said, trying to calm me down. "Like I said, just keep this between you and me."

Annette must have sensed that we knew she was keeping something important from us because she began to find ways to avoid any kind of confrontation.

She was rarely home for meals, citing her need to spend more time at the Juvenile Detention Center and library to do research.

Then she announced that she needed to return to Champaign, Illinois, to resume work on her PhD.

"Alex has missed me terribly, and I've felt the same way," she said, hastily throwing a few things together before her ride showed up.

I knew this would bother Anna because she hated the not knowing.

"If she was having some kind of difficulty, why wouldn't she just confide in us?" Anna wondered aloud.

"Maybe we're imagining something that just isn't there," I suggested.

"Maybe so, but my gut tells me there is something going on that she doesn't want us to know about," said Anna.

"Hey, she's a big girl. If she wants our help, she'll ask for it. Otherwise, we probably need to give her some space on this one," I suggested. "Whatever it is, I'd bet the house she's not pregnant."

I believed Anna was right but didn't want to put our daughter in a position of feeling cornered. She would come to us when she needed help. She likely saw Alex as the one who could help her most.

I resumed my duties at Colonial Bread, thankful I was working again. I was nearly at the end of the route when my cell phone alerted me that I had a call. I noticed that it was none other than Tim Brown.

"Hey, what a welcome surprise," I said. "What's up, Tim?"

"What's up? Are you serious?" came a voice that sounded furious.

"What's wrong? Did someone give you a rotten story lead or something?"

Tim was becoming agitated over the memory of the call, shifting his weight from side to side, punctuating his uneasiness with a heavy sigh.

"You know, we really don't need to go over this," he said. "I do remember the conversation, you know."

"I thought it might be important to go over it as part of my explanation," I said. He nodded.

"Okay, but it might make things worse."

"I hope not. What's wrong?" I asked.

He sounded livid when he answered, "You've got to be kidding me."

I couldn't figure out what he was talking about.

"Tim, slow down. Tell me what's bothering you," I said.

"I'll tell you what's bothering me," you shouted. "I was just informed that the St. Louis Cardinals have revoked our press box privileges for the rest of the year and maybe longer. Would you like to explain what you and your wife did at the Cubs game to warrant this kind of punishment?"

"Oh, actually something came up and I gave the passes to a couple of friends," I explained.

"Listen to me. The people you gave those passes to embarrassed themselves in front of the entire press corps to the extent that we will likely never get a pass in a couple of years. But that's not all. I've just been informed by my boss that I will be suspended without pay for a week because of what they called poor judgment."

"Oh, Tim, I'm so sorry," I said. "I had no idea they—"

"Before I could finish, you hung up. I tried to call you back but only got a recording to leave a message at the beep."

"No need to take this further," insisted Tim.

"No, I want to tell you something," I said. "I betrayed a quality friend in the cheapest way, gambling with his career as if it were

171

nothing more than a wild card in a poker game. We won an award for an investigative story that took us more than a month to convert into a series on gangs.

"I felt like we bonded as colleagues and friends while working on that painstaking project. As a journalist, you are aware there are areas that are sacrosanct. The press box is one of those areas. God, how could I have done something so stupid?"

Tim took this in then said, "Okay, if this is to get absolution, it's yours."

"No, it's not," I argued. "What I wanted to tell you is my fall from grace came at such a heavy price. It's not just about me. It's about the friends and family I continually let down."

Tim was shaking his head.

"How many times must you go over this?" he protested.

"Wait, just hear me out," I said.

"I knew there was no forgiving or forgetting, only a chance to grow from it. But I couldn't do that until you knew how screwed up I was when it happened. I want you to know about the entire journey, including the trip to Cape."

"Fair enough," he said. "Go on."

I immediately called Matt Moreland.

"Hey, Doug, you ready to get back into the swing of things?" he said. "I'm ready to take a swing at you for what Toby did in the press box," I screamed. "Oh no, what did he do this time?"

"I don't know the details, but it was bad enough that my friend not only got humiliated in front of his peers at the newspaper, but he's been suspended for a week without pay."

"Damn. Look, I can fix this," he said.

"You are a fucking idiot! You can't fix something like this. The damage is done," I shouted and hung up. To make sure I didn't get a callback from him or anyone else, I shut my phone off.

I could hear my heart pounding against my ribs. I had planned on going straight home after work, but now I knew I was too upset to do that. If Anna saw me in this condition, she would want to know the source of my angst. I needed to find a haven to settle down.

Smitty's seemed to be the perfect place. It was always my oasis from the troubles the outside world presented.

I realized I hadn't taken a drink since just before the surgery.

The working crowd was just beginning to trickle in. One of the barmaids sidled up to me and gave me a warm hug.

"We missed you, sugar," said Alicia, a tall brunette with a compelling smile and a lithe body so hot, I always gave the best tips to her.

A part-time aerobics instructor, Alicia was the very definition of fitness.

"Heard you had issues with your eyes," she said with a look of concern.

"Yeah, but that's all taken care of now," I assured her.

"Yeah? Does that mean you can see the wrinkles on my face?" she joked.

"No, what it means is I'll have to bring more money with me because you look even better than I remember," I said with a wink.

"Yeah? Well maybe we should send more regulars to that eye doctor of yours," she said with a flirtatious wink back.

I was enough of a regular that I didn't have to tell them what I wanted to drink. A draft beer was already in front of me before I sat down at the bar.

I noticed the owner, Jerry Smith, was at the other end of the bar, telling what sounded like one of his better jokes.

I seemed to have this penchant for showing up just before Jerry was about to deliver the punch line.

This time it was, "I told him I had just about enough of his bullshit. When he asked me exactly what kind of bullshit I was talking about, I said, 'You know, the kind that burps my skunk.'"

This elicited a roar from the cluster of patrons listening to Jerry spin another of his famous yarns.

The more I learned about Jerry's past, the more fascinated I became of just what kind of guy he really was. He was a Navy Seal during the Vietnam War yet chose to keep what happened in Southeast Asia to himself. That is unless you were a veteran. Then he would take you to the side and whisper a few things, and that would be that.

I would have loved to do a feature on Jerry. He stood six feet four or six-five and probably weighed 270 or 280. His bushy eyebrows looked like they weighed a pound apiece.

There was a picture situated behind the bar of Jerry with his arms around some of his buddies from the war. When I asked Jerry about that picture, he said that it was a long time ago and indicated with bunched lips he wasn't interested in adding to that.

I made the mistake one night when I was feeling no pain to ask Jerry what really happened in Vietnam. I heard rumors of some horrific scenes that Jerry vowed never to reveal to anyone who was not there.

That was the recurring phrase "Were you there? Well then, you don't know, do you?"

That's the phrase he gave me to shut me up. I think he knew I was a former journalist. I could see how he might suspect me of wanting to dig up something to revive my career. That wasn't my motivation. I was simply fascinated with him as a human being.

The only person Jerry seemed to trust with his stories was Bob Haskins, who served in Vietnam as a member of the Marine Corps. Jerry asked Bob about the protest movement and what it was like being a cop.

"It's like this," said Bob, leaning in closer to keep from being overheard. When Bob recounted experiences on the police force, he sometimes got carried away and didn't realize that he was talking loud enough for everyone at the bar to hear.

"I met a cop from New Jersey during a police convention in the late '80s. This guy was on both ends of the spectrum. As a young guy, he was a protester, carrying a sign and chanting 'No justice, no peace.'"

He paused, took a sip of his beer, and continued, "Anyway, the guy ends up becoming a cop. He knows what's going on in a black man's head. He told me to the protester a cop doesn't have a face, just a badge. He represents a symbol of authority. You know a cop has the power to do two things even the president of the United States can't do: take liberty and life."

Jerry was so drawn into Bob's story, he seemed oblivious to the number of patrons waiting for him to serve them a drink. When Jerry decided to tell a joke or listen to someone's story, he would take a towel and sling it over his shoulder. This meant someone else needed to relieve him. The towel was over the shoulder.

"Now the way I see it and the way this guy from New Jersey saw it, any cop who doesn't look at that power as a serious responsibility. He doesn't deserve to wear the badge. He should turn it in," said Bob with conviction, reaching for another sip before continuing. "The cop told me city officials and the police department realized there was a serious breakdown both in communication and understanding between civilian and police officer. So they went into high schools and civic organizations and offered to explain their side. And they listened to the people. What a lot of people don't understand is that the worst thing you can do when you get pulled over is to start talking. The first thing I hear from most people is 'What did I do wrong?' I've just pulled you over, I don't know who you are yet, and already there's the threat of a possible confrontation and for that to escalate into something neither of us wants. The best thing you can do is hand over your license and proof of insurance, keep your hands visible, and let the cop follow procedure. A lot of bloodshed could be eliminated if we had that dialogue between civilian and cop more often."

"Very interesting," said Jerry. "I think you should take that to the governor, the police chief, or whoever you think will listen and propose that very thing. We need that kind of dialogue today."

Bob finished his drink, nodded politely after paying his tab, and left.

I couldn't help thinking that would have been a great story for the next day's newspaper edition.

My only glimpse of Jerry's soul occurred one night when he downed more than a few shots of scotch.

"You look around this room and know that everyone here has at least one dark secret, maybe many more," he opined. "We'd fight to the death to protect those secrets. And yet if someone offered to spill the dirt on our friends and neighbors, we pay for the privilege of hearing all about it. I don't know what the term is, but we seem to take comfort in knowing it's someone else, not us."

As cynical as that sounded, I had to admit what he said had relevance.

After a few beers, I devised a plan. I would apologize to Tim and perhaps return the money he lost via suspension.

Before I could do that, however, I needed to find out exactly what Toby and his girlfriend did to get kicked out of the press box.

I remembered Sam Blackman, who worked for the *Southern Illinoisan*. Although the *Illinoisan* competed with the Cape Girardeau newspaper I worked for, we struck up a friendship when we covered Cardinal games. I still had his cell number, so I went outside Smitty's to place the call.

"Sam, hey, it's Doug," I said when he answered.

"Doug, Doug, oh this sounds like the Doug I remember from the baseball games," he said.

"The very one," I assured him.

"Say, Sam, I was wondering if you covered the Cardinal game against the Cubs a week or so ago."

"Oh, if you're talking about the game where the press box turned into a strip club, uh, hah, yeah I was there."

I wondered if he was talking about the same game.

"The reason I remember, other than the guy and his girlfriend getting kicked out, is that your name was on the credentials. I walked over to say hi and was surprised to see this guy and his girlfriend sitting in what I thought were your seats."

"Okay, I guess we're talking about the same game. It turned out that I gave the passes to a friend of mine, who then gave them to a nephew and his girlfriend," I explained.

"Yeah, well anyway, it turns out that the gal your nephew was with couldn't hold her booze. They were drinking so much beer, they had cups stacked up to their chins. When the Cardinals rallied in the ninth, she jumped up and shouted that she was 'so freakin' wasted.'"

My heart sank. How could they embarrass me like this?

"Then she decides to give her boyfriend, your friend's nephew, a lap dance. I tell you in all my years in a press box, I never saw anything like that."

I thanked Sam for the information and hung up.

I was furious. How could I ever apologize for something as awful as that? I vowed to never use someone like that, and now it's done. I've failed a great friend.

There had to be a way to make this right. First thing I needed to figure out was how I was going to come up with the money Tim lost.

Before I knew it, I was surrounded by regulars I hadn't seen in weeks. I explained why I was gone for so long, and that elicited free beers from just about everyone I talked to.

By the time the guys from the poker game arrived, I was feeling a strong buzz.

I told Bob Haskins what happened in the press box.

"Whoa, that trumps some of my best stories as a cop," he said with a laugh.

"I can see why you're pissed at Matt, but I gotta tell you that he's going through a rough time right now," said Bob, his jovial demeanor turning serious.

"What do you mean?"

"You know his wife had a bout with breast cancer, and we all thought she beat it. I mean she was in remission. Well, the cancer is back, and she's not expected to live much longer," he said grimly.

"Oh hell, I wish I would have known that," I said, feeling ashamed. "I mean I'm still pissed, but I wouldn't have gone off on him like that if I'd known about Cindy. Maybe that's why he was so quiet when I asked him if anything was bothering him."

"My advice would be to leave him alone for a little while," suggested Bob.

"No, I need to tell him I just didn't know," I insisted. "What's going on with his wife is a bigger deal than what happened with his nephew. He probably had no idea something like that would happen."

I needed time to think about how I could make amends. I decided to retreat to the men's room and focus on some sort of plan.

While I stood over the stall, I noticed a flyer with a picture of a man in military fatigues surrounded by what looked like his family.

Beneath the photo was a plea for help. Julio Gonzales was in dire need of financial help due to the medical expenses he incurred after being struck by a hit-and-run driver. That was the same hit-and-run on the news when I was at the hospital.

I knew this was important to Jerry because the guy in woeful financial straits was a veteran. Also, Jerry was not someone who allowed flyers of this kind to be tacked onto his walls without his approval.

When I returned to the bar, I asked Jerry about the flyer.

"Tough deal," he said with a sober demeanor. "His daughter told me he did a tour in Iraq and Afghanistan and was exposed to shrapnel from an IED. I guess you know that stands for 'improvised explosive device.' Well, he's dealt with post-traumatic disorder and multiple psychological issues. He was homeless at the time he was struck by a car. If you would have seen the proud yet strained look on her face, your heart would have gone out to her the same way mine did. I don't have a daughter, but if that woman were mine, I'd be damn proud to say so. If you know anything or can help in any way, I'd appreciate it," he said.

"Sure," I quickly replied, not knowing what else to say. I wasn't able to help him financially, but I was moved by Jerry's compassion for his plight.

Ironically, the very place in which I sought refuge from the outside world only compounded my list of complicated issues.

I left a message with Matt apologizing profusely for my horrible behavior and asking him to forgive me.

"Honestly, I had no idea what was going on with Cindy," I confessed.

"And our friendship over the years has to mean more than for me to just go off on you like that. I should have known that Toby didn't realize there would be rules to abide by in the press box."

Well, the next order of business was to find a way to give Tim the money lost from the weeklong suspension.

The answer to that problem came in the form of a return call from Matt. I apologized once again and asked how Cindy was doing.

"It's been a rough couple of weeks, but as long as she keeps fighting, there's always hope that we can beat this thing," he said.

"That's good to hear," I said, glad that we were at least on even terms once again.

"Look, Doug, I should apologize for what Toby and his girl-friend did. I should have known that it was a risk because I didn't have a clue what the gal was like. I've already talked to Toby about it, and he's assured me that he will come up with the money to take care of your friend's loss of pay from the suspension."

I tried to assure him that it was my responsibility to pay my friend Tim back, but Matt insisted it was already a done deal.

"Okay, let me explain," he stated emphatically. "It's not really coming out of Toby's pocket. Well, it is, and it isn't. You see, he plays in this fantasy sports league where they bid on players and so forth. So now you can go online and do the same thing, only for money. It's like a legal gambling venue online. As it turns out Toby has a friend who works for one of the companies that offers this type of betting. He gets inside info on injuries to key players before they're made public, if you know what I mean. So he has an edge on the average guy. They come up with what they call cripples. They're games where the money is stacked heavily on one team. Because Toby's friend knows what others don't, he can advise for or against jumping on the band wagon. Toby hit the jackpot about a week ago, and he's still cruising on his winnings. So let him ease his guilt and pay your friend at the same time."

It sounded too good to be true, but it was such an easy solution to what was once a complex problem, I decided to relent.

There was still the $300 I owed Matt for my losses at the poker table. Perhaps I could use Toby's plan to make enough money to pay back Matt and have some left over for myself.

I had to figure out where I could come up with betting capital.

I thought of the rainy-day fund but quickly dismissed that notion. If I lost the bet, Anna would never forgive me, especially if it was made without her knowledge.

I was so distressed by all the dilemmas that hammered away at my brain, I felt overwhelmed.

19

Digging Deeper

I went home to sleep it off. The alcohol was clouding my thoughts to the point of complete confusion and exhaustion. Then I drifted off into a quiescent state.

I'm sitting there, trying to decide if I want one or two cards. I've got a chance at the best hand I've had all night. The room feels warmer. The lights are so bright I can barely focus on my cards. In the distance, I can see Anna, Annette, and Danny, their arms outstretched as if they're pleading for me to come to their aid. But I'm in the middle of a poker game with a chance to bring home one of the largest pots of the night.

I try to block out their faces, but there's no way to eliminate the desperate sounds of their pleas for help.

"Doug, Doug, it's your turn," comes the voice from the table. First one player then two, three, and four. My heart begins to palpitate, and my hands become so sweaty, I can barely hold onto the cards.

Then I wake to find the familiar arc of sweat on my T-shirt after having another bad dream.

When I woke, Anna was already gone. She was intent on impressing her office manager by being one of the first through the door to begin a new workday. Danny was off to school, and Annette was on her way back to the University of Illinois to resume work on her doctorate.

For some reason, I kept thinking about what Matt said about the cripple and how easy it would be to score some quick cash. I scoured the sports section and found a game that looked like a sure thing. Atlanta, which was 5–0, was playing the New Orleans Saints, who were mired in last place in their division with a 1–4 record. I checked the points scored and allowed and could see that New Orleans was having a dismal year both offensively and defensively.

Atlanta was on the rise with a new coach and some top draft picks who were coming through at the right time. I decided to check the shoe box to make sure the $1,200 was still there.

When I reached in the back of the closet, however, the box appeared to have been moved. I ran my hand along the other end and found it with the top halfway open.

As a joke, Anna and I put a mark with a felt-tipped pen at the end of the shoe box lid and another just below that on the box. We were the only ones who knew about the money and the marks on the box, so if the kids discovered it and put it back, they would likely close the box without aligning both marks at the same end.

The mark from the top didn't match the mark on the box so I knew someone had been in there since the last check. When I counted the money, there was only $1,000 instead of $1,200.

I counted it three times to make sure I was not mistaken.

Someone had taken $200. The only one who knew about the contents was Anna, and I couldn't see her taking it without coming to me first.

That left the kids. Danny made enough money mowing lawns during the summer and doing odd jobs for neighbors, so he was an unlikely suspect. That left Annette. She seemed agitated about something. Maybe it was money problems. I was sure we told her more than once we were good for a loan if money was tight at school.

Then again, maybe she didn't want to explain why she needed $200.

I was reluctant to say anything to Anna because I was thinking of using some of the money for a sports bet.

If I was going to bet on the New Orleans game against Atlanta, I would have to get it in soon because the game was scheduled for the next day.

I decided to place a $500 bet on the Falcons. The point spread was six, which meant I had to win by more than a touchdown over the Saints.

Even if I lost, I could temporarily replace the money with the guilt payment from Toby.

Right after I placed the bet online, I had this feeling that something might go wrong. What if Drew Brees, the Saints' quarterback, had one of those crazy nights like in the past? He seemed to have a penchant for coming up big in nationally televised games.

The next night, I witnessed one of the most incredible passing displays ever. The only problem was it was by the New Orleans Saints instead of the Atlanta Falcons. Brees was connecting on just about every angle imaginable. He kept passing to his tight end and the guy snared pass after pass as if the ball had glue on it.

The Atlanta defense seemed incapable of stopping the pass to the tight end.

The Saints went on to win by ten points, and I was out $500. When I found an envelope in the doorway with my name on it, I knew this was from Toby. He had six crisp $100 bills with a note of apology.

"I'm sorry for my terrible behavior, Mr. Anderson," he wrote. "I just hope you will forgive me."

I quickly put $500 back in the shoe box and pocketed the $100. I considered that I still had money to make another bet, but if I failed on what seemed like a sure thing, what would I do with a fifty-fifty game?

I had to think about this. There was still the money I needed to give Tim plus money I wanted to donate for the Julio Gonzales family fund.

Usually when I needed to think, I would go to the river, but this was one night when I felt like being around people. I decided to take a chance that some of the locals would be at Smitty's.

The place was nearly empty. The few that inhabited the bar were strangers. I drank a few beers and motioned to the waitress to bring my tab when Bob Haskins slid into the seat next to me.

"Bob, how's it goin'?"

"Oh, okay, I guess," he said with a grim demeanor.

"What's wrong?"

"Ah, it's a family matter," he said with a strained look. Upon further consideration, he added, "Well, I guess we know each other well enough. My brother called me to ask me about this thing that kids are taking these days. They call it spike or spice. Another name is K2. Anyway, it's a synthetic form of marijuana. It's real cheap, but the bad thing is they never know how strong it's going to be or where it came from. Well, his son was apparently taking it, and he ended up in the emergency room. He damn near died. Can you believe that? I guess every generation has something to experiment with, but this is so dangerous."

I was hoping he was going to recover, but I had to ask to be sure.

"Is he . . . I mean, will he be okay?"

"Yeah, but my brother is worried this is a sign that the kid is having a lot of problems he's not talking about. I mean, why would he even want to take a chance like that unless he was unhappy with his life?"

I empathized with his dilemma yet found some comfort in the notion that my kids never felt like they needed to resort to anything as drastic as that.

Bob took a few sips from his beer and said he needed to go to his brother's house and talk about what was going on. He paused then said, "I don't have any kids, so I can't say I know what he's going through, but you've got two. Do you ever worry about them?"

"Sure, I mean, I hope that they're safe and all that, but honestly, I never really thought that drugs would be a problem for either one. They just seem very well adjusted," I said. "I don't take credit for that. Anna is the one who has done an excellent job with them."

"Yeah, well anyway, I'll talk to you later," he said and took a slow walk out of the bar.

I felt like having one more beer before heading home. I began to think about what he said. What if the $200 had something to do with Danny or Annette being in trouble like Bob's nephew? Maybe they got caught up in something that was too big for them to handle by themselves.

Then again, I surely would have noticed something. I dismissed the dark thoughts as more evidence of my tendency to worry about things unnecessarily.

I still had money for another bet if I could just find the right game. Then it occurred to me as I looked beyond the television screen. There was a game of keno. I bought two $5 tickets with numbers connected to birthdays and my favorite athletes. I chose 53 because it was the year I was born. Then 45 because it was the number of my favorite pitcher, Bob Gibson. I selected 6 because it was Stan Musial's number.

I bombed on the first two tries. I decided to double the bet on the third try with a $10 ticket. To my surprise, it came back a winner.

"Damn, you won $1,200," said a young woman seated at the bar. She was right. When I looked at my ticket, I realized I had matched all the numbers.

I was so excited and in need of sharing my euphoria, I stuffed the money into my jacket pocket and began hugging the woman who declared me a winner.

She was wearing a perfume that traveled to my libido with such force, I wanted to go beyond the polite hug.

"This calls for a celebration," she declared, shaking her lustrous brown hair in a way that made the moment feel electric. Her blue jeans were so tight, I could see every contour of her shapely legs and ass.

If flirtation were an art, she had the gift to make masterful, hypnotic strokes.

She had to be at least twenty years younger than me. I was mindful that were it not for the $1,200, she probably wouldn't have joined me for a shot of whiskey.

"You do seem to have the magic touch," she said with a wink. "How good is that touch anyway?"

I sensed she was coming on to me, but I wasn't sure. She could have meant nothing more than to be playful with the whiskey doing the talking. But she started to go beyond mere flirtation, stroking the inside of my leg.

Her tan looked like it came from many hours spent outdoors in a warm climate.

"Are you from here?" I said, trying to get some idea who I was dealing with.

"Oh, actually, I moved here from Florida," she said softly, staring at the floor when she talked. "My brother and his wife are starting a new business, and they wanted to talk to me about getting in on the ground floor, so to speak," she said, pulling a cigarette out of her purse. "I really need a smoke, but they don't let you light up inside. How about joining me outside," she suggested, arching her back to highlight the contour of her breasts.

"Sure," I said, welcoming the chance to get away from the eyes of regulars who knew Anna. "I just need to use the ladies' room, so do *not* go away or anything," she said, squeezing my arm in a playful manner.

"Oh, I won't," I promised.

When we went outside, she grabbed me and kissed me hard on the mouth.

I was overwhelmed by a powerful sexual urge. I returned the kiss and began to grab her breasts. She didn't seem to mind.

"Should we go somewhere?" I suggested.

"What do you have in mind, sugar?" she said with a slight giggle.

Before I could respond, a car pulled up to where we were standing, and two men jumped out.

"Hey, Melissa, get in the car. Tommy wouldn't want to hear about what we're lookin' at," shouted a man who looked like he could tear me apart if he wanted.

"Tommy doesn't own me," she shouted back. I knew this was trouble. I separated myself from the confrontation and went inside. I quickly paid my tab and used the back door to avoid any trouble with Melissa and her two goons.

It became clear that I was being set up. When she went to the bathroom, she likely used a cell phone to call for the goon squad. All they had to do was grab me and steal the money, and I would have been in no position to call the police.

God, I was such a dope. When I dug into my coat pocket to make sure I still had the money, my heart stopped beating. It was gone. That manipulative, sex-driven bitch. She probably lifted it from my pocket when she hugged me. Boy, was I duped. They were probably still laughing at how easy a mark I was.

The hope that a woman half my age could find me as attractive as any of her contemporaries was the source of my temporary blindness.

I heard from some wise barfly that if you frequent any drinking establishment often enough, two things would happen: the patrons would all eventually know your name as well as your shame.

I stumbled home, took a shower to remove any trace of Melissa's perfume, and threw my clothes into the laundry basket. Anna was asleep, and Danny's bedroom door was closed. I decided to get back to a normal work routine and devise a plan that had a better chance of success.

Once again, I felt like a rat. And for the second or third time, I had dodged another bullet. How much Russian roulette could I afford to play before my luck ran out?

The game was over as far as I was concerned. It had to be. Anna never found out about the first one. I felt as much a victim as Shannon claimed to be. It all came together so easily. The ambitious intern at the university who pretended to hang on my every word. Each week she seemed to search for ways to volunteer for projects that included me. The languorous poses to gauge the length and breadth of my interest.

She could tell by my intense stares and willingness to play along with whatever ruse she invented that this could be pushed to the next level.

The way she brushed her long blond hair back, jostling her head then finishing it off with a mischievous grin, told me she was no novice.

The Saturday she just happened to stop by to pick up a jacket she purposely left behind on Friday emboldened me to make a move.

Grabbing a piece of power or celebrity was like a tempting drug that some people just had to have to prove they could go beyond the mundane and into the magnificent.

The damning event finally happened when I grabbed her in the elevator and tried to plant a hard kiss on those red lips.

She squealed like a little girl feeling trapped by a mouse for the first time.

What followed is still a blur. Did I hit her in the mouth or merely try to stop the screaming by placing my hand over her mouth? She bit down hard on my hand, thereby creating evidence I couldn't refute.

The upshot was an agreement that I leave the university quietly to avoid any scandalous story from the local media. What an ironic twist that was.

I distinctly remember asking for a favorable reference to allow me to continue working as a journalist. That was assured via a verbal assent. However, I now know that the verbal promise was never kept because I never got another journalism job from that point on.

But neither Anna nor Annette ever found out about the misdeeds performed by their husband and father. Oh, the steps I was willing to take to keep them from learning about the lecherous rat that I am.

In a strange way, I considered the scam with the $1,200 to be a blessing in disguise. I was through with this game. I had to be, or I would lose my wife, son, and daughter in one terrible stroke, and I probably couldn't live with myself if that happened.

I wasn't sure how I would come up with the money to pay Tim. I knew if I didn't find a solution soon, it would eat away at me the same way the memory of my mistakes with young women tormented me.

20

Truth Be Told

O ctober was nearly over, and I barely took time to stop and take in the kaleidoscope of richly colored leaves and array of pumpkins on porches and in stores.

I still remember the fall day Anna remarked that the burned-orange sun seemed to linger like a shy schoolboy hoping to work up enough nerve to ask the girl who dominated his thoughts for the last slow dance. The sky was turning gray, clouds were darkening ominously, and my thoughts moved on to other issues.

The streets would soon be illuminated with holiday lights and stores littered with reminders that Thanksgiving was just around the corner. I wondered how many people would be at our table this year.

My sisters hinted they might come, but I figured whenever they said Thanksgiving, they really meant Christmas. That's the way it usually worked when we were kids. If they said they would help raking the leaves this week, it meant they would be available next week or the week after that.

I found out there would be at least one more place to set at the table when Anna got a call from Annette late at night.

"Honey, look, it's not that bad. Whatever is troubling you can't be that bad," insisted Anna. "Just calm down and tell me what's going on."

For the next several minutes, Anna just listened.

"Okay, look. The best thing for you to do is come here and we'll talk about it," said Anna with the gentle, reassuring tone that a mother instinctively employs during a crisis.

Annette agreed to come home and seemed to indicate that she would stay for Thanksgiving. This made Anna happy enough to want to clean the house and even plan to get a real tree for Christmas.

"We can afford it," she declared, mindful that there was more money coming in from her job.

"Did she tell you what was making her so upset?" I asked, feeling left out.

"No, she was so hysterical, I couldn't even get coherent sentences out of her," said Anna, her brows pinching the middle of her forehead. "I can only guess here, but I think it has something to do with her and Alex. Maybe they broke up, or maybe they're just going through a rough patch."

I suspected there was more to it than that. Anna had a way of protecting her daughter the same way I seemed to want to shelter Danny from the rough stuff until he was old enough to deal with it.

I found myself in just that situation a few days later when I was awakened by what sounded like an intruder. Someone or something was making noise in the living room. Anna was still asleep, so I went downstairs to find out what was going on.

Danny was pacing the floor and stabbing the air as if he were being assailed by ghosts.

"Danny, what's going on?" I said as softly as possible. He kept pacing and stabbing the air vigorously as if possessed by an unknown demon. I finally grabbed him and pulled him toward me. "It's okay, son. I'm here," I whispered, peering hard into his dilated eyes.

He collapsed in the La-Z-Boy chair and began sobbing like I've never seen before.

"Tell me what is wrong," I pleaded.

"Tell them to go away," he uttered with a weary breath.

"Tell who to go away? Tell who?" I demanded.

"Them. Them," he cried repeatedly. Something clicked in my head. This reminded me of a bad LSD trip I had when I was in college.

The desultory phrases and the irrational behavior all fit. But surely Danny wasn't taking acid.

"Son, did you take something?" I finally said, hoping he would say no.

"It's called a bunch of things: mojo, scooby snax, black mamba, something like that," he said when he was able to calm down.

"What is that?"

He stared at me with a look of sheer fright and replied, "I have no idea. They said it was harmless marijuana."

"Who, who said this?" I demanded.

"I don't know. I just don't know anything," he insisted. I managed to settle him down enough to stretch out on the couch. I knew he wouldn't sleep much, but he needed to know that he was safe, and I was there if he wanted to talk. We stayed like that until morning.

Catching glimpses of him throughout the night, I felt closer and more needed as a father.

I recalled the day he looked so defenseless and innocent as a baby. I never thought a disaster could fill a void, but in this case, it had a way of closing off some distance.

I lifted him up and carried him to his bedroom and decided that this would be something between the two of us. Anna had enough to deal with after taking the frantic call from Annette.

The next day, Danny said he wasn't feeling well and needed to stay home from school.

We both knew it wasn't the flu, but that was the best excuse we could come up with until I could talk to him after I came home from work.

"We're going to go over this," I insisted before I left for work. He merely nodded meekly and went back to bed.

I suspected that there could be a connection between Danny's ordeal and what Bob was talking about. I called to check.

"Bob, you mentioned something about synthetic marijuana the other night. Do you know if this K2, spice, or spike has any other names?"

"Sure, it's sometimes called mojo, scooby snax, black mamba," he replied. "There are any number of names for the same thing: poison."

My heart beat like a trip hammer, and my pulse raced upon hearing this. I should have known better than to leave Danny alone. If this drug had a hallucinatory affect, he could easily become paranoid and even suicidal.

I called my boss and told him I needed to take the day off. I raced home and ran up the stairs to his room. He wasn't there. I looked in Annette's room then room to room until I found him in the basement, rocking himself back and forth with a blanket covering his head and body.

"Danny, what are you . . ." He continued rocking back and forth as if he didn't hear me. When I searched his eyes, he appeared on the brink of hysteria.

"Can't sleep, must . . . not . . . sleep," he repeated.

"Danny, what is going on?" I screamed, trying desperately to get him to realize I was there.

"Sleep is death, death is sleep," he mumbled.

This was not something that was going to go away like a hangover. He needed professional help. I tried to pick him up, but he resisted, hitting my chest with his fists. I let him fight me until he grew weak. I managed to get him into the back seat of the car, locked the doors, and headed to the emergency room.

When the nurse in the emergency room asked if I knew what he took, I said it was likely some form of synthetic marijuana. She called for help, and they rolled him into an area where a doctor could examine him.

"This is a real problem," said the female doctor, who looked not much older than Annette. She explained further that spice, spike, K2, and many other titles for this synthetic drug was coated with synthetic cannabinoids, a family of over seven hundred research chemicals. "It looks like dried marijuana, but it's much more dangerous and can have different effects, depending on how it affects brain receptors," she added.

After a thorough examination, it was determined that Danny would be okay, but he would have to remain in the hospital overnight for an extended observation period.

I called Anna and explained what happened. She sounded stunned, saying over and over, "How could this be? Our Danny? A Boy Scout, a member of the chess club. How could this be? I want some answers, damn it."

"Look, Anna, he did something stupid. Now is not the time to run him through a police interrogation. I should know."

"What does that mean?" she screamed.

"I, uh, well, some guys in my dorm room once took something they shouldn't have, and it screwed with their heads, and they realized they never wanted to do it again," I lied.

"They what?"

She sounded hysterical.

"They were young, like Danny, and they took a tab of acid. I never said anything when we first met because you weren't from that kind of crowd, and it never made any sense to go into it," I explained, hoping she would find this plausible.

"So much for not having any secrets," she fumed. I got her to calm down enough to talk about how we would proceed.

"Okay, I'm on my way. I promise I won't pass judgment, but I think we need to find out who gave him this drug or whatever it is he took to put him in this situation," she said.

"I'll be here."

I expected Anna to be furious. Instead she seemed somewhat calm and did what any mother might; she hugged him.

"Thank God, you're okay," she said. Before she could say another word, I got a call on my cell phone. I was going to ignore it, but I noticed it was from my boss at the bread company.

"I should take this to find out what Justin wants," I said.

"Go ahead," said Anna, whose posture as an irate mother somehow transformed into a supportive parent. "Doug, I'm short two drivers," said Justin, sounding desperate. "I know you're involved in a family situation, but if there's any way you can break free, just for about three hours, it would really help me."

I explained what the problem was, and Anna gave me the okay. "We'll be fine," she said. "I'll see you when you get home."

When I was completing my route, I began thinking of Michael, a boy who inspired one of my columns. I met him on the Little League baseball field. He was born with just three fingers on one hand and would need to have extensive surgery to stretch his legs so he could grow into an adult's body. When I asked his parents, Rob and Robin, if it was okay to talk to Michael, his mother looked me squarely in the eye and said, "Why don't you ask Michael?"

I was struck by this. They were treating him as if he were much older than ten. For good reason. He would have to deal with medical issues that most kids didn't even know existed. His femur, the largest bone in the leg, had inexplicably stopped growing. Michael and his parents were considering whether or not he would want to endure the pain from multiple surgeries.

When I crouched down to ask Michael if he would grant me an interview, I saw sage eyes that didn't belong to a little boy. They reflected a river of calm, a mature form of stability and strength you might expect from someone who has dealt with more than a few of life's harshest moments. But then wasn't that the case with Michael?

He nodded, and we talked about the fact that he was not only playing baseball but had just struck out the last batter he faced. I asked about his instinct to comfort a teammate who had just dropped an easy pop fly.

"We're a team," he explained. "That's what teammates do."

I remember feeling the hairs on the back of my neck standing at attention. I wondered if I could ever become the kind of father Michael had. And now I had to measure what kind of job I was doing with my own son. Considering what just transpired, I'd have to say not even adequate. It certainly paled in comparison with what Rob and Robin had done with their son.

When I returned home that night, Anna was still awake.

"So how did it go at the hospital?"

"Actually, he told me things I didn't know. Did you know he took money from the rainy-day fund? And that he quit the chess club and started hanging around kids from a different school? He broke down crying and begged me to forgive him. After that I think we had a good talk," she said, looking somewhat contented.

"I told him how much of a scare he put into us and all that, then he asked me about Shirley."

I hadn't heard that name in a long time.

"Your friend who died in the car accident," I said, wondering why Danny would bring that up.

"Yes, well, he reminded me of that time when he was a kid and was having problems making friends and he wanted to know more about her, so I told him. He said he wanted nothing to do with the kids who introduced him to the K2 or whatever they call it and was focusing on getting back to work on his essay for Christmas."

"That's good to hear," I said, relieved she didn't want to go back to what I said about witnessing friends taking LSD. "I realized tonight that instead of punishing him, we need to take more time really talking to him," she said calmly. "I mean adult to adult instead of parent to child."

I agreed and hugged her while whispering repeatedly how much I loved her.

"You haven't forgotten how to charm the shirt off my back, have you?" she whispered.

We made love that night. It wasn't spectacular, but it was tender and intimate and much needed. I slept better that night than I had in months.

I made sure Danny knew how I felt about what transpired.

"Your mother told you how scared we were," I said, knowing how much worse it could have been. He nodded and stared at the floor.

"Danny," I said, determined to get his full attention.

To my surprise, instead of turning away, he quickly lifted his head up and looked me in the eye.

"I'm not here to scold you or anything. I was a teenager once and made mistakes. I know what it's like to want to be like the popular kids, to be cool or hip or whatever you want to call it. I thought we talked about a kid who was considered a nerd, a freak, an outcast. His name is Jimmy."

I could tell by Danny's surprised look that this was the first time he heard about Jimmy. When I finished, Danny flashed an appreciative glance.

"That's a helpful story," he said.

"What I also want to tell you is that when you get ready to write your essay, think of it as a story you've always wanted to tell but were afraid what people would think or say." A look of recognition creased his face.

"I was younger than you when I was assigned to write an essay. It was a school assignment. We were supposed to write about what we did over our summer vacation. I was ashamed to admit that we were too poor to take a trip to a national park or go to a city much larger than St. Louis. All your grandfather could afford was a trip up and down the Mississippi on the SS *Admiral*.

"The *Admiral*, you mean the casino?" said Danny, appearing amused.

"Yeah, well, at that time, it was a steamship that offered excursions up the river for an hour and back down for another hour," I said.

"I looked forward to that trip in the spring and into the early part of summer. But I didn't want anyone to know that's all we got. So I made up a ridiculous story that made everyone laugh. When I saw how a story could make the entire class break out into laughter, I thought I created magic. What I realized is that I merely made an ass of myself. My teacher, Mrs. Fant, explained that the truth, even if it looks threadbare and difficult to admit, has more substance than a dazzling tale that isn't real. The mistake I made was thinking I was fooling my audience. The realization later was that the only fool was the one telling the false story.

"If you have the courage to stay true to what you honestly think and feel and never worry about acceptance or failure from the outside world, the most meaningful story will be told. That's when a sense of self gets stronger."

As much as I wanted to claim that advice as my own, it was something I overheard Tim Brown telling a young reporter in Cape Girardeau.

Danny never averted his gaze, revealing a look of increased curiosity.

"Okay, I get what you're saying, and that's fine if I've settled on what I want to write about," he said, vigorously running his hands through his thick dark hair. I read something interesting in his body language. The compressed brow and knotted facial features, all revealing an intense struggle to understand fully what was being said. His thoughts and emotions were likely tangled up, fighting to push forward to formulate a synapse. Only then would he start the journey that would lead to a clear understanding of what he wanted to accomplish. "I'm still not sure which parts to include and which ones to leave out," he said with a look of frustration. "I seem to have a knack for telling long-winded stories."

"Don't let that hold you back," I advised, thrilled that my son was not only taking me seriously as a source of information; he wanted to know more. Anna was right: talking to him as an adult brought us into a more respectful, mature conversation.

I had another thought.

"You might want to also try this," I said. "Ask Annette to interview you as if she were a reporter chasing a story. You can give her the idea you have for your essay, and she can get you to talk at length about why that is important to you. If it happened sometime ago, you can go over what it meant then and if anything has changed over time. My best stories could be traced to quality interviews. I had to have a great quote to make a story come alive. Maybe the process will work for you."

Suddenly I detected a flicker of understanding in his eyes.

"Oh, hey, you know, that might help me explain it all better," he said with enthusiasm. "That way, Annette can tell me what answers got to the point and which ones were hard to understand."

"I had an idea what I wanted to write about. Now I'm going to try something different. It may be good, or it may stink, but it will be my story," he said with conviction. "The one that means the most to me."

"That's the one you should write," I said, encouraged by his acceptance. It thrilled me to see him make such a positive transformation.

"Thanks, Dad."

"You're welcome."

He likely had no idea how much that exchange meant to me.

21

A Storm Erupts

With all that had transpired in the last few days, I thought this was going to make Thanksgiving more than Anna wanted to deal with, but she surprised me again by warming up to the notion that we would be together as a family on a critical day of the year.

To make things easier, I suggested that we order a precooked turkey from the grocery store along with all the vegetables, salad, and desserts. Anna smiled appreciatively and said that would help her immensely.

When Annette arrived, I noticed that she looked much thinner than the last time, and her hair was somewhat disheveled. She hugged Anna then me and Danny. I realized Anna told her what happened with Danny by the way she greeted us.

"Well, it's been a long drive and I'm tired, but I want to talk to everyone after I take a short nap and we can have our Thanksgiving," said Annette, looking somewhat troubled.

The short nap lasted several hours, after which she had a long talk with Anna. I thought this would be an appropriate time to find something to do with Danny.

"You want to watch some football or something?" I suggested.

"I wanted to do some more work on my essay," he said. "When Annette is ready, I'd like to talk to her about some of the things we went over the last time she was here," he said earnestly. "Oh, and maybe go through the interview thing, the things we talked about."

"Yeah, that would be good while it's all fresh in your mind."

I picked up items for the Thanksgiving dinner so I could relax later and watch a few football games.

Before we sat down to dinner, Anna told me that Annette had something to say to the family.

"Please be supportive," she urged. There was that motherly look I grew to love so much.

"I will do that, absolutely," I said, wondering where this was headed.

"Thank you," she replied.

When we gathered around the table, Annette asked if she could say something before we started our prayer.

"In the last few weeks, I felt very alone," she said nervously. "I think Mom probably guessed that I was pregnant."

I couldn't believe what I was hearing. I could feel my blood pressure escalating. My hands were clenched under the table, and my head throbbed.

Anna must have noticed how angry I was becoming because she slowly shook her head as if to warn against an outburst.

Annette paused then continued when she saw that I elected to remain silent.

"Instead of sharing that with everybody, I kept it to myself. It wasn't so much that I didn't want you to know. Rather, I was torn over what to do. I mean, Alex was so focused on his medical career, it was clear he wasn't ready to become a father. I have to admit, I was in the same frame of mind. With my career in psychology, motherhood didn't seem to fit into the plans.

"But the longer I felt that child in my body, the more I began to think of how spectacular it would be to have a baby to nurture and love as my own. A miscarriage took whatever decision I thought I had away.

"It hurt to lose the baby, but what caused more pain and anguish is the fact that I tried to work this out on my own without coming to the most important group I'll ever know: my family. I'm sorry I didn't trust you enough to simply say what was going on and believe that the final decision would be mine."

Anna was in tears as soon as she heard the word *miscarriage*.

"Oh, honey, thank you for sharing that, and I am so sorry for your loss," said Anna, her face stricken with anxiety.

"I'm also sorry for your loss, but for God's sake, Annette," I shouted, unable to hold back the disappointment I felt upon hearing such an announcement. Anna looked deeply disappointed at my reaction. I could see her reaching out to settle me down to avert a family argument. But there was no preventing me from reaching the boiling point. I was already there.

"You're working on a PhD, and you said yourself this was really serious. What would keep you from being protected?"

"Doug, we're past that now. Let's just deal with what is in front of us," cautioned Anna.

"You," roared Annette, glaring at me in a way I only remember once when she saw her mother and me in a heated argument. "What makes you Mr. Moral? God, what a freakin' hypocrite."

I looked at Annette, who appeared stunned. I felt like the walls were closing in on me.

"Oh, honey, you don't mean . . .," uttered Anna, looking disoriented.

"Oh yes, I do," said Annette.

Danny stared at the table, appearing at a loss for words.

Annette bolted from the table and slammed the bedroom door shut.

Anna was unable to talk her into coming back out. I apologized to Danny and Anna and asked that we just eat our meal in peace. Anna picked at her food and left the table in disgust.

"So, Danny, what's new?"

"Dad, what did she mean when she called you a hypocrite?" said Danny with a pained expression. Was he thinking about the talk we had about revering the truth?

"Oh, you know, sometimes people say things they don't mean . . . in the heat of the moment so to speak," I said. Danny shrank back as if insulted by such a response.

Annette and Danny were simply too smart to be hoodwinked by my stock lies.

Danny shook his head and said he wasn't feeling well. I finished the meal alone, tormented by what the immediate future might entail. If this was Thanksgiving, what was Christmas going to be like?

Was dysfunctional behavior something I inherited?

Later on, I could hear the soft murmur of Annette as she intercepted Danny in the hallway.

"Danny, I apologize for ruining your Thanksgiving," she said, barely above a whisper.

"Oh no, it's not a big deal," he said with a reassuring tone. "I'm really sorry you lost the baby."

"Thanks," she said, her voice sounding hoarse. "I'm sorry to hear what happened with the K2," she said with a comforting tone. "I wasn't here, but I could have warned you about that stuff. I'd be happy to help you with your essay if you like."

"That would be great," he said with a trace of excitement. "I've got a few ideas that I need to organize into a coherent pattern, if that makes any sense."

"Absolutely," she said.

I couldn't let the clash with Annette go without saying something. After several minutes, she finally answered my knock and let me in.

"Look, I may have reacted the wrong way, but I still had to say what I felt," I said, trying to keep the tone civil.

"Yeah, well, given some of the things I know about you, I had to say what I felt as well," she said with a tear running down the side of her face.

"What are you talking about?"

"Who's MH?"

My heart was beating so wildly, I felt like I was on the losing end of a wild chase. Where did that come from? How could she know about that?

"Would you like to tell me what you're getting at?"

"I was going to send an email using your computer when I saw you had a message. When I read it, I knew it wasn't from somebody Mom knows because it was signed MH. Who is that?"

"I don't even remember that," I lied.

"Yeah, well, your face looks guilty as hell," she said with a penetrating stare. "I'm aware of some of the facial features when a person is not telling the truth," she stated with the conviction of a savvy courtroom lawyer closing in on a confession. "Remember, I'm in psychology. And it's not Psych 101."

She had tapped into an area I thought was beyond her reach. I was trapped and there was no way out.

"Okay, it was something I did that was stupid, and nothing really came of it. If you want to tell Anna, you can, but you should know that it never turned into an affair or anything."

"I won't tell Mom, but it really hurt to think you would do such a thing, all the while telling her how important she is."

"Well, she is important. I love her as much today as I did when we met, maybe more so."

"Look, Dad, I don't want to go over this anymore. I just want you to know that you can't take the high moral ground with someone when you do things like that. It's fucking hypocritical."

God, I hated to hear her phrase it like that.

"Well, you know what they say: judge not lest ye be judged."

I didn't want to resort to something like that. It was a self-defense mechanism Sister Gordiana used when the moment of truth was upon her.

"Oh, that is rich," said Annette with a scornful expression. "What do you call what you did when I tried to explain what happened? You judged me as if I were a cheap whore. Dad don't use stuff like that on me," she uttered with disdain. "You are so . . ."

"Go ahead. Finish it. What?" I challenged.

"So . . . so narcissistic." I was stunned into speechlessness.

How long had she suppressed these thoughts? And how many more stinging accusations was she prepared to launch?

"Narcissistic, oh, that's a good one. Did you pick that up in Psych 102?" As soon as I uttered such a stupid line, I knew I was digging a bigger hole from which I could never climb out of with any degree of dignity.

I looked into her eyes and saw a wounded soul lashing out instinctively to preserve what she knew had to be kept whole.

"No, I picked it up each time we had to move to a new city so the Big Man in the house could win another award," she shot back, directing a look of disgust that nearly brought me to my knees. "Each time a new friend asked me what city we lived in before the current one, I'd have to make sure I had them all in the correct order. I was tempted to say we were in the witness protection program after my Dad fingered a powerful crime boss in the East Coast, anything but being the family with a father so self-absorbed, he rarely stopped to think what this rootless existence was doing to our lives."

"Okay, fair enough," I said, feeling as if I had been pushed into a corner. My sense of self-preservation took over. "You can call it narcissistic or selfish or whatever," I said. "I'd call it ambition, and it took me a long time to get that."

Annette directed a hard stare then replied, "When you were chasing the ideal, we were stuck dealing with the real."

"You don't . . . you don't know all of my real," I cried, unable to keep from her what I swore she would never know.

"All of your . . ." She stopped herself and appeared to have realized something because the intensity in her face relaxed somewhat. Then she started to back off, admitting she likely didn't know all of my past.

Thankfully, exhaustion took over.

We found a way to let the issue go for the time being, and I said good night. Annette turned her back and closed the door.

I was right about one thing: the appreciative look she gave Annette after praising her for the nurturing phase was not meant to include me.

Narcissistic. All I could think of was the Greek play I saw in college in which the character Narcissus fell in love with his reflection while staring into the pool of water. Was that how my daughter saw me all those years and now?

She knew me more than I wanted to admit. I was after more layers of success while Danny, Annette, and Anna were forced to cope with the consequences of my ambition.

When I returned to our bedroom, Anna was visibly upset.

"You couldn't see that she was distraught over the whole thing," she said, shaking her head. "Whenever you two get into an argument, there's never a civil ending."

"Look, I apologize for what I did," I said, feeling a knot in my stomach tighten. "We ended it on a civil note. At least I think we did. Anyway, our daughter said that I'm nothing more than a narcissistic hypocrite. How do you like that?"

Anna looked like there was a thought about to cross her quivering lips, but she kept silent and went to sleep.

What a great prelude to the Christmas holiday, I lamented. I wonder what I could do for an encore.

22

Honesty Heals, Forgives, Unites

I feared my confrontation with Annette might influence Danny's essay in a negative way. The timing of our dysfunctional skirmish could only cause confusion. Given my advice about never wavering from the truth and not worrying about acceptance or failure, how could he produce anything but a dark, fatalistic outlook on friends and family? Were we about to be set up for public scorn?

We would find out soon enough.

I was surprised, however, that there were no physical or emotional signs of angst in Danny's behavior during the days leading up to the deadline.

Danny seemed satisfied with what he wrote for the contest and decided to turn it in without letting anyone read it.

"Maybe I'm superstitious, but I'd rather just send it in. If it bombs, then that's that," he said with solemn gravity. "If it is better than that, then you'll hear it for the first time in a few days."

Annette seemed especially pleased with the essay, but even she didn't get to read the final draft.

Anna appeared nervous as we filed into the auditorium. Annette and I found a way to keep our distance to avoid another outburst. We were doing our best to be supportive on what was essentially Danny's day.

When Anna struck up a conversation with a former teaching colleague, Annette moved to the seat next to me.

"I said some harsh things that I now regret," she said in a hushed, rueful tone. "Mom told me about your childhood. Doesn't sound like Disney had a hand in writing that script."

"I didn't want to bring that into your world," I said with an even temper. "No, it wasn't the best thing on the planet, but it definitely wasn't the worst."

She moved closer to hug me. I never felt so unburdened by a hug as I did at that moment.

"I apologize for the things I said on Thanksgiving," I said when we separated.

"No apology necessary," she stated firmly. "Anyway, I just wanted to tell you that the idea of having me interview Danny really worked. He started slowly, but after we turned it into more of a conversation, he got some great ideas," she said with noticeable enthusiasm. "I don't know what the final draft looked like, but no matter what the judges think, it was a good learning experience for him, and I learned from it as well."

"I'm glad to hear that," I said, grateful that we were speaking once again.

Danny made such a positive transformation from the drug experience to this, I hoped he wouldn't be crestfallen if they didn't announce his name when time came to reveal the winner.

As it turned out, I had nothing to worry about.

The scoutmaster asked for everyone's attention as he held the winning essay.

"This year's winner has put together a very fine essay," he beamed. "It is something we can all look at and feel proud that this individual is a product of the Boy Scouts and a citizen of this country. This year's winner is Daniel Anderson."

Anna covered her mouth to avoid screaming. Annette pumped her fist into the air, and I leaned back and felt a shiver go up and down my spine. The timing of making amends with Annette and the surge of euphoria from such an announcement caused tears to temporarily blur my vision. I was eager to hear what he had written.

"This year's winning essay is titled 'Two for the Seesaw,'" declared the scoutmaster "Please hold your applause until the end of the reading."

The seesaw has always fascinated me. It's just a simple piece of wood balanced on a support in the middle, but one of the most important aspects is that its purpose is for use by more than one person. I think that is what drew me to it in the first place.

Our family moved three times in the span of ten years, and it was sometimes hard to break into a new neighborhood. When you're the new kid, you get measured and tested to see where you fit in. No matter how many times you go through it, it never gets easier. I've always wanted to fit in, to be accepted, to be as normal as any other kid.

One day my dad took me to the local park when I was starting school. I noticed a kid staring at the jungle gym. He had the kind of bashful look that told me he was lonely but didn't want to admit it. I knew that look because I'd worn it on more than one occasion.

On this day, I didn't care to admit it either, but I was on the lookout for a new friend. I walked up to him and asked if he tried the seesaw. He looked down at the ground then over to his mother, who was sitting on a bench.

She seemed to signal that it was okay. "You can play with this kid if you want."

"I don't know what's so great about the seesaw," he said.

"Well, it doesn't cost anything to use, and I can't think of anything that makes you feel taller than you really are," I said, hoping this might persuade him.

"Okay, I guess I could try it," he said with a look of indifference.

Since we were about the same size, it worked out just fine. When I was the one lifted into the air, I declared that I was emperor of the world, captain of the sea. When he was lifted up high, he shouted that he was a pirate who was now in charge of the sea.

We laughed and invented new titles and roles for ourselves and had a great time. I found out that Tommy was going to the same school in the fall. We became good friends. If I went to Tommy's house one weekend, he'd come to ours the next weekend.

Then I started to get to know other kids at school. One of the most popular was a kid named Charlie. His dad was an executive for a big company and made enough money to give Charlie the idea that practically nothing was unaffordable.

If there was a new gadget in the stores, Charlie was the first to bring one to school so his friends could try it out. Tommy was not as outgoing as me and didn't seem to care if Charlie wanted to include him in this tight-knit circle he seemed to hold sway over.

So I took it upon myself to mention to Charlie that if we were going to go to the movies, I'd like to include my friend Tommy. Charlie immediately dismissed this idea.

"Nah, not Tommy," scowled Charlie. "No towel heads on this expedition."

I didn't know what he meant, but I knew there was something about Tommy that he was never going to warm up to, and that was that.

I tried as hard as I could to figure out why I could be Charlie's friend but Tommy couldn't. After all, we were so much alike. Weren't we all, deep down, just kids?

That was when I learned about the ugly side of race and religion. I never stopped to think there was anything wrong with Tommy because his parents were Muslim and mine were Catholic. To me white and brown or white and black went together like an assortment of cookies in the same jar. My parents taught me that the only way to judge someone is from the inside out. That will tell you what's in their heart.

I think my Mom put it best when she said the person who generates enough warmth for everyone to share is a teacher and a student at the same time.

I'm still working on the full meaning of that. I guess so far I've noticed that being friendly, or warm, opens doors, and being mean seems to close them.

Anyway, it became clear that if I was going to be accepted into Charlie's circle of friends, I would have to dump Tommy.

Charlie not only had access to the newest gadgets, he also seemed to attract a lot of girls. One girl I couldn't take my eyes off of was Amanda. She was someone who always seemed to hang around Charlie. I would have given anything to get a chance to talk to her, but I couldn't think what to say. Charlie was someone who could introduce us.

I went home and tried to come up with a solution to this problem. On one hand, I still wanted to be Tommy's friend, and on the other, I didn't want to break ties with Charlie and all of his pals.

My mom noticed Tommy wasn't coming around as much and asked me why. I explained my problem. That's when she told me a story about someone she knew when she was young. Her name was Shirley. My mom met Shirley at school. They both played saxophone in the high school band. They decided that they should practice on their own so they could get good enough to form their own band and play the music they liked most.

When Shirley invited my mom to her neighborhood, one of the locals confronted them.

"What's this honky doin' here?" blurted a man who emerged from a group.

"She's not a honky," protested Shirley. "She's my friend, something you wouldn't understand."

Mom said that the look the man gave her was so steeped in hatred, she felt her knees shake. All she could think about was getting out of that neighborhood and back to where she was comfortable.

When Mom's mother found out that her daughter was in an all-black neighborhood, she said it was forbidden for her to ever go back there.

From that point on, the friendship between Mom and Shirley took a dramatic change. They joined different clubs and drifted apart.

It wasn't until something tragic happened that Mom realized she lost her best friend. Shirley was killed in a car accident on her way home from a dance.

Mom told me that as an only child, she often wondered what it would have been like to have a sister. She told me that Shirley was her sister, her best friend. She didn't realize that until it was too late. She would never be able to tell her how important she was, how much she loved her.

Mom told me that I was the one to decide who was worth having as a friend, not someone else. She said to deny the chance to meet someone extraordinary simply because they don't look or act like you is a pitiful excuse for exclusion.

Just recently I discovered how much truth there is in that. I have a greater appreciation for the importance of family, friendship, honesty, and loyalty.

My dad told me that to have all of those is something you should never take for granted. He told me about Jimmy, a kid he knew in grade school. Jimmy had a good family. He knew he was loved by his family and that they wanted to do what they could to give him a better life than theirs.

But all the love Jimmy's family could give him still couldn't solve his problem. Because they were poor, Jimmy's parents could only afford one school uniform. When it was ripped during the games Jimmy played at recess, his Mom had to sew a patch to make it presentable for the next day. When he came home with another rip, he was told to stop playing the rough games. From that point on, Jimmy was looked at as an outsider. What made it worse was the old nun who mistook Jimmy's curiosity for mischief. He was disciplined by an authority figure and shut out by his peers. Dad told me that Jimmy became a target for bullying. Even when he attempted to stand up to the bullies, he was outnumbered and finally humiliated to the point that he never wanted to return to school.

Dad told me Jimmy thought the reason he was so lonely, so unable to fit in, was because he was poor. His wish was to invent something that would enable him to become a millionaire. Then everyone would take notice and give him the respect he saw others get so easily. Dad eventually learned that human worth was different than net worth measured by bankers and stock brokers. Jimmy may never have understood this. At least not then.

I overheard my parents talking one night when we were living in Ohio. They were discussing a birthday party Dad was planning to attend with Mom. The day of the party, I became sick. A doctor said

I had a viral infection in my lungs and needed plenty of rest and to not return to school until I took all the meds prescribed. Because of my illness, Dad said he wasn't going to the party. I could tell he was nervous about something because he kept getting up and pacing then sitting down again. Mom told him if this was his friend, he should go to the party. No sense in two people watching over me when one could do the same job, she reasoned.

"These are the first friends who happen to be black," Dad said. "I know I'm going to say something that comes off as dumb."

Mom told him to relax.

"Just be yourself and everything will be fine," she said.

Dad when to the party, and when he came home, he told mom that all his misgivings about not having a good time had to do with ignorance.

"I had all these preconceived notions being uncomfortable as one of the few white people in a mostly black party that I went into that house stiff as a board," he said. "I feared I'd say something stupid like, 'This is good. Is it soul food?' Or 'I heard on National Public Radio that if Chaucer were alive today, he'd definitely be a rapper?'

"Then Cassandra, who turned fifty and was the reason for the party, came up to me and said, 'I didn't invite you here to stand in the corner. Let me introduce you to some of my friends.'"

From that point on, he said he had such an enjoyable time, he didn't even realize he was there for more than four hours. He told Mom he followed her advice and was glad he did. With an open mind and an interest in other cultures, your circle of friends will not only expand but become more extraordinary. Diversity is the key to widening and enhancing the circle.

I can honestly say that Tommy proved that point. I only wish Jimmy would have been able to benefit from that.

Having a family that loves you but no friends is like sitting on a seesaw alone. You're always safe, on solid ground, but without the friend on the other end, you're never going to have a look at yourself and others from a different angle, to have that feeling of soaring past time and place. With a friend, you can unleash your inner thoughts and know the relief that comes with that.

The seesaw, like friends and family, teaches you the laws of gravity: what goes up must come down. Life is full of ups and downs. It also demonstrates the importance of balance. When you're around people who truly care about you for yourself and not some ulterior motive, you can relax and explore who you are and what you would like to become instead of trying to be someone you're not. On your worst day, a friend will never abandon you. If it's a great friend, this person will offer the help and support that will elevate you from your lowest point and provide a fresh perspective. What once seemed like a horrific problem is suddenly something that can be solved.

Family can also become as important as the safety net trapeze artists rely on when they attempt the critical hand grip after floating from one side of the tent to the other. When we watched acrobats do triple flips and attempt the exchange, the crowd fell silent, mindful of the danger. Then the last exchange failed, and an acrobat plunged downward. It was such a relief to see the trapeze artist bounce up after hitting the net. There are going to be times when we reach for something beyond our grasp and must rely on family and friends to help us rebound. I made a foolish choice and could have suffered terrible consequences. But it was the undying support, love, and patience of family that enabled me to recover. If you think of family as intertwining threads that keep the unit whole, it's something to behold. I just wonder what would happen if the net were to widen to include neighbors and adjoining townships with the same supportive spirit, how cool would that be.

When I was down, my family enabled me to develop a plan to get back up. For that I am grateful. No matter how difficult life becomes, I know I will always have a haven, a warm retreat not only to recover but to strive for excellence. Tommy was the best friend I ever had.

I hope I can find out where his family moved to so I can tell him that. I hope I can meet more people as genuine and warmhearted as Tommy.

The audience applauded and gave Danny a standing ovation.

I couldn't believe it, a standing O. I won more than a dozen awards and never got something like that.

I was so moved by Danny's essay, I felt a flood of emotions welling up from within. When I looked at Anna, there were already tears slowly rolling down her cheeks.

When she caught me staring at her, she instinctively wiped away the tears. For a second, she looked so serious, I thought she was sad.

"That was beautiful," I said.

"Oh my god, it was better than anything I ever expected," she said, squeezing my hand with fervor.

"Oh, for a second I thought you were disappointed," I said, still confused. "I mean our son got a standing O."

"Oh no, it's just a lot of emotions coming at me at once," she explained.

We congratulated Danny at the auditorium and told him how proud we were.

"It's not every day a crowd is moved to stand as one on your behalf," I said, glowing with pride. Danny seemed to take the roaring approval in stride, not even commenting on it beyond what I just told him. His most eloquent statement came not in words but in action.

"Thanks, Dad," he said, first offering his hand then moving closer for a hug that rivaled the one we had when he was recovering from the effects of K2.

Tim looked as if he had discovered the answer to a complex riddle.

"Hmm, so that was the test," he beamed. "That was it, the advice you gave Danny before he wrote the essay. That was the test. You saved your best punch for the round that counted."

"Very good, and . . . um, well, thank you. There's still more," I warned.

"I'm in for the long haul," he said with a nod. "Continue."

On the way home, Anna seemed surprisingly quiet.

"Danny, you really put a lot of thought into that essay," I said, hoping once I broke the silence, Anna would jump in and add to the conversation. She didn't.

She kept staring out the window. I noticed Danny's look of concern when I caught a glimpse from the rearview mirror. Annette's brows were furrowed.

"Mom, I was hoping we could trim the Christmas tree together the way we did when we were kids," she said, her eyes searching for some sign.

"Oh sure, I mean, you guys can handle that. I'm probably going to lie down for a few hours," said Anna with what looked like a grimace.

I cringed thinking of my mother doing the same thing during Christmas. She had a penchant for ruining my favorite time of the year just when I was getting into the spirit of the holidays.

"Are you feeling ill?" said Annette with concern.

"No, just tired," said Anna in a weak tone. "I've been working a lot of hours lately. A little rest will do me some good."

When we reached home, I encouraged Anna to get as much rest as she needed.

"I can help the kids with the tree," I said.

"Thanks," she said, sounding exhausted.

That night I asked Anna if anything was wrong.

I could tell she had been crying.

"Just tell me," I pleaded. "If Danny's essay meant anything, it's that as a family, we can handle just about anything."

Anna stared at me then looked away. Whenever she did this, it was something she had difficulty facing.

"I didn't tell the full story to Danny about Shirley," she confessed. "The reason she was in a car crash was because of me. I killed Shirley." As she said this, her eyebrows twitched, and her eyes blinked repeatedly. Releasing this fact to the surface after years of suppression must have sent her body into a temporary state of shock.

"I don't understand," I said, feeling more confused than ever.

"I went to the same dance that night," she said, her hands clenched and her voice cracking. "For some reason, I decided to take a swig from one of the flasks they were passing around in the parking lot. It tasted bitter and went down hard, but I wanted to shake this image of being a Goody Two-shoes. Shirley had to be home earlier than me, and said she needed to get going. I told her I'd take her home. She asked me if I was okay to drive. I said I was fine, not knowing the true effect of the alcohol. A slow rain gathered momentum and became a steady downpour by the time we hit the highway. Shirley asked again if I felt sober enough to drive. Before I could reply, our favorite song was playing on the radio.

It was "Walk on By," a song by Dionne Warwick we knew by heart. We both broke up with our boyfriends at the same time, so the tune seemed appropriate.

"I will never forget the lyrics:

> If you see me walking down the street and I start
> to cry each time we meet, walk on by.
> Make believe that you don't see the tears.
> Just let me grieve in private 'cause each time I see
> you I break down and cry,
> I just can't get over losing you and so I seem bro-
> ken and blue.
> Walk on by.

"When I took the off-ramp, we skidded and ran into a ditch. At first, I thought Shirley was unconscious and would wake up when the ambulance arrived. They took us in separate ambulances, so I had no idea she would never wake up.

"My parents found a way to keep me from being charged with a DWI and manslaughter. Dad used his connections as a lawyer in a prestigious firm, and all of a sudden it was like it never happened. I tried to apologize to Shirley's family, but they wouldn't listen. 'You killed my daughter and all her dreams of helping people,' her mother repeated over and over. I heard those words in my sleep. She was right, I took her daughter's life.

"Shirley always wanted to be a teacher. I wasn't sure what I wanted to do. From that day on, however, I knew exactly what I needed to do."

Anna's face was streaked with tears. Her hair was disheveled, and her hands trembled so severely, she folded her arms against her body to keep them out of sight.

I realized the cruel irony of those lyrics after she revealed what had happened.

"What you've accomplished as a teacher must count for something," I said, wanting desperately to alleviate her pain. "Didn't you become as great a teacher as . . . I mean haven't you more than made up for . . . ?"

Anna held up her hands as if to stop that line of thinking.

"Life doesn't let us keep score the way sports does," she said grimly. "I don't think it's as simple as that. If only it were."

I went to hold Anna, to comfort her, but Anna signaled she wasn't finished.

"I know your sisters are coming for Christmas. I don't want to ruin the holidays for anyone. Please don't tell the kids about this. I've had to live with it for so many years. A few more days won't really mean that much."

I promised I would keep her secret from the kids for at least a few more days.

Given what she just told me, I had to think this made my secret even worse. How could I tell her about the transgressions that led to my fall from grace as a writer and journalist?

"I could call Cynthia and Claire and tell them we're not up to having a full house for the holidays," I suggested.

"No, please don't do that," she objected. "I would feel even worse for spoiling the holidays for everyone. I know how much you resented your mother for doing that to you over and over as a kid," she said, her face creased with anguish.

I forgot having told her that.

"Okay, well, we need to share the cooking and cleaning so you don't have to do all of that by yourself," I insisted.

23

Less Than Picture Perfect

Cynthia and Claire arrived looking resplendent in Christmas dresses. Claire topped off her red and white holiday ensemble with a Santa hat. Cynthia topped off her green dress with harp-shaped earrings, always the artist.

Their enthusiasm seemed to breathe new life into a house that sorely needed a lift. It was good to see both brothers-in-law and all the kids, Sam, Erin, Matt, and Ron.

I made sure everyone knew about Danny's essay.

"Looks like we've got another writer in the family," declared Cynthia, brimming with pride. Danny merely shook that off and said it was a once-in-a-lifetime effort.

"I got a lot of help from Mom, Dad and, Annette," he noted. "Dad got me started on the right path, Mom told me a story that related to something from my past, and Annette showed me how to organize these thoughts. Annette's interview made the process work better than anything I could have done on my own," he confessed.

"Well, you don't win first place without have a terrific idea, so at least take credit for that," said Cynthia.

"Yeah, sure," said Danny, looking somewhat embarrassed to be the focus of attention.

Anna picked up on the change in the overall mood of the house and did her best to add to the festive weekend as much as possible.

Annette did much of the cooking and was helped by my sisters as soon as they realized that Anna was feeling less than 100 percent.

After dinner we moved into the living room to be by the Christmas tree. Cynthia whispered to me that she was glad they made the trip from California.

"It's good for us to be together again," she said with a soft, contented smile.

When we were all in the living room, Cynthia suggested taking a group picture.

"I forgot my phone," she said. "Doug, you've got a smart phone, don't you?"

I handed her my phone, and she went about the task of moving everyone into a tight group so she could snap a photo. Then I took a photo of Cynthia with the rest of the family.

"We take one of these at least once every decade, so give me your best smile, folks. Everyone ready?" I shouted then snapped the picture. Cynthia took the next picture, this time with me included.

Cynthia and I viewed the results.

"Oh, you're going to have to email this to me," beamed Cynthia. "Claire, look at this handsome group."

When I saw the photo that included me, I was nearly reduced to tears. It was a great shot of our family, but I didn't look like I belonged. It was as if I had crashed the party, pretending to be someone I wasn't and found a way to blend into the background out of a last-second feeling of shame. When I peered at the photo, I wondered who that impostor really was.

I thought of what Annette said. She was right. I let my insatiable hunger for fame push aside the more mature ambition of becoming a selfless father and faithful husband.

I considered the damage I caused. Tim's career was in an esteemed, comfortable position before I brought it into the gutter. When Matt was dealing with his wife's medical condition, I lashed out at him as if he were a mere acquaintance. Although at the time I didn't know she was suffering, I did little after I was aware of the onset of another bout with cancer.

I was so lucky to have a wife who understood my drive to excel as a journalist, sacrificing her own ambitions to test her writing ability. And yet she still found a way to help so many students.

Next to Danny's essay, my accomplishments paled in comparison. Everywhere I looked, there were honest people doing the best they could with the talents bestowed on them.

I remembered what Dad said to me when I asked him about whether or not it was a sin to be poor. He told me if I was able to help someone in need, I should do so. I thought of the woman who made such a strong impression on Smitty.

All she wanted was for her family to be together again. Was there some way I could help them?

Couldn't I find a way to use my skills as a writer to ease the financial burden created by the hit-and-run accident?

A paroxysm of doubt clouded my thoughts. I couldn't even develop a workable plot for a novel. How was I going to accomplish something as real as coming to the aid of a family in financial straits? Maybe I was nothing more than a dreamer, a hapless modern-day Walter Mitty.

I managed to get through the rest of the evening without revealing the churning inside.

I hugged Claire and her kids and told them how much I appreciated the effort they made to be with us on Christmas. When I went to hug Cynthia, she must have sensed my angst because she reflected a look of stark concern.

"You okay?" she queried, the area between her eyes pinched.

"Yeah, I guess I'm a little tired," I bluffed.

"Hmm. I'd say it's more than that," she whispered as we hugged. "Give me a call when you feel like talking."

"Okay," I said, trying to assure her it was nothing more than the onset of holiday fatigue.

24

A Call to Action

I remembered that Anna said she tried to reach out to Shirley's family. Perhaps that was something I could do for the Gonzales family. I went to Smitty's and jotted down the phone number that was on the flyer. When I called, a voice that sounded young and female said hello. When I explained who I was and how I learned about the hit-and-run, she thanked me for my concern.

"I'm not sure why you're calling," she said.

"I guess I just wanted to say that if there's a way I could help your family, I'd like to do that," I said, not exactly sure how.

"Unless you can get the hospital to stop sending bills, I'm not sure how you can," she said, her voice barely audible.

"I'm not either," I said. "But if there's a way, I'm going to help."

She thanked me and said my concern meant a great deal to her.

"It's not every day that someone I don't even know is kind enough to offer help to someone who is homeless," she stated with a stronger tone.

"May I call back if I have a way to help?"

"Yes," she said solemnly.

I drove to the Mississippi River to think about what I wanted to do for her and Julio. I must have stared at the river and the barges that inched their way past me for hours before I came up with something.

I found a notebook in the glove compartment and began writing.

I wrote about the void I felt until Danny's bout with K2 and Annette's accusations, all of which were true. Then Anna's confession brought it home to me. We were a family splintered by our individual frailties. But it was our love for one another and the understanding that blood keeps us forever linked that allowed us to find ways to recover and bond. Danny's essay made me realize what the pursuit of honesty and truth can do for one's character. Annette used her skills to bring him into uncharted territory. But once he secured a footing, he willed his way through it, and the result was a magnificent declaration.

Couldn't I use my skills as a writer to help the Gonzales family and many others? Of course. I could do that by writing a grant proposal that would help the homeless get back the self-respect they once likely took for granted. Didn't all conditions matter, regardless of class, color, or religion?

I knew I couldn't say all of this with a phone call. I should put it in a letter and have it delivered to the Gonzales family.

I drove back to Smitty's and asked for the owner.

"Smitty's out of town, but I can give this to him," said one of the barmaids.

"I want this to go to the family of the hit-and-run victim," I stated with conviction.

"Oh well, Carmella, that's Julio's daughter, is coming in either today or tomorrow to collect the money we raised," she said. "I could give this to her when she comes in."

"Oh yes, that would be great," I said, grateful that I could be clearer about my resolve to help.

"No problem," she said, storing the envelope in a drawer behind the bar.

I walked out of Smitty's feeling better than when I entered the bar. At least I was prepared to do more than pay lip service to performing an altruistic deed.

I would still need to tell my family, but I wanted to wait until I heard back from Julio's daughter Carmella.

A week went by, and there was no indication from anyone I talked to at Smitty's that the daughter had a response.

"Are you sure she received the envelope?" I pestered.

Each person I asked said the same thing.

"I know she received it because she took it with the envelope that included the money we raised," said the barmaid who accepted my envelope.

Then one day when I was sitting at the end of the bar, staring at a football game I didn't really care about, Smitty handed me an envelope. My hands were shaking as I took it and stared at it.

There was no writing on the outside. I opened the envelope and read with a racing heart what it said.

> Mr. Anderson, I appreciate your letter. You said you might call, but when I didn't hear from you, my mother and I had to deal with the death of my father. We are still devastated by our loss. My mother and I have decided to move to California to live with my uncle Mario. He owns a landscaping business and is able to help us get back on our feet.
>
> We are going to use the money from Smitty's and some other charity benefits to start over.
>
> I'm still not sure how your idea of writing a grant proposal would have helped, but I'm convinced your heart was in the right place. For that I am truly grateful.
>
> If you want to do something to honor my father's life, you could volunteer your time at a homeless shelter. You could also use your talents to make life easier for veterans returning home after suffering debilitating injuries. Julio had many problems before a coward sent him to the hospital. Many of those problems came from his experiences and injuries suffered during his time in the military.

You could find an agency that helps veterans get their lives back together and volunteer your time there.

Look for ways to help people who are unable to fend for themselves. I was moved by the way your family worked to heal and become whole. Not everyone is as fortunate.

There are people who have family but are too ashamed of where they are in life to go back to them and try to heal as a unit.

Our family was one of those—a family shattered by something like this may never get back to where it once was, not without some help from people who have the means to give them a timely boost.

Again, thank you for wanting to help. There should be more people like you.

Carmella

She was right. I needed to do something to help people who couldn't fend for themselves. But first I needed to go to Cape Girardeau and find a way to make amends for what I did to Tim's standing with the newspaper.

Then I needed to bare my soul in front of Anna and the rest of the family.

This was the time to tell them what I had done in Ohio. It had already cost me my career.

Maybe it would turn my family away from me. I had to confess before it was too late.

I had to do it before Annette returned to Champaign to resume work on her doctorate.

I would gather everyone and tell them without any chance to rehearse.

Would they still want me as a father and husband? Or would they tell me to just walk on by?

They deserved to know the truth.

I scribbled a note to Anna, telling her I needed to take care of an obligation in Cape Girardeau and would be back as soon as that was finished to discuss something important.

I threw some clothes in a duffel bag and left before anyone stirred.

As I drove the hundred-mile distance to Cape Girardeau, I began to formulate a plan. Our favorite haunt was a Cajun restaurant called Broussard's, located on Main Street. The caricature of an alligator chasing a lobster with a meat cleaver was the restaurant's classic signature icon and among my favorite in any town.

I hoped the inside, decorated in neon with murals on the walls reflecting Mardi Gras themes, was the same as I remembered it.

"Tim, you recall how we gravitated to Broussard's to discuss stories and talk about sports and our families. You talked about Patti like she was the greatest thing to ever happen to you. There was one thing that struck me. I think it was with the birthday cards."

"Yeah," said Tim. "We had this way of picking each other up when times seemed bleak. There was no set formula. Something would occur to us, and we'd go with it. Well, one year I was in a slump. I wasn't getting any response back from the resumes I sent out, and I feared I would be stuck in a job I hated. Then the recession hit, and it really looked bad. Patti left a birthday card with this message: 'On what looks like our darkest day, we still have each other. Doesn't that make us rich beyond our wildest dreams?' There was a soothing kind of tenderness and a touch of humor all rolled into that simple statement. The timing was perfect. It anointed her as genius for a day.

"I asked her how long it took to come up with such a brilliant message, and she said, with a deadpan expression, 'Oh, pretty long, like a minute or two.'

"From that point on, I made sure that the birthday card I bought for Patti had more than a quaint message written for the masses. It would have to be blank, so I penned the message.

"After that important moment, things started to fall into place. A month later, I got a call from the *Southeast Missouri Bulletin Journal*, and not much later than that, we formed a pretty good investigative team."

"Oh, okay. I remember that story now," I said. "It doesn't get any better than that."

I was jealous. Anna and I never rescued each other in that way.

I steered the conversation away from birthday cards.

"You didn't have any children, but you spoiled nieces and nephews as if they were their own," I noted.

Tim nodded.

"Yes, we did. You know we thought about adopting and came close to getting a child from Russia, but it fell through, and Patti said she didn't want to go through that again," he said.

"Well, tell me more about your trip to Cape."

25

An Unburdening Discovery

When I reached the edge of Cape, I slowed down during the predawn stillness to see if the town changed. I was immediately struck by a feeling of unwanted detachment. The cold feeling stemmed from the fact that I no longer drew pay here, nor did I have a phone number or address that would link me to the city. Even when I listened to the birds chirp away, it didn't sound lyrical the way I remembered when I inched my way toward the newspaper parking lot each morning.

The crisp staccato sounds that routinely lifted Cape out of its final drowsy hours appeared foreign, somehow encoded with a message meant only for locals, not visitors like myself.

Broadway seemed the same. The fast-food restaurants were still there, a McDonald's, Hardees, and Burger King within a short distance of each other.

When I drove past Capaha Park, a flood of memories surfaced. The time Southeast Missouri State Baseball Coach Joe Uhls taught me that a milestone such as win number five hundred can be celebrated in private.

"What do you want me to do, jump up and down or something?" he said annoyingly.

I spent countless hours covering high school, college, and American Legion baseball games there, sitting in the grandstands with a book to keep score and an imagination to recount the accomplishments as well as disappointments that would shape young boys and usher them into quality adult lives.

I remember the summer games most because they were played by individuals whose love of the game was tested in many ways.

The sun beat down with such ferocity, you could see heat vapors rising from the infield grass. And there were extra-inning marathons that ended in a draw because the game went past the park curfew. There were times when the burned-orange sun would descend languorously, seemingly allowing the audience to get a last look before it went to bed.

As I continued down Broadway the tired, unimaginative array of fast-food establishments were replaced by downtown images I remembered fondly. The downtown streets, although still mostly dark, were festooned with holiday lights and ornaments that could be seen by barges inching along the Mississippi. Businesses like My Daddy's Cheesecake and bars like Celebrations were still apparently thriving. There were a few new ones I didn't recognize: Katy O'Ferrell's Publick House and The Library.

"What kind of charm and innocent mischief would I find inside the Irish pub?" I wondered. And the Library looked interesting enough to pay a visit.

There was still plenty of character to be found in this Bootheel town after all.

It was too early for Broussard's to open, so I parked on the corner of Main Street and Themis and leaned back to take a nap. I couldn't help noticing the town clock, which kept time for the city and its courthouse directly in its path. Rick Benson, a reporter who just joined the staff, earned the dubious distinction of generating the wildest typographical error when he referred to the town clock minus the *L* in the lede paragraph.

I felt the early rays of morning sun tiptoe across my face. The town was beginning a new day, and I hoped to take care of a problem that was gnawing at my soul.

The first person I recognized was Cookie, a mainstay in Broussard's kitchen for as long as anybody could remember. Her real name was Cecelia, but everyone who frequented the restaurant just called her Cookie. She couldn't have been taller than five-one or five-two, but the fierce look of those piercing blue eyes gave customers who thought of causing a scene reason enough to move along quietly.

Tim you used to say it would take a steamroller to make this Cookie crumble.

"Well, if it isn't the long-lost journalist," said Cookie with a wry smile. "Did you come back to show us your novel?"

"No, no novel," I admitted dryly.

"Hey, Cookie, what's the special of the day?" I said, eager to change the subject.

"Well, let's see, I guess it would be your favorite: bayou breaded frog legs and onion blossom," she replied.

"You have a terrific memory," I said.

"Don't forget that luscious Cajun shrimp with the memorable sauce that was surely concocted in heaven."

"Ah, you were always one of my favorite customers," she said with a captivating smile.

"Speaking of favorites, when do you expect Tim Brown to stumble in here?"

Cookie's smile was replaced by a sober expression.

"You won't be seeing Tim here anymore."

I couldn't believe it.

"Are you serious? What happened? Did he find a new restaurant or something?"

"Nah, there's none better than this one," she said with conviction. "No, Tim was offered an early retirement, and he took it. He moved to Colorado to be closer to his brother and sister."

"How long ago was this?" I said, finding such a quick departure hard to believe.

"They left about a week and a half ago," she said with a dejected look. "I'm gonna miss him. We all will."

A profound feeling of sadness swept over me.

Tim's last professional memory of Cape Girardeau would not be some ceremonial thanks for the journalistic excellence he practiced there. Instead it would be the sanitized business deal, neatly folded and packaged into severance form to usher his nondescript exit."

"Did he say anything about me?" I said, hopeful I wasn't setting myself up for another fall. She started to respond then hesitated. I felt compelled to speak.

"The reason I came down here was to apologize for something I unintentionally did to hurt his standing with the newspaper. Did he say anything about that?" I said, searching for some evidence in Cookie's demeanor of how he regarded me before he left.

"No, he didn't say anything bad about you, if that's what you mean," she said, showing no sign of pretense. Then, as if the questions triggered the memory of something, she added, "Tim was upset about something. He said he screwed up by trusting somebody he never thought would let him down. He never said who that was though."

Her face quickly brightened when she thought of something else.

"He always said you two were a great one-two punch when it came to investigative stories."

God, that meant so much to me. I was nearly reduced to tears just hearing that.

"I guess I'd have to go to the newspaper to get a forwarding address," I said, hoping she might say she already had that.

"I don't think you'd find anybody you recognize," she said. "Tim's not the only one who was offered an early retirement. You remember John Ramsey? He left too. It's a young bunch of reporters that run the paper today."

"John Ramsey," I said wistfully, remembering his signature handlebar mustache. "Is he still living in Cape?"

"Nah, he decided to go back to his hometown of DeMoines, Iowa," she said. "John's wife found out he was runnin' around with a coed from the university. Bev said that was enough. No more. She left him."

"How did she find out?" I asked, feeling my stomach churn.

"John decided to tell her himself. Big mistake," she said, shaking her head while bunching her lips. "If you can't fix what was done in the past, it's sometimes better to just focus on the present and future," she added sagely. "John ended the affair and felt it was only right to fess up to what he did. It ended up costing him his marriage. He was not a happy camper when he left town."

"I can't believe how much has changed since I left," I said, somewhat bewildered over the sad news she was giving me.

"You've been gone for . . . what . . . a decade or so?" she said.

"Yeah, it's been over twelve years," I corrected.

"A lot can happen in twelve years, even in a small town like this."

"You haven't lost your wisdom," I declared, nodding to show appreciation for the exchange.

"I know nothing about wisdom," she declared. "My hope is that if I leave behind nothing more than an ounce of inspiration, it will grow into a pound of prosperity and happiness. That would validate my time on the planet."

She didn't know it, but that statement applied balm to a wound festering inside of me for a long time. I was humbled by such an eloquent proclamation.

"You're right," I shouted back. "You're right, Cookie. Thank you."

I had planned on stopping at the newspaper to talk to some of the veteran reporters, but that now seemed like a bad idea. But the statement about someone you trusted letting you down stayed with me.

It was after 8:00 a.m., so the paper would be getting ready to cover another day of news. I was glad to see Donna Crawford was still the receptionist. She looked thinner than I remember.

"Wow, look at you," she cried out with excitement. "How have you been?"

"Oh, okay, I guess," I said flatly.

"Come on now. The last thing I heard about you was that you were working on a novel," she prodded. Is that true?"

"No, I'm not sure where that got started," I said, relieved I was no longer clinging to that lie. "Truth is I'm driving a bread truck."

She looked like I had just told her my dog was run over by a bus.

"Oh, well, everybody needs someone to deliver their daily bread, right?" she said, looking uncomfortable as she said this.

"Yeah, I guess so. Look, Donna, I heard there have been some changes around here, and Tim Brown is no longer here," I said.

"Yeah, a lot of the older . . . I mean veteran reporters were offered buyouts," she said glumly.

"Okay, well, I did a terrible thing to tarnish Tim's reputation, and I need to set the record straight. Is the publisher in yet?"

"No, he's actually in New York," she said. "Won't be back for another week."

"Well, who's the editor now?"

"It's Joe Wolfe," she said with a poker face.

"Joe? Oh, okay, he was just getting started when I was here, but he seemed like a good reporter and was definitely ambitious. Is he here yet?"

A look of concern creased her face.

"He's here but they're in a meeting," she warned. "I can't let anybody in there. It's a rule he said can't be broken. I could get into a lot of—"

I didn't wait for her to finish. I knew where the meeting room was. I knocked on the door, and suddenly the voices inside came to an abrupt halt. I waited for several seconds and opened the door. The frozen faces sitting at a circular table took in my intrusion with stunned silence.

"We're in a meeting here," barked Joe annoyingly, showing no recognition.

"Joe, you probably don't remember me, but I'm Doug Anderson," I said. "I used to work here."

Suddenly a look of acknowledgment surfaced.

"Doug, okay, sorry, it's been a long time," he said placatingly.

"Just give me a few minutes of your time," I said.

"Okay, I'll be right back," he said to the reporters who stared at me as if I just announced my name was Jesse James and I was there to rob the place.

He motioned for us to take the conversation into the hallway.

"Look, Joe, I did a terrible thing to Tim Brown, and I want to set the record straight," I said.

"Tim did the terrible thing from where I'm sitting," he insisted.

"No, I'm to blame for the press pass," I said, determined to set the record straight. I explained what I told you Tim and what actually happened.

"Well, that does change my understanding of what really happened, but nothing can be done about it now," he said with an angry tone. "Tim's gone."

"Yeah, but he's not dead," I stated. "I'll talk to the person in charge of public relations for the Cardinals if I have to."

"No, that's not necessary," he insisted. "We had a conference call with them, and they're going to reinstate our press box privileges on a probationary basis."

"Oh, okay. Well, I still need to get in touch with Tim. Is there anybody here who has his forwarding address?"

"Yes, Donna has that. I'm sure she'd be happy to give that to you," he said. "Look, I've got to get back in there," he said with an anxious look.

"Oh sure, well, good luck to you," I said.

"Sure, same to you," he said with what sounded like false sincerity.

Donna gave me Tim's address and wished me luck, not so much as a reflexive gesture but like I really needed some.

"He said his phone number would be different, but I don't have the new one," she said.

I looked at the slip of paper she handed me. Tim was now living in Colorado Springs. Wasn't that where Olympic hopefuls train?

26

A Journey Comes Full Circle

I returned to my car and headed North on I-55. When I saw the sign that read "St. Louis 90 miles," I felt relieved there was a home and a family that was still intact.

I was more confused than ever. Should I risk what befell John Ramsey when he confessed to his wife about the affair?

I never really had an affair in Ohio. It was more a series of flirtatious fantasies over what might be instead of a serious romance. Same thing with Mary Henderson.

But the incident in Ohio cost me a career I loved. It came with harsh consequences because it also meant we had to move to another city.

When I walked through the front door, I smelled coffee brewing. The day's news was emanating from National Public Radio.

Danny was on the phone, talking to what sounded like a girl.

"Where's Annette?" I said to the woman who radiated so much warmth and kindness. She looked ethereal, like a celestial gift wrapped in a pink robe.

"She's on her way back to Champaign," said Anna, the delicate lines on her face revealing character and wisdom instead of age and stress.

"So what was the obligation you had to take care of in Cape?" she said, her brows furrowed with a look of deep concern.

"Oh, it turns out that the guy I owed money to, Tim Brown, has moved on to Colorado Springs. And I think I should move on as well."

"What on earth do you mean by that?" she said as if stricken with a fearful premonition.

"I mean I need to make a career change," I explained.

"Is that what you meant by talking about something important?" she said, relief replacing the tension in her face. "That's what the note said."

"Note?"

"Yeah, the note you left before you went to Cape," she said.

"Oh, I had this idea that maybe driving for the Colonial Bread Company isn't such a good idea anymore," I said.

"Yeah, what will you do?" she queried with a look of intense concern.

"I'd like to learn how to write grant proposals," I said.

"You see, it's taken me a long time to realize that I've been using my ability in a selfish way."

Anna's face blossomed into an appreciative smile.

"Oh, I think you're onto something there," she said.

"Well, you know I said I'd tell the kids about what happened the night Shirley died," she reminded.

"Yeah," I said, feeling anxious over what she might say next.

"I don't think that's such a good idea," she said with a slight quiver.

"You know, I think you're right," I said with relief.

"Yeah?"

"Yeah, and maybe one day, when we're better off financially, we can take a trip, say to Colorado Springs . . . to see the US Olympic Training Center, things like that," I suggested.

"That's for the future," she said. "For now, we can take it slow and easy and deal with the here and now for a while. Matt called to say Cindy was feeling better. Maybe we could invite them over for a barbecue."

"Good idea. I've got to settle a debt with Matt," I said. "Poker game that I had no business playing in," I said in anticipation of her question. "I'm done with that for a while."

"Wonderful idea," she said. "Oh, speaking of ideas, I had a good talk with Annette before she left for Champaign, and she said open communication can do wonders for the soul. Maybe we need to talk more, like we used to."

"I think you're right," I said. "You're always right."

"No, not always," she said with a reproachful smile.

"No? Well, how about this," I said with a gush of enthusiasm. "A wise person told me that if you can leave behind just an ounce of inspiration, it could grow into a pound of prosperity and happiness. And that would validate your time on the planet. Well hell, you've already done a ton of that."

Anna appeared at a loss for words as she pressed a trembling hand to her mouth.

"Is that from the novel?" she said.

"No novel," I said. "It's from here," I said, tapping the left side of my chest. "It's from this," I said, expanding my hands to indicate the length and breadth of the home we lived in.

"Once again, you've charmed me into another welcome home," she said, opening her arms wide. "I'm not waiting forever."

I let her arms close around me and accepted a much-needed hug, thankful her robe was thick enough to absorb the amount of moisture cascading down my face.

"Yes, welcome home."

We Are One with Each Other

Tim selected a restaurant on the outskirts of town. It had a rustic look that elicited an appreciative smile from Anna. How did they know we were especially drawn to places like this? I wondered.

"I hope you like this place," said Patti, who looked as if she hadn't aged in the years that separated us.

"You know we do," assured Anna.

The waiter recited the specials flawlessly and said he would be back with our drinks.

Then, as if he read something in our faces that piqued his curiosity, he said, "Special occasion?"

"Reunion," replied Tim. "First of many."

Everyone agreed that was a good idea.

"You two had a long talk last night," noted Patti with a searching gaze.

"Yeah, I thought you were solving the problems of the world," said Anna with a curious expression.

"Not the problems of the world," said Tim with a knowing expression "Just a reminder of how important you two are and how blessed we've been over the years. Friends and family—you should never take that for granted," he added wistfully.

"Not for a second," I agreed.

Tim lifted his glass.

"I learned something this weekend. If we applied the same instincts of survival to friendship, family, and community, the quality of life would increase dramatically."

"Maybe you should explain that a little more," I said, viewing the puzzled looks from across the table.

"Okay, we know the difference between a suntan and a sunburn. It comes from our understanding of moderation. We know the benefits from a gentle breeze and the destructive nature of a hurricane. That comes from our knowledge of force. We know the difference between pleasure and pain, comfort and discomfort. We know which one we prefer.

"We can't control the forces of nature, but we can have a say in the nature of our thoughts and actions. We can develop the discipline, the sensitivity to listen, to understand, to open our minds to the hopes and dreams of our neighbors as well as our friends and family. Wouldn't that make us feel as wonderfully connected as we do right now? Here's to spreading some of that around on a more consistent basis," he said. "Cheers."

I felt my heart expand as I looked at the faces around me. The scene was rich. I was truly blessed.

The euphoric moment was cut short by a disquieting vibration emanating from my pocket. It was a phone call from Matt. I excused myself from the table to call him back. I noticed there was a voice message.

"Doug, just wanted to let you know Cindy is back in the hospital. Hopefully a false alarm. I'll let you know more later."

I told Anna about the message. We decided to drive back immediately.

"You have to leave so soon?" said Patti with a look of disappointment.

"A friend is fighting cancer," said Anna. "We need to be with her and her family."

Patti and Tim accepted the news with deep concern and an understanding look that needed nothing further.

Good friends and family know all of what that means.

As we drove through a mountainous terrain, I noticed a billboard with an ad for lemonade. I thought I was the only one who noticed it, but I was wrong. Anna offered a knowing grin. We looked at each other and erupted into laughter. The wordless moment felt intimate, poetic, rich. She leaned her head against the car seat and closed her eyes. I couldn't wait to jot down how she looked, what it all felt like. There would be more images and vague thoughts sluicing through nerve tissue, electrical impulses zipping through neural pathways, taking synapsed flight and willing their way to the surface. This followed by the compulsive need to recruit apt words that will unite and find their place to form a lean, intelligible sentence. The need to stop everything to get it all down was growing stronger. I wanted to believe I was looking at the specter of an old friend who dared advance out of the shadows of memory and step confidently into a world I could touch and feel. Is that you, raison d'être?

About the Author

B ill Heitland spent fourteen years as sports editor, columnist, and news reporter for newspapers in Southeast Missouri. He won numerous awards, including first place for column, feature, and investigative reporting. He was also a senior publications editor for a university in Ohio.

He currently lives in St. Louis, Missouri.

CPSIA information can be obtained
at www.ICGtesting.com
Printed in the USA
BVHW031255180619
551319BV00001B/22/P